NOTHING GOLD CAN STAY

Also by Dana Stabenow

The Liam Campbell Series

The Kate Shugak Series

The Star Svensdotter Series

DANA STABENOW

NOTHING GOLD CAN STAY

A LIAM CAMPBELL MYSTERY

A DUTTON BOOK

DUTTON
Published by the Penguin Group
Penguin Putnam Inc., 375 Hudson Street, New York, New York 10014, U.S.A.
Penguin Books Ltd, 27 Wrights Lane, London W8 5TZ, England
Penguin Books Australia Ltd, Ringwood, Victoria, Australia
Penguin Books Canada Ltd, 10 Alcorn Avenue, Toronto, Ontario, Canada M4V 3B2
Penguin Books (N.Z.) Ltd, 182–190 Wairau Road, Auckland 10, New Zealand

Penguin Books Ltd, Registered Offices:
Harmondsworth, Middlesex, England

First published by Dutton, a member of Penguin Putnam Inc.

First Printing, October, 2000
10 9 8 7 6 5 4 3 2 1

 REGISTERED TRADEMARK — MARCA REGISTRADA

LIBRARY OF CONGRESS CATALOGING-IN-PUBLICATION DATA:

Stabenow, Dana.
Nothing gold can stay : a Liam Campbell mystery / Dana Stabenow.
p. cm.
ISBN 0-525-94559-8
1. Campbell, Liam (Fictitious character) — Fiction. 2. Police — Alaska — Fiction.
3. Serial murders — Fiction. 4. Alaska — Fiction. I. Title.
PS3569.T1249 N68 2000
813'.54 — dc21   00–022610

Printed in the United States of America
Set in Cochin
Designed by Leonard Telesca

PUBLISHER'S NOTE
This is a work of fiction. Names, characters, places, and incidents either are the products of
the author's imagination or are used fictitiously, and any resemblance to actual persons, living
or dead, business establishments, events, or locales is entirely coincidental.

for Dawn
the perfect niece

ACKNOWLEDGMENTS

As always, I have taken a high and free hand with the geography of Alaska. Some of the place names are right, but few of the names are in the right places. Storyteller's privilege.

My thanks to Dennis Lopez, for teaching me the difference between boy trucks and girl trucks. My education is now complete.

My thanks to Mary Kallenberg, for so generously buying a Jayco popup for Liam.

My thanks to Jim Kemper, World's Greatest Meteorologist, for the storm.

As for Uuiliriq, his is a story I first heard from Mary Ann Chaney, who spent seven years of her childhood in Manokotak, a Yupik village forty miles west of Dillingham. Her parents, Van and Alice, were Bush teachers who believed strongly in the incorporation of the local culture into the curriculum. Whenever Van had to leave town on school business, he asked Yupik elder Simeon Bartman to take over his classes. Simeon's method of teaching was to tell stories, a medley of Yupik history and legend. The students didn't know it then, but he was passing on an oral tradition that goes back centuries. So, my very special thanks to Simeon Bartman, whose memory casts a long shadow.

NOTHING GOLD CAN STAY

ONE

A seven-foot Jayco popup camper perched unsteadily in the back of a Ford F250 truck is not the best of all possible beds for a six-foot-two-inch man. Even sleeping corner to corner, Liam's feet still stuck over the edge. There was no toilet, no shower and no place to hang his clothes, in particular his uniform, which, to uphold the dignity of the Alaska State Troopers, maintain the authority of the judicial system and invoke the might and majesty of the law, should at least begin the day unwrinkled.

On the other hand, the Ford F250 was parked in the driveway of Wyanet Chouinard. He had free access to Wy's kitchen, Wy's laundry room and Wy's bathroom. He had free access to Wy, when Tim wasn't home, as the door to Wy's bedroom was six feet down the hall from Wy's bathroom. Even if the bed in that bedroom was smaller than the one in the Jayco popup, Wy was in that bed, and he didn't really give a damn if his knees stuck out over one end of it and his head and shoulders the other.

Of course, Tim was home now, having returned from fish camp the day before to start school the day after Labor Day, so nights in Wy's bed, comfortable or not, would be severely curtailed. She'd made that clear last night. "No hanky-panky with the boy in the house."

1

"Is it hanky-panky if we're married?"

"We aren't married."

"Then let's get married."

"Not yet" was all she would say. "Not yet."

He rolled over on his back and stared at the ceiling fourteen inches from his nose, thinking of her less than fifty feet away, waking up in her bed. She slept in T-shirts, no panties. Handy, as he woke up with an erection pretty much every morning. He'd certainly put it to good use during the last month.

Not this morning. He cursed his way out of bed, stamped his legs into sweats and let himself out of the camper. He stretched and examined the southeastern horizon, where most of Newenham's weather came from. Partly cloudy, looked like. He lowered his eyes and stood for a moment regarding the Ford F250. At least it was a boy truck.

"A boy truck?" Wy had said.

"As opposed to a girl truck," Liam said.

"And a girl truck is—?"

"A smaller truck. Like a Ford Ranger, or a Dakota Sport."

She looked from the big brown truck to the little gray truck parked next to it. "Like my truck, do you mean? My truck's a girl truck?"

"No, your truck's an old man's truck."

"Why?"

"Because it's rusty and all the bumpers are dented and it needs a ring job and a front-end alignment and you have to hold the door on the canopy open with a bungee cord and add a quart of oil with every second or third gas tank, but it still runs. That makes it an old man's truck."

"Ah. So big trucks are boy trucks and little trucks are girl trucks, except for little trucks that need paint jobs, which are old men's trucks."

"Yes," he said. "Except for any truck of any size painted banana yellow."

"Oh."

"Or lipstick red."

"Uh-huh," she said.

"Then it's a girl truck."

"Right."

Except for the subject matter, it had been a repeat of one of those nothing and everything conversations they had so delighted in when they had first met, three years and a lifetime ago. In the interim, he had lost his wife and his son to a drunken driver, and very nearly his job as well, and she had acquired a new home, an air taxi and an adolescent son. They were still getting to know each other, feeling their way, on a direct heading, he hoped, for a permanent relationship, formalized by the local magistrate and vows, the whole nine yards. *Grow old along with me! The best is yet to be, The last of life, for which the first was made.* Browning, not his favorite poet, but this time right on the mark.

The front door of the house was unlocked, and he padded down the hall.

Someone was already in the bathroom. He looked around and saw that Tim's door was still closed. Employing the covert tactics taught him at the trooper academy in Sitka, he opened Tim's door and saw the boy deeply asleep beneath a tangle of blankets, a book open on the floor next to his bed, noise coming from a set of headphones that had slipped from his ears.

He grinned and closed the door.

The bathroom door locked from the inside. "Tim?" Wy's voice came from behind the shower curtain.

Liam stepped out of his sweats and pulled the curtain to one side. Wy blinked at him through the water running down her face. "Liam!"

He stepped into the tub and pulled her against him.

"You can't be in here!"

He lifted her and kneed her legs apart.

"Tim is right down the —"

He kissed her and slipped inside her in the same moment.

3

"—haaaaaall," she said. Her other leg came up to wrap around his waist. "Liam," she whispered.

"Wy," he whispered back.

"We shouldn't be doing this," she said weakly, and arched her back to take him all the way inside her. "Tim might wake up. He could come in, he might—"

He paused. "Want me to stop?" He kissed her, the water running warm down his back. "I'll stop," he whispered.

"Noooooo," she said, and after that they didn't talk.

Liam and Wy were both late for work, and Wy was later because on a whim, she had reversed back into the driveway and run into the house to put on her gold hoop earrings. Liam had given her those hoops during a four-day trip to Anchorage three years before. The trip hadn't ended well and she hadn't worn them since. Today seemed like a good day to resurrect them. She was unaware of just how complacent the smile on her face was when she left home for the second time that morning, headed for Mad Trapper Memorial Airport and the headquarters for Nushagak Air Taxi Service, which business consisted of one Piper Super Cub, one Cessna 180, one small shack and Wy, owner and chief pilot.

Nushagak Air Taxi held the contract to deliver the U.S. mail north of Newenham, to settlements scattered along and to the west of the Nushagak River. Bristol Bay Air Freight held the contract for the east side of the river and for the communities south and west from Newenham to Togiak. Dagfinn Grant, the owner and operator of Bristol Bay Air Freight and Wy's direct competitor, had been her nemesis ever since the United States Postal Service had decided to spread governmental largesse around and carved off a slice of Grant's mail route to award to Wy. It was only ten villages, with mail service once a week year-round, but to Wy's one-woman operation it meant the difference between paying attorney fees for Tim's adoption or letting Tim be remanded to the custody of his mother, who had nearly killed him the last time he was in her care.

4

To Finn Grant, it meant war. When Wy was approached by potential passengers on a day that was booked solid, she directed them to Bristol Bay Air Freight. When Grant was approached by potential passengers on a day that was booked solid, they were told that there were no other air taxis in Newenham and that he'd try to squeeze them in sometime later in the week. Grant's pilots were forbidden, on pain of instant dismissal, to give Wy any information about weather or strip conditions anywhere in their mutual flying area, and Grant's mechanic had been docked a day's pay when he sold Wy an oil filter at cost.

Mechanics by nature being contrary, cantankerous and fiercely independent creatures, this one had told Grant to take his job and put it where the sun don't shine and marched across the primary Newenham runway beneath the nose of a taxiing Alaska Airlines 737, there to offer his services to Wy, at a discount. She couldn't afford to hire him on full-time, but she was grateful for the offer, and when he set up his own shop she'd directed pilots his way. Troy Gillis had been servicing her Piper Super Cub and her Cessna 180 for a year now. The engines on both planes had never sounded better, and when a boat skipper with more malice than brains had ripped up the fabric of the wings on her Cub that spring, Troy had had them recovered in two weeks.

Of course, this was just something else for Finn Grant to hold against Wy. She kept sending him her overflow business in hopes that in time he would come to realize how ridiculous the feud was. He ran a single Otter and two Beavers. With her Super Cub, she could get into strips for which his aircraft were too big, and her Cessna hauled only a maximum of six people. Finn could haul twelve in the Otter alone.

They should have been working together because there was certainly enough business to go around. Wy had toyed with the notion of adding a second Cessna to her fleet, but that would have meant hiring on another pilot, and that would mean she would have to start a payroll and find a group health insurance provider and begin paying Social Security and unemployment. It might have been the smart thing to do as far as the business was concerned, but it would be the top of a slippery slope toward a desk for her, and from the age of sixteen, when she had first stepped into the cockpit of an aircraft, all she had ever wanted to do was fly. Her parents had wanted her to be a teacher, like them; fine, she had completed her degree in education, and the day after she had received her diploma had enrolled in flight school. They had sighed in disappointment but they hadn't stopped her. As her mother said to her father, she thought out of Wy's hearing, "She can teach from a wheelchair if she has to."

The postmaster, a short, bull-necked man with a too-tight collar and a red face, met her at the freight door. "You're late," he said.

"I know, I'm sorry, I got held up at home." Wy walked around to the back of her pickup and lowered the tailgate, and without further pleasantries helped the postmaster load the mail. Forms were signed in quadruplicate, and without another word the postmaster disappeared into the bowels of the big square building with the coppery-colored plastic siding. She cut him slack for his brusque manner; he was new to the job. The previous postmaster's wife had pled guilty to murder that summer, her very fancy lawyer having engineered a sentence that would have her out in eighteen months. Unable to hold his head up under the shame and disgrace of it all, her husband had given up the job of postmaster and joined the missionary corps of his church. Last Wy heard, he was on his way to Zimbabwe. She hoped the Zimbabweans were tolerant people.

She made it to the airport, calculated the weight of the freight and had to choose: two trips in the Cub or one trip in the Cessna. The Cessna was too big to get into two of the villages; the Cub too small to take all the mail at one go. Plus, she had a passenger scheduled, if he ever showed up.

Each destination had its own brown leather bag, strapped and locked; Kagati Lake had two and the two heaviest, but then that bunch of hard-core Bush dwellers had made an art form out of shipping everything by U.S. mail. Wy still remembered delivering cinder blocks for the foundation of a house, one at a time.

There was a single, small bag for Akamanuk. By its shape and weight, there was a prescription included with the letters. Probably Ted Gustafson's insulin, which came in every three months. Akamanuk's strip wasn't big enough for the Cessna, but she could get around that. Russell she could mail bomb, too. One trip and the Cessna it was, so long as her passenger didn't weigh three hundred pounds. She backed the Ranger LT around until the tailgate faced the cargo door. She had pulled the rear seats the night before and 68 Kilo was refueled and ready for loading.

She was topping off the tanks when she heard a car drive up and looked around to see Betty Reynolds pull her Ford Airstream van with the "Taxi" sign in the window up to the Chevron fuel pump.

"How you doing, Betty?"

"Hey, Wy. Got your passenger here. Sorry we're late, had to get help to get Rodney Graham out of the back."

"He passed out?"

Betty, a short, rotund woman with a square-cut bob of straight, fine brown hair and an unfiltered Camel fixed permanently to her lower lip, made a disgusted face. "My fault, I left the doors unlocked. He must have decided home was too far to crawl." The radio bolted to the dash crackled, and she answered briefly. "Gotta go. Good flying."

"Thanks."

Her passenger was a man with thinning gray hair combed carefully across his bald spot. He was carrying a buckled leather case that looked, she was pleased to see, heavier than he was. "Mr. Glanville?" she said, descending the stepladder.

"Ms. Chouinard?"

"Yes." They shook hands. "That van smelled vile," he said.

"I'm sure it did. Ready to go?"

Mr. Frederick Glanville of the Internal Revenue Service

looked apprehensively at 68 Kilo, and was clearly rethinking the attraction of the vile-smelling van. "Is this little plane what we're going in?"

"Yes."

"And you're the pilot?"

"I am, and we're late," Wy said briskly, "so let's get a move on."

Glanville climbed in, clutching his briefcase on his knees. She removed it, helped him fasten his seat belt, stowed the case next to the survival kit (water, matches, mosquito dope, a compass, flares, two Kit Kat bars and half a dozen paperbacks; another month and it would be water, matches, compass, flares, parka, bunny boots, a Sterno stove, a couple of aluminum pouches of freeze-dried food, an itty bitty booklight and half a dozen paperbacks), and in ten minutes they were airborne and headed northwest. It was ten a.m. and she was behind schedule, but she had a nice little ten-knot tailwind and she'd make up some time in the air.

Her first stop was Mable Mountain, a hop of forty miles, and Drake Henderson was waiting at the end of the strip with his truck and as much attitude as the Newenham postmaster. Next came the ranger station on Four Lake. She buzzed the station before landing so they would meet her at the strip. They'd be coming out for the winter in a week's time, but they'd be coming out with Dagfinn Grant, so she didn't have to dawdle while they made plans.

Next up was a zig to Akamanuk, perching precariously on the edge of the Nushagak River two big bends above Newenham. She buzzed the homestead, two buildings, a short airstrip crowded with trees and a tilled rectangle of earth with what looked like a very healthy crop of potatoes. Ted came out and peered skyward. She turned, banked, dropped down to fifty feet and opened the window, straining a little against the force of the air generated by their forward motion. Wind roared through the cabin and the sound of the engine doubled in decibel level. Over the headphones Wy heard Mr. Glanville, silent until now, whimper the tiniest bit, but he made no other sound and she wouldn't have listened if he had. First pass she dropped a half-used roll of toilet paper, the end straggling free, the roll falling about ninety feet from Ted's front door. She could do better than that, and turning and banking again, she came around for a second pass, this time waiting another fifteen seconds before she dropped the mailbag.

It thudded onto the ground ten feet in front of Ted. She painted a lazy eight in the sky while he fetched it and checked the contents. She'd included a box of sugar-free chocolates, his favorite ballast, and he waved his thanks. She waggled her wings in reply and zagged north, following the river to another river community, Kokwok, this one with a bigger strip, where she deposited a relieved Mr. Glanville along with Kokwok's mailbag.

Between Warehouse Mountain and Kemuk she buzzed the mining camp on Nenevok Creek and dropped another bundle of magazines neatly in front of the shack, but no one had come out before she had to pull up and get out of the way of any one of three mountains that were trying to snag the Cessna by the wing. It had been a long summer for the miner's wife, and Wy could still remember the forlorn look on her face the last time Wy had dropped off a load of freight. But they would be coming out, along with the rangers, the following weekend. Wy bet the wife was counting the seconds.

Next stop Rainbow, where Pete Cole had left the mail to be picked up in a bag leaning against a stump at the end of the strip, surely a violation of the Postal Code, but who was going to tell? Certainly not her, and she had no intention of remonstrating with Pete, either. Pete didn't like visitors, women or engine noise, in that order and without discrimination. How he'd managed to become postmaster for Rainbow remained a mystery, considering he sorted the mail in the little shack he'd constructed at the extreme edge of his property for that purpose, and left the door unlocked so that no one would come up to the cabin bothering him for the mail. Probably Rainbow wasn't on the postal inspector's regular route. She traded the outgoing mailbag for the incoming one and was in the air in ten minutes.

Weary River next, in and out in twenty minutes, then a flyover of Russell, where she just missed putting the mailbag onto Devon Russell's roof. Devon shook a friendly fist at her, and Wy ran up and back on the prop pitch in reply. It would have to be the Super Cub next Wednesday, when the mail had to be picked up as well as dropped off.

Then the longest hop, north by northwest fifty miles to Kagati Lake. Half an hour on the ground and she could head for home. She checked her airspeed and then her watch, and grinned. She'd be back in Newenham by five o'clock.

Banker's hours.

Liam drove to work in a distracted frame of mind, mostly because he'd left his mind at home. Living with Wy did that to him. Or not living with Wy, or whatever the hell it was they were doing.

Take the books. They were all over the house. There was a copy of *Harry Potter and the Prisoner of Azkaban* in the bathroom, which she and Tim were reading simultaneously, different-colored sticky notes marking each other's places. *The Human Factor* by David Beattie sat on the kitchen counter, a book that after the first careless perusal Liam never picked up again, as it dealt with the hazards of planes and the flying of. On the coffee table in the living room sat a beat-up British paperback edition of *Round the Bend*, a book that in spite of also being about flying Liam liked very much, possibly because the narrator was a mechanic and a good one and worked very hard to see that the planes he worked on never broke in the air. Liam was convinced that every plane he was on was going to break in the air.

In the bedroom there were *Ethan Frome, In the Electric Mist with Confederate Dead*, and *Persuasion*, from evidence of bookmarks being read simultaneously.

Liam read a lot, too, mostly history and poetry, but he'd never had books stacked back to back all going at once the way Wy did. He was pretty sure she had kept every book she'd ever read, too; there were bookcases in every room of the house including the bathroom, all flavors, essays by Carl Sagan, historical romances by Thomas B. Costain, the entire Oz collection.

He'd found her weeping one day the previous week, huddled over a much-thumbed copy of a mystery, one of a series. In this one the heroine's lover had died. She took it as a personal affront—"I can't believe she did that! How could she do that?"—and threw the book across the room, only to retrieve it a moment later and force him to listen to her read the death scene out loud. He was amazed at how involved she became in the story, and a little amused, but he was afraid that if he made some smart remark the next time she'd throw the book at him, so he kept his mouth shut.

It was something else to know about her, something they hadn't gotten around to sharing in that brief time they had had together three years before, something he could add to his growing store of information. He wanted to know everything about her, every single thing, from the way her toes curled when he bit the sole of her foot to the way she played air mandolin with John Hiatt, to the way she mothered Tim, the adopted son in the room down the hall.

A green Chevy Suburban pulled out suddenly from a side street and wavered from center line to shoulder, put on a brief spurt of speed, slowed down, speeded up again.

Well, hell. Liam hit the lights and the siren.

The Suburban put on another burst of speed and, just about the time he thought he might have a Hollywood car chase on his hands, screeched over to the side of the road and slammed on the brakes, skidding another four feet in the loose gravel before coming to a halt somewhat perpendicular to the line of traffic.

Liam got out of the Blazer. The driver got out of the Suburban. "Stay in your vehicle, ma'am," Liam said, but she ignored him, walking toward him with a step as straight as the course she had been driving.

He sighed. But this day had begun with such promise, he thought, struggling to master a reminiscent grin when the woman reached him. The smell of alcohol got to him first.

She stopped four feet away, glaring at him and weaving a little on her feet. This time he had no trouble holding back a smile. "Amelia, did you have breakfast at the Breeze Inn again?"

"Damn right," she said, blinking rapidly, as if trying and failing to focus. "I can do anything I wanna, I'm the councilman's wife."

"Yes, you are," Liam said, taking her by one arm.

She pulled free. "You know which councilman?" she said belligerently.

"Yes," he said, taking her arm again.

"That's Councilman Darren Gearhart," she said. "*H-a-r-t.* No *e.*"

"Yes," he said. This time she followed him to the passenger door of the Blazer.

"I'm his wife," she said as he sat her down. She leaned back against the headrest and fell asleep as easily and instantly as a child.

"Amelia, Amelia, Amelia," he said. "What the hell am I going to do with you?"

The letter of the law required that he take her into custody.

So he took her to Bill.

TWO

Kagati Lake, September 1

Opal Nunapitchuk was a happy woman. Fifty-six years old, with three children and eight grandchildren, she was the postmistress of the tiny (population thirty-four in summer) village of Kagati Lake. A corner of her living room, furnished with a wooden counter polished smooth by forty years of elbows and a cubby-holed shelf fixed to the wall, was devoted to the getting and sending of letters, magazine subscriptions, bank statements, utility bills, Mother's Day cards and birthday and Christmas packages between the citizens of Kagati Lake and the outside world, and to the upholding of the generally fine standards of the United States Postal Service. People could sneer all they wanted to, but in Opal's opinion the best federal service her taxes provided was the post office and priority mail (delivery guaranteed in two days for three dollars and twenty cents). She loved being the bearer of good tidings, and she was ready with Russian tea and Yupik sympathy when the tidings were bad. She was a thoroughly round peg in a thoroughly round hole and she knew it.

The residents of Kagati Lake, like those of any small Bush village, relied almost entirely on the United States Postal Service to keep them in touch with their friends and families and, indeed, with the rest of the nation and the world itself. Frequently it sup-

13

plied more than that, in ways the Inspector General of the Postal Service had never dreamed. Mark Pestrikoff had engaged himself to be married and, deciding a one-room plywood and tarpaper shack might not put his best foot forward with his new bride, had flown into Anchorage, bought the makings for a two-bedroom, one-bathroom house and mailed it home. He didn't have time for the Nushagak River to thaw, he'd told Opal, and postage was cheaper than freight anyway. Construction on the house had lasted longer than the marriage. Mark was still working on the former. Opal had just yesterday taken shipment of two five-gallon buckets of Sheetrock mud, C.O.D., and they sat on Opal's porch, tagged and waiting for Mark to pick them up.

Dave Aragon called his orders into Johnson Tire by radio, and in due course tires appeared at the post office, studded snow tires for winter driving and street tires for summer, although the only road in Kagati Lake was the ten-mile stretch between the lake and the dump, and it was neither paved nor maintained during the winter, so Dave didn't really need the snow tires. Hell, he didn't really need the truck, as the village sat right on the lake. People got around in boats during the summer and on snow machines during the winter. Half the people in Kagati Lake had no driver's license.

And of course groceries came in by air. You could always tell when someone had made a Costco run to Anchorage by the way boxes of Campbell's soup and pilot bread flooded in, always with the General Mail Facility's postmark on them. Opal spared a sympathetic thought for the people at the post office at Anchorage International Airport. They were people who earned their paychecks. She'd heard that on April 15 they dedicated employees full-time to standing on the road leading into the post office just to accept income tax filings. After that, she started staying open late on April 15 herself, so she wouldn't feel like a slacker.

Opal sprayed Pledge on the counter and paused for a moment to admire the flex of muscle in her upper arm. Not many women her age could display a muscle that firm, an upper arm that toned. No sagging, no spare flesh, just a smooth covering of muscle and bone. She flexed once more, shook her shining cap of hair into place and swept the dustcloth over the counter. It had been made of burlwood from a gnarled old spruce felled on Josh Demske's homestead, and hand-hewn by her father into the counter she sold stamps over today. She was proud of the workmanship, and of the family history embodied in the dark brown sheen of the wood.

Her living room was filled with mementos of family and friends, most of them Alaskan in origin and some very valuable. There was the pair of ivory tusks carved with walrus heads and polished to a high gloss, yellowing now with age. A nugget of gold out of Kagati Creek, a rough lump the size of her youngest grandchild's fist. A series of Yupik, Aleut and Inupiat masks, wonderfully carved and adorned with beads and feathers, human spirits laughing out of animal eyes. There was an upright, glass-fronted case filled with old rifles, too; one of which was said to have been brought north by Wyatt Earp when he took the marshal's job in Nome. A mustard-yellow upright piano, ivory keys worn to the touch, occupied the place of honor in one corner.

Of all her children, her daughter Pearl was the nearest to her heart, and the most accomplished on the piano. She was with the rest of the family at fish camp now, and would not be home for long before going Outside to school. Opal sighed, sad and worried at once. She and Leonard had done their best; home schooling with an insistence of a B or better average, a firm grounding in the Methodist faith. Each of the children could skin a beaver, roast a moose heart, kill a bear, reduce the trajectory of a bullet fired from a .30-06 rifle to mathematical formula, even allowing for drift. They could bake bread, grow potatoes, keep a radio schedule, perform CPR, read. Opal just didn't know how many of those skills would prove useful to Pearl Outside. The boys had chosen to remain home and take up the subsistence lifestyle of their parents, fishing, hunting, trapping. Andy and Joe had married girls from Koliganek and Newenham, respectively, although Newenham was an awfully big city compared to Kagati Lake and Opal and Leonard worried over how Sarah would settle in. Both boys had built homes north of their parents' homestead, proving up on their state land in three years instead of the required seven. She was proud of them both, although she tried not to show it too much. She didn't want the boys to get swelled heads.

She tried not to think of Ruby, her second daughter and fourth child, and as always, she failed. So she was glad when the door to the living room opened. She looked up. "Come on, you know the mail plane won't be here until eleven, I—oh."

A man she had never seen before stood in the doorway, short, stocky, dressed in faded blue jeans and a dark blue windbreaker. A red bandanna was tied round his forehead in a failed attempt to discipline a tremendous bush of dirty grayish blond hair that repeated itself in tufts curling out from the neck of his shirt and the cuffs of his sleeves. He carried a dark blue interior frame pack, fabric stained and worn at the seams with long use, with a shot gun in a sheath fastened to the back.

Opal was used to waiting on hermits, as this area of the Bush supported more than its share, and she smiled, teeth very white in her tanned and healthy face. "Hi there," she said. "What can I do for you?"

He looked around the room slowly and carefully, missing nothing, and suddenly the hair on the back of her neck stood up.

"Nice place you've got here." His voice was rough, almost rusty-sounding, as if he didn't talk much and wasn't used to it when he did.

"Thanks," she said, watching him. "My father built it. Felled the logs, finished them, built the place from the ground up."

"He the collector?" The man walked over to the nugget, sitting in a place of honor on a little table of its own.

It was nothing a hundred other people hadn't done over the years, but all at once Opal was realizing that she was all alone in the house, and pretty much alone in the village, as most people were at fish camp, waiting for the last salmon of the season to make it this far north. Her husband and children weren't due back until the weekend. "Yes. What can I help you with? Did you want to check general delivery for mail? I'll need to see some identification."

He touched the nugget with one forefinger, moved on to a hair clasp made from ivory and baleen in the shape of a whale. "No, you won't have to do that." He swung his pack down from his shoulders and pulled out a pistol. He didn't aim it at her, or even in her general direction, let it hang at the end of his arm, dangling at his side.

"You have to come with me," he said, and smiled at her.

Newenham, September 1

Bill's Bar and Grill was one of those prefabricated buildings common in the Alaskan Bush, housing post offices, ranger stations, grocery stores, trooper posts and not a few private homes. The roof was always tin, the siding always plastic in blue or green or brown, the front porch always cedar that weathered gray in a year. Insulation was problematic at best, as during winter the metal siding contracted and shrank from doors and window frames alike, resulting in enormous heating bills. In summer, windows had the occasional alarming habit of bursting unexpectedly from their frames, and doors either wouldn't open in the first place or wouldn't close again if they did.

September was a good time for the prefabs, neither too cold nor too hot. Bill's had a chipper, almost cheerful air. The front porch was swept, the windows clean, the neon beer signs glowing and the last of the nasturtiums bursting into bloom next to the porch. Liam escorted Amelia Gearhart up the stairs and in the door. Bill was washing glasses behind the bar. "Oh hell," she said when she saw them coming. She was over sixty, silver of hair, blue of eye and zaftig. She knew it, too, and today had chosen to accent her manifest charms with blue jeans cinched in at the waist by a woven leather belt and a tight pink T-shirt which purported to advertise last May's Jazz Festival in New Orleans but which really was advertising Bill.

Moses Alakuyak sat at the bar. Too tall for a Yupik, eyes too Asian for a white, he was a mongrel and gloried in it. "Ever see a purebred dog, missy?" he'd been heard to tell some poor tourist who had wandered in off the Newenham street. "Nervous, stupid, half the time got them some epilepsy or hip problems or some other goddamn thing. Always barking, always jumping on you or whoever else is in range, can't trust them around kids or anybody else, either. Give me a good old Heinz 57 mutt every time for smarts and good manners." He'd glared down at the hapless tourist. "Same goes for people. Mongrel horde, my ass. We'll inherit the earth, not the goddamn meek."

The tourist had murmured something soothing and drifted slowly but surely out the door. Anyone in Newenham could have told her she was in no danger; Mount Moses in full eruption was a common sight, worthy of attention and respect, but it was never necessary to get the women and children off the streets.

"Married five months," Moses said, looking at Amelia, "and now she's drinking her breakfast." He said something in Yupik that sounded less than complimentary. Amelia wasn't too drunk to understand, and colored to the roots of her hair.

"Knock it off, Moses," Bill said. She looked at Liam. "What do you want to do, Liam?"

He sighed and looked around the bar. It was empty except for them, but it was going on ten-thirty and it wouldn't be long before the lunch crowd showed. "Hell, Bill, I don't know. This is the third time this week."

"Want to swear out an arrest warrant?"

An arrest warrant. State of Alaska, plaintiff, versus Amelia Gearhart, defendant. To any peace officer or other authorized person, you are commanded to arrest the defendant and bring the defendant before the nearest available judicial officer without unnecessary delay to answer to a complaint/information/indictment charging the defendant with violation of Alaska Statute 28.35.030, driving a motor vehicle while under the influence of alcohol. If Liam requested one, Bill would sign it; hell, she wouldn't even have to take Liam's oath, Amelia was her own worst prosecution witness. The criminal process would begin, he would arrest Amelia, Bill would set bail and order Amelia to court, and she would be charged, arraigned, tried, convicted and sentenced. DWI was a Class A misdemeanor and carried a mandatory sentence and fine. More important, she would have a record, and penalties escalated for repeat offenders.

He looked at her. She was just a kid, seventeen years old, a devout Moravian who had dropped out of school to marry without her parents' approval. Her husband saw no reason for marriage to interfere with his previous lifestyle, which had included the determined chasing of skirts as far up the Nushagak as Butch Mountain. He spent more time in the bag than out of it and never refused a fight, and Liam knew it was only a matter of time before he had to pick up Darren on his own DWI. He'd won election to the city council by standing rounds for the regulars at Bill's and the Breeze for a week straight before the voters went to the polls, and had thus far spent most of his time in office trying to change the local ordinance governing bar closing hours, at present set at two a.m., to five a.m.

Amelia stumbled in place, and her hair fell back from one cheek. Moses' lips tightened into a thin line, and Liam stretched out a hand to raise Amelia's chin, revealing a bruise high up on her left cheek. "Did Darren hit you, Amelia?" he said.

She pulled away. "I'm the councilman's wife," she said, enunciating her words with care.

"Yeah, yeah, you're the councilman's wife," Moses said, and stood up to grab her and muscle her into a chair. "You're not gonna arrest her," he told Liam shortly, "and you're not gonna charge her," he said to Bill, "so don't stand around with your thumbs up your asses like you are."

"You have an alternative suggestion?" Bill said, irritated.

"She's going to hurt herself eventually, Moses," Liam said.

"She did that when she married the jerk," Moses replied.

Liam remembered the evening in Bill's in May, the first day he met the shaman, when Amelia and Darren had come to Moses for his blessing. Moses, drunk and verbally abusive, had withheld any such thing, and at the time Liam had thought him harsh. "The problem is, she might hurt somebody else at the same time," he said now.

"I'll handle it," Moses said.

"How?" Bill said.

"I said I'll handle it!"

Bill refused to be outshouted. "HOW?"

Moses glared at her. "I'll take her up to fish camp, dry her out, talk some sense into her."

If it were possible for Bill to pout, she would have pouted. "But you just got back."

Moses' expression changed. "Turn the bar over to Dottie and Paul, and come with."

Bill stood very still for a moment, and then leaned across the bar and swept Moses into a lavish kiss, to which he responded wholeheartedly.

Liam examined the king net hanging from the ceiling for holes and found it in himself to be grateful there was a bar between Moses and Bill. For two people who were older than God and who woke up nearly every morning in the same bed, their enthusiasm for each other never seemed to wane.

He thought of Wy, of waking up in the same bed every morning with her, and found himself looking forward to being older than God himself.

Bill pulled back, her face flushed. "Well, fish camp ain't New Orleans, but it's not a bad second best."

Moses responded with what could only be described as a salacious grin. "We'll have to boat you home, lady, because you won't be able to walk."

❊   ❊   ❊

20

When Liam got to the post, Prince was already there and in his chair, typing up a report. He nodded at the computer. "What have you got?"

She made a face. "Elizabeth Katelnikoff got off the night shift at AC this morning at eight a.m. like she always does, and got home to find Art Inga and Dave Iverson wedged into the window of her bedroom, half in, half out."

"What, they were stuck?"

"You could say that," Prince said, considering the matter with judicial impartiality. "Seems they'd had a little too much to drink last night at a party at Tatiana Anayuk's. You know about the permanent party at Tatiana's, don't you?"

"Been invited a time or two."

"Yeah, me, too," said Prince, who'd only been assigned to Newenham two months before, but appeared to be integrating into the local population without strain. "Anyway, Art and Dave decide they're both in love with Elizabeth and fight a duel to see who gets her. Tatiana—who was not happy to be woken up at ten this morning, and from whom you may receive a complaint later today—says nobody won, and after that she closed the party down."

"What time?"

"About four a.m., she said. Art and Dave staggered off, she thought down to their boat in the harbor."

"But no," Liam said.

"But no," Prince agreed. She was a tall, lithe woman with deep blue eyes and short dark curls. She was slim enough to look good in a uniform, and on duty, at least, had a crisp, formal manner that did little to conceal her enthusiasm for the job. Fresh out of the academy, she was ready, willing and eager to serve and to protect, preferably at gunpoint.

She'd also had a thing going with Liam's father during Charles' visit to Newenham in July, but that was something Liam preferred not to think about if he could possibly avoid it, which he couldn't. It was hell when your father's sex life was better than your own. Although that wasn't the case now, he thought, and had to repress that grin again. "How did they wind up stuck in Elizabeth's window?"

"Near as they can remember, they thought it would be a dandy idea to serenade her. When she didn't come out, understandable as she was stocking shelves at AC at the time, they decided to crawl in. They made it halfway, and passed out cold."

Liam didn't bother to hide the grin this time. "Must be a little window."

"Nah. Both Art and Dave could stand to lose a little weight."

"Why didn't the local police respond to it?"

"Roger Raymo's in Anchorage testifying at trial, and Cliff Berg just pulled a thirty-six-hour shift and his wife says he's in bed and staying there."

"Where have you got them?"

"Over to the city jail."

"You going to arrest them?"

She looked surprised. "Of course. Drunk and disorderly, breaking and entering, resisting arrest."

"Art Inga resisted arrest?"

Prince grinned. "Well, I don't think he would have if Dave hadn't shoved him so hard he fell backwards out of the window when I woke them up. He did come up swinging, though."

Liam hung up his hat. "Is Elizabeth pressing charges?"

"She was kind of lukewarm about it at first, but then Art tried to kiss her, and since he'd thrown up at some point during the night on the floor beneath her window, she wasn't pleased." She saved the file and hit the print button. He motioned her up and out of his chair and took her place. The printer coughed into awareness and he reached over to turn it off before it began to print.

"Sir?"

Liam sat back. "There's the letter of the law, Prince, and there's the spirit. Art Inga and Dave Iverson have been in love with Elizabeth Katelnikoff since all three of them were in high school together."

"So?"

"So she can't make up her mind, she goes out with one and then the other and then switches back and then switches back again."

"What's that got to do with them breaking into her house?" Prince demanded. "They did break into her house. Sir."

"Yes, they did, but this charge will never make it to trial. Elizabeth will never testify against them, and besides, you won't get an arrest warrant out of Bill because she'll laugh you out of her bar first."

A short silence. "Drunk and disorderly?" she said, almost pleadingly.

"Sorry." Liam shook his head, and deleted Prince's report. "Unless Tatiana made a complaint?"

Reluctantly, she shook her head.

Liam cocked an interrogatory eyebrow.

There was a brief pause.

"Hell," Prince said.

"Relax," Liam said dryly, "you had eight solved murders on your record before you'd been in town a week."

"I know," she said glumly.

"Even somebody named for Wonder Woman ought to be happy with that."

"Up yours," she said, still glum.

He grinned at her. "We'll try to scare up another one for you sometime soon."

Later, he would remember saying those words, and curse himself for a fool. Now he said, "Anything else?"

"Yeah, the phone was ringing when I walked in the door. Some guy, name of Montgomery, looking for—"

"Lyle Montgomery, looking for his daughter," Liam said with a sigh, and glanced at the calendar. First of September, first of the month. Right on schedule.

"You know him?"

"He's got a daughter missing. Name of Cheryl." Liam opened

one of the desk drawers and rummaged through it, producing a file. "She was canoeing alone through the Wood-Tikchik State Park. Finn Grant dropped her off at the Four Lakes Ranger Station. She had a full load of supplies, plus the canoe. The rangers gave her a map and the standard warnings. She left around noon of that day, with the stated intention of camping her way up to Outuchiwenet Mountain Lodge. She had scheduled a fly-out from there with Grant at noon two weeks from the day he put her down."

"And she didn't show?"

"No."

"When was that?"

"August."

"Just last month?"

"No, that's the problem. August 1997."

"Oh." Prince was silent for a moment. "And her father's been calling ever since?"

"He's called the first of the month every month since I got here. I assume he had been doing so before. Corcoran didn't stick around long enough after I showed up to fill me in."

"Doesn't it say in the file?"

He took a last look at the photograph stapled inside the folder. She was a looker, Cheryl Montgomery, a long fall of straight fair hair, large blue eyes with ridiculously long lashes, a dimple in her right cheek. Born in Juneau, a graduate of the University of Alaska at Fairbanks, she had been a wildlife biologist working for the Alaska Department of Fish and Game in Anchorage. Twenty-six years old. A daughter who at the very least deserved a phone call once a month.

Just another overconfident backpacker swallowed up by the Alaskan wilderness. He closed the file and tossed it to Prince. "Corcoran wasn't into keeping up with the paperwork. I talked to John Barton about it, and he said the family was all over the Wood-Tikchik for four months. They fought us suspending the search. And they fought the presumptive death hearing."

"And now her father calls us the first of every month, checking to see if we've found her."

"Yeah."

Prince closed the file and tossed it back. "Okay, you can be boss."

"Gee, thanks," Liam said, but he knew what she meant. Next to domestic disputes, reporting deaths to surviving family and friends was the law officer's least favorite job.

The phone rang and they were called out to a shooting at a home eleven miles up the road to Icky, which turned out to be an accidental discharge by a thirty-six-year-old man who shot himself in the hand with a .401 shotgun while taking it down from an overcrowded gun rack. His five-year-old daughter had been standing next to him at the time, and had caught some buckshot in her shoulder. Joe Gould, Newenham's local and it would seem only paramedic, judging from the many crime scenes where Liam had encountered him, was already there, soothing the girl with a cherry Tootsie Roll Pop as he picked pellets out of her shoulder with surgical tweezers. She was sitting on her mother's lap. The mother would occasionally glare over her shoulder at the father, who sat in a corner, largely ignored, weeping and wailing over a hand that would never pull the trigger on a weapon again.

Prince got the story out of the man (between sobs) and observed to Liam, "I'd call this a violation of basic safety rules, wouldn't you, sir?"

"I would, and I'd arrest him for it, too," Liam said, so they did and brought him before Bill for arraignment. Bill flayed what skin the guy had left with a blistering indictment of his lack of judgment, and they delivered him into the tender hands of Mamie Hagemeister at the local jail, who turned out to be a bosom buddy of the guy's wife and godmother to his daughter. They found out later that she didn't feed him for two days.

Meanwhile, back at the post, the door opened and a woman walked in. She was short, with the thick-waisted build of the Bay Yupik. Her eyes were dark and narrow, her expression wary. She was dressed in shabby slacks and a windbreaker, wore no makeup, and her long black hair was clean and neatly combed.

Prince strode forward, every inch the trooper. "Yes, ma'am? How may we help you?"

The woman pulled a piece of paper from her windbreaker pocket. "I have this court order," she said. "From Anchorage."

"What's your name, ma'am?" Prince said, and took the paper.

"Natalie Gosuk," the woman replied, and Liam stopped lounging back in his chair and sat up straight. "That paper says I get to see my son."

Prince finished reading the order. "Yes, it does," she said, and passed it off to Liam.

He scanned it briefly. Judge Renee Legere had signed the order. It was legal, all right. He folded the order and handed it back to Natalie Gosuk, taking his first real look at the woman. She wasn't saying much, letting the court order speak for her. She kept her eyes lowered, but the curve of her mouth was set and resentful.

Four times she'd been accused of assaulting a minor child, and Judge Legere had allowed visitation anyway. It was so easy in Anchorage, looking at the perp across a room, a perp cleaned up and sobered up and scared into something approaching civil behavior, it was so easy to judge them human and worthy of the rights of other humans, of second, third, fourth, fifth chances, and besides, the jails were all full. So what if she smacked her kid around a little? She was rehabilitated, look at her standing there next to her lawyer, all neat and tidy and vowing repentance and an ache in her heart for the son lost to her.

Out here, where the human rubber met the road, there was a different view. Here one lived next to the victims, broken, bleeding, bloodied, terrified, most of them so intimidated they couldn't even be brought to testify.

Since it didn't look like he was going to say anything, Prince stepped in. "Was there a problem with the order, Ms. Gosuk?"

"She won't let me see him."

"Who won't?"

"The woman my son lives with. She won't let me in the door of the house. I want you to make her let me in."

Prince looked at Liam. When he said nothing, she asked the woman, "Have you shown her this document?"

Natalie Gosuk hesitated. "Not yet."

"Show it to her," Prince advised. "If she won't let you see the boy, come to us."

"This paper says she has to," Natalie Gosuk insisted.

"Yes," Prince said. "It does. Limited, supervised visitation. It means you can see him but you can't take him out of the house and you can't see him alone."

The woman's eyes shifted. "They told me."

"Call us if you have any trouble."

The door closed behind her with a soft sigh. Prince looked at Liam. "Domestic disputes," she said with loathing. "God, how I hate them. Give me an old-fashioned ax murder any day." He remained silent. "Whose kid was she talking about, do you know? Who's the 'she' in 'she won't let me see him'?"

Liam looked at Prince. "Go on down to the jail and give Art and Dave a talking-to and turn them loose."

"We could leave them where they are until their twenty-four is up." Suspects had to be released after twenty-four hours if no arrest warrant had been sworn out against them.

He pointed a finger at her. "Better." He stood and reached for his hat. "I've got a few errands to run. I'll take lunch and then come back and relieve you for yours." He paused at the door and grinned at her. "Monthly report's due today." She groaned, and he added, "Hey, I'm the corporal, you're the trooper. Low man does the paperwork."

The answering smile on her face faded as soon as the door closed behind him, and Prince was left to wonder what had produced the lines of strain around her boss's eyes, lines that hadn't been there when he first walked in the door.

THREE

Nuklunek Bluff, September 1

John Kvichak and Teddy Engebretsen had been sworn companions since kindergarten. They'd studied grammar together beneath the beady eye of Mrs. Johnson in the fourth grade, stood shoulder to shoulder against the bully boys in the seventh grade, they'd lusted after the same girls in high school and they'd graduated together attired beneath their caps and gowns in the same jeans and gray sweatshirts, ready to party as soon as the diplomas were given out and the caps tossed into the air. They fished salmon together, hunted caribou and moose together, trapped beaver together. When they reached legal age, they drank together. It was said in Newenham, their hometown, that they would never marry because they could never find a woman capable of putting up with both of them, and although the saying began as a joke, there was probably some truth to it.

They owned a drift netter together now, the *Isabella Rose*, named for both of their mothers. Isabella, Teddy's mom, won the coin toss for whose name came first. Rose, John's mom, took it well, frying up a panful of bread and bringing it down to the christening. Of course, it was all charred to a crisp. Isabella laughed and laughed, and made John and Teddy eat up every bite.

Each fall, after the fishing season was over and the *Isabella Rose* was hosed down and put into dry dock for the winter, John and Teddy would go hunting together in the Wood River Mountains. They concentrated on moose and caribou, but took time out on occasion to bring out the shotguns and go for geese, ptarmigan and spruce hens.

Neither one of them was a pilot, so they chartered Wy Chouinard to fly them into their preferred hunting area, the long, level plateau between the broad plain that sloped down into the Nushagak River in the east and the Wood River Mountains in the west, where a small but fecund herd of caribou fattened on lichen, where the occasional moose wandered up the narrow chasms and canyons. Birdlife was plentiful, and one year Teddy even brought down a brown bear with a beautiful coat, which now hung in a place of honor on his mother's living room wall.

So long as they stayed sober they were responsible hunters, harvesting what they killed, packing out the meat, taking no more than they could eat in a winter, in no way giving Newenham's fish and game trooper Charlene Taylor cause to arrest them for violating the wanton waste law.

They had, however, come to feel somewhat proprietary about the bluff: the Kvichak-Engebretsen Private Hunting Preserve. Hikers and campers, thinking they were well within the boundaries of the Wood River-Tikchik State Park, had occasionally run across John and Teddy's path and been apprised of their error. Once a couple had returned from a hike up Kanuktik Ridge to find their tent slashed and all their belongings scattered in the creek. "Could have been a bear," Charlene told Liam. Two others had had their canoe shot out from under them on Three Lake. "Probably not a bear," Liam told Charlene. A group of Great White Hunters in the tender care of Dagfinn Grant had been in hot pursuit of a bull moose sporting what looked like a record rack when suddenly gunshots fired from an unknown source had spooked the bull, who was last seen heading across the Middle Fork at a clip that would put a four-wheeler to shame.

29

Charlene had been waiting for John and Teddy at the airport that time, alongside a steaming Finn Grant, mustache crawling down either side of his mouth like Fu Manchu's. "Gosh," Teddy said, eyes wide, "I didn't hear anything. Did you hear anything, John?"

John shook his head. "Nope."

Teddy turned to Grant. "Sorry we can't help, Finn. I think it's just awful the way some people go around popping off guns in the woods, don't you? Somebody could get hurt out there."

Grant threw a punch at him, which Charlene stepped in to block, and for a few halcyon moments Teddy and John basked in the delightful prospect of pressing charges for assault. "Don't push your luck, boys," Charlene said dryly, so they loaded John's pickup with meat and headed into town to distribute their haul, to the loud hosannas of both families. Times were tough in Newenham, the salmon catch down and down again for two years running. For some families, if they didn't get their moose they didn't eat meat that winter.

It was serious business, providing meat for their families, and John and Teddy took it seriously. Mostly. Which meant that sometimes they took beer, and sometimes they didn't.

This time they had.

That morning they had dropped a bull that would provide them with six hundred pounds of meat, dressed, something to celebrate, John said, and Teddy agreed. They'd already got their caribou, hanging in quarters now from trees around camp. There were four dozen ptarmigan in canvas bags, and another dozen geese, gutted but not plucked.

"We deserve a beer," John said, standing and stretching. The moose was gutted and skinned and hanging next to the caribou. The heart, tongue and liver were set to one side and steamed gently in the crisp fall air. Liver and onions tonight, he thought, smacking his lips, and pictured his mother's face when he came in the door. "You're a good boy, John," she always said, whether he brought home the meat or not. This fall, he felt he'd earned it.

"Hell," Teddy said, "we deserve six," and opened the case of Miller Genuine Draft with bloodstained hands.

Newenham, September 1

Liam did what he had to do without compunction, without reconsideration, without, in fact, any thought of his sworn oath to uphold the law and constitution and parental rights. He ordered his usual fatburger and fries at Bill's and ate them to the accompaniment of Bill's countdown of Things to Be Done While I'm Gone. The recipient of all this good advice, Dottie Takak, took it as she took most things in life, stolidly, silently, without question or expression on her wide brown face. She'd been cooking for Bill for nine years, she'd subbed for Bill when Bill went on Costco runs to Anchorage, when Bill and Moses took time out for trysts during walrus hunts or purse seining or New Year's jaunts to the Kenai Princess Lodge, where once Bill claimed she had actually talked Moses onto cross-country skis. Dottie listened stoically as Bill told her not to forget to restock the beer, wash the glasses, sweep the floor, unplug the jukebox (currently floating Ivan Neville's "Why Can't I Fall in Love" out over the room, definitely not one of Liam's many problems, so he tuned it out), scrub the grill, take out the trash and lock the doors, the front and the safe's. Count the till each night, keep each day's take in a separate envelope, messages should be entered in the Daily Diary for Bill to peruse when she chose to return. As far as magistrating went, she'd keep a schedule at ten a.m. every morning on the shortwave at the fish camp; tell the hyperventilating to call her there. If there was a murder, she might come back. Otherwise, they could wait.

Finally Bill ran down. Dottie, still silent, took the list and vanished into the kitchen. Bill looked at Liam. "You weren't gone long." She found a saltshaker and passed it over the counter.

He anointed his fries. Could never have too much salt on potatoes and popcorn. He could feel Bill's eyes on his face as he continued to eat.

"What happened?" she said.

He rubbed a fry in the pile of salt on his plate. "Case I've got."

"You weren't gone long enough to acquire a new case," she said. "Must be one of the old ones."

He ate the fry.

"What, I'm supposed to guess?"

"No," he said, swallowing. He put half his burger down, his appetite gone. "Just this woman, beat up on her son, she came back into town carrying a court order says she can visit him. It's limited, supervised, but . . ."

"What pea-brain judge signed that order?"

"Legere."

Bill's snort said that she shared Liam's opinion of the jurist in question.

"The kid's terrified of her, doesn't want to have anything to do with her, and he's just starting to settle in where he's at now. This is really going to shake him up."

"Who's got him?"

Liam raised his eyes. "Wy."

There was a long silence. Liam watched Bill's face as realization dawned. "Natalie Gosuk's the one with the court order?"

He nodded. "She's sober, too, who knows how long. But she's got the order, she knows what it means and she's going to use it. I think she'll run off with him first chance she gets."

Bill's eyes narrowed.

"Sooner or later, she'll start drinking again, like she always does. But for the moment, she's here, and she'll be knocking on Wy's door, wanting to see Tim." He looked down at his plate. "Too bad Moses brought him in from fish camp. School doesn't start until Monday, and Natalie never lasts longer in town than three or four days."

She spoke carefully and deliberately. "You miserable, manipulative, Machiavellian son of a bitch."

He nodded with no particular pleasure.

She tossed the bar rag and turned to go. Over her shoulder she said, "You want to be a social worker, you better lose the trooper uniform."

FOUR

Nenevok Creek, September 1

Rebecca Hanover was a reluctant gold miner.

"I like to knit," she had told her friend Nina in Anchorage in April. "I like to bead and quilt and cross-stitch."

"You can do all those things at the mine."

"Yes, but I like to do all those things in front of a roaring fire in a stone fireplace with an episode of *Buffy the Vampire Slayer* on the television. I like getting up during the commercials and going to a bathroom that has a flush toilet."

"Ah. Then it isn't beading you like, it's indoor plumbing."

Rebecca refused to be diverted. "I like meeting you for coffee and canella at City Market on Saturday mornings." She raised her cup and gestured at the large room full of loud cheerful voices and the mingled aromas of Kaladi Brothers coffee, Italian sausage sandwiches and spicy sesame chicken. In the parking lot cars were idling, waiting for an empty space. "I like people. I like eavesdropping on their conversations. Like that guy?" She pointed with her chin. "He's a superior court judge, and that isn't his wife. Before you got here they were planning a weekend in Seattle, until he remembered that was the weekend of his anniversary. She hasn't spoken to him since."

Nina shifted in her chair and managed a covert, over-the-shoulder look. "Isn't that Shelby Arvidson, the anchor on Channel 6?"

"Yes, it is, and you'll notice, she's still here."

"Your point being?"

"The weekend may still be on, anniversary or no. And you see the couple in the corner? The dark woman in the red T-shirt with the tall blond guy?"

"Uh-huh."

"That's Lois Barcott."

"The defense lawyer?"

"Yeah. And that's Harry Arner, the district attorney. I bet they're cutting a deal on the Baldridge case."

"I love having a friend who's a legal secretary," Nina said. "Who's Baldridge?"

"Used to be a banker, accused of embezzlement and fraud. He made nine million dollars in unsecured loans to people who turned out to be close personal friends of his."

Nina did her best to look shocked. "Goodness me."

"The bank went under. The trouble is the state has a lousy case, no witnesses and a lot of boring paperwork. I bet Arner holds out for dismissal of all charges. But, like I was saying."

"Rebecca. I thought you told me Mark was really excited about this placer mine you'd bought."

"He bought it," Rebecca said, an edge to her voice.

"Ah." Nina examined the coffee in her cup with close attention.

"Without even asking me if I wanted to spend the whole summer out there, he goes and buys a gold mine. God, Nina, I don't even know where it is."

"Did he say?"

"West of Anchorage, north of Bristol Bay."

"That takes in a lot of territory. Is there a town nearby?"

Rebecca gave her head a gloomy shake, her fine blond hair escaping its ponytail to fall into wisps around a face that had been described variously as an angel's (her mother), Hayley Mills' (her father), Grace Kelly's (Nina, enviously), and "fucking drop-dead gorgeous" (Mark). Her figure had been described as "a little too plump, dear" (her mother), "healthy" (her father), "stacked" (Nina, enviously), "built like a brick shithouse" (Dale, her roommate before she married Mark) and "it's like Christmas every time I unwrap you" (Mark, although he hadn't said that in months).

"I like going to two movies on a rainy Sunday afternoon," Rebecca said. "I like biking the Coastal Trail, and hiking Near Point. I especially like it that there is a hot shower and a soft bed at the end of a day of biking and hiking." She raised her cup ceilingward. "I like lights that turn on with the flip of a switch."

"There's no electricity? How do you get the gold out?"

"How should I know? By gold pan, I guess."

"I thought they only painted on gold pans these days."

"Me, too, but Mark brought home half a dozen yesterday. Plastic ones. They're green or black, so they show the gold more, and the bottom of the pans are riffled, you know, little ridges? So the gold falls down between them and is trapped when you rinse the dirt out. Because it's lighter."

"Lighter than what?"

"The gold."

"Oh. Sounds like you know something about it."

"I don't have a choice. It's all he talks about anymore."

There was a short silence. "You want a refill?"

"Sure. Heavy on the half-and-half. Which I also have to give up. No cows in the Bush, I bet."

Nina returned with full cups the color of café au lait, and Rebecca accepted hers with the air of one who was determined to savor every drop as if it were her last.

"Rebecca, you don't have to go," Nina said. "Just say no."

Rebecca sighed. "He's been working double shifts all winter to save up for time off this summer. He's got nine weeks coming, plus his regular two weeks off, plus the week he won at the Christmas party. Twelve weeks in all. He'll be out there the whole summer, Nina."

"Let him be."

It wasn't as if she hadn't thought of it herself. "I can't."

"What about your job?"

"He wants me to quit."

"Rebecca. You love being a legal secretary, and you love your boss."

"Yes," Rebecca said mournfully, thinking of the bright, bustling office on the seventh floor of 710 K Street. "I do."

"He can't ask you to do that."

"He's my husband," Rebecca said. She tried to smile. "Forsaking all others, and all that. You know."

Nina, who had never been married, didn't know, but she was that good and rare friend who listened without judging and so she sipped her coffee and smiled. "You know what's wrong with Mark?"

"What?"

"He's too good in the sack," Nina said, and grinned.

Rebecca rose to Nina's obvious expectations and made an elaborate show of bristling. "And you would know this—how?"

Nina toasted her. "Only by reputation, girlfriend. Only by reputation."

They laughed and changed the subject.

And now here Rebecca was, five months later, waking up in a one-room shack deep in a canyon somewhere in the Wood River Mountains, part of the southwestern curve of the Alaska Range. The mine sat on a creek in a deep, narrow crevice formed between three mountains four, five and six thousand feet in height. The sun could have been up till midnight but Rebecca couldn't swear to it; the only time the mining camp got direct sunlight was between the hours of ten and two. It might as well be December. There was even snow packed into various hollows on the north-facing slopes of the peaks.

It had not been a fun summer. Not only was there no electricity, there was no running water, and the plumbing consisted of a teetery outhouse with bear hair stuck to the outside where the local grizzlies had come to scratch. With the advent of salmon up Nenevok Creek, the bears had come for more than scratching their backs. And if there weren't bears, there were moose, mama moose with babies and attitude. One day a porcupine had wandered into the outhouse and frightened her outside. Mark had come running at the sound of her shrieks and roared with laughter at the sight of her hobbling around with her pants down around her ankles.

Mark had bought her a .357, which nearly knocked her flat the first time she'd shot it, and she wore it faithfully whenever she stepped out the door, but guns made her nervous and she preferred to remain inside, beading and knitting by the soft glow of the kerosene lamp. Mark had gotten a little tight-lipped when she had run out of kerosene for the second time, but that nice woman pilot with Nushagak Air Taxi had dropped off two five-gallon cans on a trip from Newenham to the fishing lodge at Outuchiwenet Mountain. The three Danish fly fishermen on board had taken one look at Rebecca and tried to persuade the pilot to leave them there, too. They spoke little English, but Rebecca, starved for conversation in any language, had been reluctant to let them go.

The pilot had also brought in a bundle of magazines, *Newsweek*s and *Time*s and *Smithsonian*s and *Cosmopolitan*s, and Rebecca had been moved nearly to tears. The pilot, a leggy woman in jeans with dark blond hair stuffed carelessly through the back of a Chevron baseball cap, could not quite conceal her sympathy. Rebecca, who had her pride, pulled herself together enough to express her thanks, wished the fishermen luck and helped push the tail of the plane around, yet another skill she had acquired this summer. The Cessna blew dust into her eyes as the engines revved up for takeoff, but she stood where she was, watching as it barely cleared the birch trees at the end of the rudimentary little airstrip with the uphill grade and the surface made of rocks rubbed smooth from a hundred years of tumbling in Nenevok Creek. The engine roared a protest in the thin mountain air as the pilot hauled on the yoke and the plane slipped through the minuscule space between Mounts Pistok and Atshichlut. Rebecca had tears in her eyes from more than the dust.

And now here it was, September 1, a Wednesday. On September 6, Labor Day by the calendar but Christmas, New Year's and her birthday all rolled into one for Rebecca, Nushagak Air Taxi was scheduled to fly into the Nenevok Creek airstrip and pick up Mark and Rebecca and fly them back to Newenham, where they would board an Alaska Airlines 737 (until this summer the smallest plane Rebecca had been on). In a little over an hour, they would land in Anchorage. Nina was meeting them, with orders to have in hand at the gate a grande cup of the day from Kaladi Brothers, with half-and-half and a packet of Equal already stirred in. Rebecca could almost taste it, and looked up from the watchband she was beading for her grandmother to the calendar on the wall, as if by doing so she could make the days, the hours, the minutes go faster. Dinner at Villa Nova, she thought, or maybe Simon's, or Yamato Ya, or Thai Kitchen. She was so sick of salmon. She was a good cook, but there were only so many ways to prepare fish, and she had tried them all.

Maybe a trip to the Alaska State Fair in Palmer, she thought, examining her palette and selecting a number 11 seed bead in lime green. Rain or shine, the fair was always crowded over the Labor Day weekend, kids standing in line for their last Octopus ride before school started, serious, tight-lipped women examining the crafts building for blue ribbons, cowboys roping calves in the arena, lumbermen rolling logs in the pond, Roscoe's Skyline Restaurant selling the best barbecued ribs this side of Texas on the Red Path. But no, Roscoe had forsaken the fair for the Sears Mall, and for that matter, Labor Day was the last day of the fair, wasn't it? She used to know these things. Fine, they could stop at Roscoe's at the Sears Mall on the way home. Rebecca's mouth watered at the thought.

No more washing dishes in cold creek water, of filtering drinking water for both sand and beaver fever. Rebecca thought of the

Amana Heavy Duty Washer, with its Extra Large Capacity and Seven Cycles, and of the Amana Heavy Duty Dryer with Nine Cycles residing in the laundry room of their home on the Hillside. No more scrubbing of clothes in the tin washtub. No more spit baths in that same washtub. No more listening to Mark complain because his jeans never dried on the line strung between the cabin and the toolshed. How were they supposed to dry without sun? It wasn't her fault he'd chosen to buy a gold claim stuck down a hole.

No more picking lettuce out of the garden, instead of buying it already picked—and washed—from City Market, like a civilized human being. She could look for a new job, a real job in a downtown office with a computer and a modem and a telephone and copy and fax machines, in an office with no mosquitoes or black flies, where she could go down to M.A.'s hot dog stand at the corner of Fourth and G and have a Polish Special on a sunny summer day, and to the Snow City Cafe for a salad sampler on a crisp winter day.

She had never felt so isolated, so abandoned, so alone.

She looked at her palette, a paper plate with piles of beads, seed, square, frosted, tubular, in shades of green and purple and gold.

"Say it," she said out loud. "So bored." She looked at the piece in her hand, which had begun to curve eastward around the vintage German teardrop, and threaded a faceted garnet onto her needle. A little splash of color in this otherwise otherworldly piece, something to draw the eye but not enough to overpower the whole. Yes, she thought. Alone, lonely, but most of all, bored.

Mark, on the other hand, was thriving. He'd pulled nineteen ounces of gold out of the creek, once he had identified a deposit and had worked out how to pan it. Rebecca thought of his salary as a BP geologist, working one week on and one week off the North Slope oil fields, and one evening took pencil in hand to figure out the dollar value of Mark's take. Gold had been selling for two hundred fifty-four dollars an ounce when they left Anchorage in June. Nineteen times two hundred fifty-four equaled four thousand eight hundred and twenty-six dollars. The mine and the surrounding five acres had cost them twenty thousand dollars, which didn't include state permits and fees, supplies and transportation, or the house sitter's fee. Mark's salary was one hundred and fourteen thousand a year, which would be cut by nearly a third because of all his time off this summer. Paid vacation time only covered three weeks.

She looked back down at her work, and sighed. One good thing to come out of this summer, she'd filled her Christmas list. A woven bead necklace for Mom, a sweater for Dad, sweatshirts with beaded designs for her niece and nephews, beaded Christmas ornaments for friends, all were done and already neatly packed away in the single box that contained her personal belongings, all that she had brought in and all she was taking out.

Mark, on the other hand, had not even begun to pack. Every available inch of space was littered with his clothes and geology books and gold pans and pickaxes and pry bars and what seemed to be hundreds of rock samples. The shack was too small for this much clutter, but Rebecca had soon given up on trying to keep Mark's gear in order. She kept the cooking area clean because they had to eat, but she left Mark's stuff strictly alone. He didn't complain, at least out loud.

She heard his step on the path to the cabin and looked up when the door opened. "You're early," she said. "I haven't even started lunch."

"I know. No, it's okay," he said when she put her work to one side and began to rise. "I wanted to talk to you."

His face was grave and her heart skipped a beat. "What about? Is something wrong?" Had Nushagak Air Taxi somehow left a message that through some unavoidable mix-up they wouldn't be picked up on Monday?

He pulled out a chair and sat down opposite her, leaning forward to place his hands on her knees.

She looked at him and some part of her thrilled yet again to his

41

dark good looks, the thick black hair curling against his collar, the dark eyes, the firm-lipped mouth. His shoulders were broad, his hips narrow, his legs long and well muscled. Naked, he looked like a god. They had made love standing in front of a mirror once, and she still marveled at the memory, dark and light, masculine and feminine, strength and softness. It remained her best orgasm to date.

He took the piece from her hands and examined it. "What's this?"

"I don't know yet."

"What do you call the method again?"

"Bead weaving."

"Right, right. Pretty, whatever it is."

She removed it from his hands, square hands with strong fingers and neatly clipped nails, permanently grimed now after three months of grubbing in the dirt. "You didn't quit work early to come in and talk about my beading. What's up?"

"Besides me?" His hands traced a firm path up her hips, urging her legs apart. It melted her, as it always did. He knelt between her legs to suck at the pulse in her throat, nibble on her earlobe, bite her nipples through the knit fabric of her T-shirt.

He raised his head and kissed her, long and slow, flirting with his tongue and his teeth. She dropped her beadwork and reached for his zipper.

He pulled back and framed her face in his hands to smile down at her. In a low, husky voice, he murmured, "What would you say if I told you I wanted to quit my job, and for us to stay out here year-round?"

Newenham, September 1

The hopelessly drunk, the terminally idiotic and the criminally inclined had for a change taken the rest of the day off, and Liam was home by five-thirty and gloriously off duty, as Prince was on call for the evening. "Tim?" he said when he stepped in the door. "Wy?"

No answer. He went out on the bluff between the house and the river and stood post for fourteen minutes, until his thighs decided enough was enough, and then went through all thirty movements of the form three times. It was thirty now instead of sixty-four, Moses had informed him a week earlier, because Liam had learned enough not to have to break each movement down into each of its component parts, and had given him a whole new set of names to memorize. Liam was fully conversant with the statutes describing assault in its various degrees, and had kept his hands in horse stance instead of fastening them around Moses' neck.

Doing form wasn't enough to soothe his conscience — Bill's "social worker" remark still rankled — but he showered and changed into jeans and unpacked the bag of groceries he'd bought on the way home. Dinner for two, with wine, no less. She couldn't be mad at him if he made her beef Stroganoff washed down with cabernet sauvignon, could she? The cabernet had cost more than all the rest of the ingredients put together.

He cut up the beef and put it into a frying pan to brown, adding a dollop of the wine for the hell of it. He poured out a glass of Glenmorangie for himself and broke into the bag of egg noodles. He was filling the pot with water when the phone rang.

"Yeah?" he said, cradling the phone between his shoulder and his ear.

Prince's voice said, "We've got a body down at Kagati Lake, sir."

He put down the noodles and turned off the burner. "Where?"

"Kagati Lake, a hundred or so miles north of here."

Something about the name niggled at the back of his mind. He carried the walk-around phone into the living room, where the one wall that didn't have a window had a map of the Bristol Bay area taped to it. He found Newenham and followed the river up. "I don't see it."

"North and west. North of the lakes," she said, and he moved his finger to the left, encountering the mail route Wy had penciled in, asterisks marking the stops. He traced it up the map, Four Lakes, Warehouse Mountain, Weary River, the names some people hung on some places. Russell—he stopped.

The route ended at Kagati Lake.

Prince had taken the floats off the Cessna and put the wheels back on the week before in anticipation of freeze-up, and they were in the air forty-five minutes later. "You sure she said she wasn't hurt?"

"I'm sure," Prince said patiently. "She found the body, is all."

On either side Newenham airport fell rapidly away from them and Liam's stomach gave its usual takeoff flip-flop. "She's going to kill me," he muttered through clenched teeth.

He hadn't meant to be heard, but the headset was a good one and Prince turned her head to stare. "Why would she be mad at you?"

The plane hit a pocket of dead air and dropped fifty feet. Liam grabbed for the edges of his seat. "Because she's done nothing but find dead bodies since I came to town."

"That's not your fault."

He forgot his terror long enough to send Prince a pitying glance. "You've never had a permanent relationship, have you, Prince? A serious one?"

Defensive now, she shook her head. "Still—"

"Still nothing," Liam said. "It doesn't matter if it's my fault or not. It will be by the time I get there."

He stared resolutely ahead, trying to ignore the thousand feet of space between himself and Mother Earth.

Prince mumbled something he couldn't hear. "What?"

"Nothing," Prince said, and tossed Liam the FAA's Airport/Facility Directory. He opened it, and found the airport sketch for Kagati Lake. "It's a gravel strip, two thousand forty-five feet long, fifty-five wide."

"Elevation?"

"Eight hundred eight feet."

"Light?"

Liam squinted down at the page. "Says it's unimproved. That mean no lights?"

"If there were lights it would say." Prince tapped the dial of a gauge on the control panel. The needle didn't move. "We'd better hustle if we're going to beat the sun."

It hadn't registered with Liam until this moment that the sun was in the act of setting. There wasn't any snow yet, piled into neat, defining berms along the sides, so it could be hard to spot an unfamiliar runway in the dark. "How long?"

"We've got a little bit of a tailwind," Prince said. "I'd say about an hour."

Liam thought of Wy, alone on the ground in Kagati Lake but for the doubtful company of a corpse. "Can we push it?"

Prince grinned beneath mirrored aviator lenses that made her look like one of the extras in *Top Gun.* "What the hell, the state's buying."

She kept the throttle all the way out and they raised Kagati Lake in fifty-nine minutes. It was still light enough to see 68 Kilo parked at the west end of the strip, near a large sprawling building that looked as if it had begun its long life as a one-room log cabin, and then had skipped the split-level phase entirely to metamorphose into something that was a cross between a plantation house and a barn. The roof was variously shingled, tarpapered and capped with sheets of corrugated plastic.

Wy emerged from beneath the wing of 68 Kilo and looked up. Prince waggled her wings. Wy didn't wave back.

"See?" Liam muttered.

The 180, which even Liam had to admit was a well-mannered beast, set down smoothly, jounced once in and out of a pothole, recovered neatly and rolled to a stop.

As always, Liam was first out. Wy was waiting for him.

"I don't want to find any more dead bodies," she said.

"I know," he said.

"I never used to find dead bodies."

"I know."

"I never, ever found a single dead body before this year."

"I know."

"No more dead bodies," she said. She was very definite. "Of any kind. Nobody I know, nobody I don't know. Not next to the fuel pump at the Newenham airport, not in the middle of the ruins of an abandoned village, and especially not at a Bush post office where I'm delivering the U.S. mail."

"Okay," Liam said.

"Good," she said. "So long as we're clear."

"Perfectly," he said.

"I mean it," she said.

"I know," he said. "I'm sorry." He could feel Prince beginning to get restive, and he said, "Tell me what happened, Wy."

"What happened?" she said. "What happened is I'm on my mail run, I'm landing at my last stop on the route, I start unloading the mail, and when Opal doesn't come out to carry it inside I go in looking for her." She swallowed. "And I found her."

"Did you know her?" Prince said.

"Of course I knew her," Wy snapped. "I knew her like I know everybody on my mail route. She was the postmistress, I talked to her once or twice a week, weather permitting."

"What did you say her name was?" Prince got out her notebook.

"Opal. Opal Nunapitchuk. Oh god." There were a couple of benches arranged around a lovely little copse of plants, shrubs and trees native to Alaska, evidence of someone's inspiration and loving care, and Wy went over and sat down hard on one of them. "Oh god," she repeated, and bent over to put her head between her knees.

"She in the house?"

Wy nodded without looking up.

"Better take a look," Liam said to Prince, and led the way up the path.

Opal Nunapitchuk lay sprawled on her back behind the counter that fenced in the corner of the room to the left of the door. Her eyes were wide open, her head at an odd angle because of the cramped quarters of the space behind the counter. Her left shoulder was shattered, a mess of white splinters of bone and congealed blood.

He looked at her face first, something he had trained himself to do from his first crime scene. He wanted to imprint the face of the victim in his memory, be able to call it up at need. He wanted the face of the victim right there as he gathered evidence, as he interviewed witnesses, as he swore out an arrest warrant, as he arrested a suspect, as he conducted the interrogation, as he testified in court. He made sure that the victim was always with him.

His first impression was how young she seemed, clear brown skin tanned from a summer in the sun, a long fall of shining black hair, a slim, muscular build that looked as if it had been vigorously active in life. There were creases in the corners of her eyes, laugh lines at the corners of her mouth, the telltale crepe beneath her jaw. Not so young, then, but a very attractive woman. Rape? No, she was still fully dressed, her jeans belted tightly around a slim waist. He looked at the wound. It seemed high, as if the shooter's aim had been off. Or she had pushed it off.

"Not a body shot," Liam said, more to himself than to Prince, but she picked up on it.

"Not aiming to kill, maybe?"

"Maybe."

Prince stooped and raised the body slightly to peer beneath. "Entrance wound. She was shot from behind."

"Bullet spun her around."

"Yeah." She stood up. "Guy pulls the gun, what, going for the cash?" She looked in a few of the half-open drawers. "Aha." She pulled out a rectangular aluminum box and opened the lid to show him. It was divided into sections for bills and change, and it was empty.

"She turns to run . . . behind the counter?" he added doubtfully.

"For a weapon?" Prince said. She reached beneath the counter. "There are clips here, I'd say for a rifle."

"But no rifle?"

"No."

"He probably took that, too."

"So, she turns to go for the rifle, he shoots, she spins around, falls. He takes the cash and the rifle and leaves."

"From the look of the wound, I'll bet the slug ricocheted off a bone," he said. "It could be anywhere." Bullets frequently had minds of their own once they impacted their target and Liam placed no dependence on their being able to find this one. Which didn't mean they wouldn't look.

A series of large V-shaped shelves took up the corner from floor to ceiling, the top half divided into square, open-ended boxes, some with mail in them, some not. The bottom half was divided into drawers, and the two were bisected by a narrow counter, also V-shaped.

"She hit her head on the way down," Prince said, pointing at a dark brown smudge on the edge of the counter.

"Twice," Liam said, looking at another smudge on the second drawer down. They checked and found blood matted in Opal's hair.

Envelopes, letter size, business size, nine-by-thirteen manilas and priority mail, were scattered across the floor, the shelves they had fallen from teetering dangerously at the edge of the desk they sat on. At least she went down fighting, they both thought.

Liam prodded Opal's arm. "Rigor's coming on." He looked at his watch. "It's going on seven o'clock." He looked up. "What would you say the temperature was in this room?"

"Fifty-five, maybe."

"Outside?"

"Temperature at Newenham airport was fifty-four when we left."

"But this is farther north, and higher up. The walls are pretty thick, not many windows. Probably didn't get above sixty-five all day in here."

"Sounds about right."

"So, she died ten, maybe twelve hours ago, you think?"

Prince shrugged. "M.E. will tell us more."

"Yeah, but I want to know how much of a head start the son of a bitch has on us, and we're going to miss the last jet to Anchorage by the time we get the body back to Newenham, which means it'll be two, three days before the M.E. has a time of death."

"Not smelling much yet."

"No. Which could mean she hasn't been here that long, or that it never warms up in here." He looked back down at the body. "Robbery, you think?"

Prince spotted a group of pictures sitting on a table, and went over to look. The dead woman was in several, surrounded by what looked like husband and children, and more than one with the house they were standing in in the background. "Could be. This is probably her home, too. We don't know what's missing." She pushed back her cap to scratch above her ear, resettled the cap. "If this were Anchorage, I'd say someone was making a hit on people's Social Security checks. But way out here . . . well, I don't see some thug hiking five hundred miles through the Bush to coldcock some old woman for her hundred-and-fifty-dollar Social Security check."

"Yeah. We'll have to find out how many were due to this post office today, how many people collect it hereabouts."

"Goody." Prince paused. "You think it was someone she knew?"

"Usually is." Liam stood up and looked around. "And this would be an awfully big house to live in alone."

It was a large, rectangular room, furnished with couches and recliners and dominated by a fireplace made of rock that boasted its own spit. Alaskan memorabilia was piled in every corner there wasn't a bookshelf, including a Japanese glass float with the net still on that looked a foot and a half in diameter. There were black-and-white pictures of tall, thin men in leather jackets and hats with chin straps standing in front of open-cockpit biplanes, interspersed with paintings in oil and watercolor, some good, some bad, and a small one of a cache on stilts in winter that could have been an original Sydney Lawrence. Considering how much Lawrence traveled around Alaska, and considering how often he painted for booze, the possibility was not at all unlikely. If that was the case, why would the robber leave something so valuable behind? Liam was fuzzy on the valuation of art, but even a small painting by Lawrence had to be worth two or three thousand dollars, and this one was a very portable size.

There was a window next to the painting and through it Liam could see a thermometer fixed to the eaves of the house. It read fifty-one degrees. That was warm for the north side of a house, which meant it might have been a lot warmer in Kagati Lake than he had originally thought. Warm temperatures delayed rigor, so Opal Nunapitchuk could have been dead longer than ten to twelve hours, which only put more time between the killer and the scene.

He looked at the table standing next to the dark green recliner. It was a slab of burlwood, sanded, polished and finished with a coat of Verathane. A trick of the fading evening sun reflected off the glass on one of the watercolor paintings and landed on the table, which was covered with a fine layer of dust, except where something sort of square had been sitting until very recently.

Scattered around the room were three other tables, one hutch and the mantelpiece. All of them needed dusting, and all of them were missing objects that had heretofore kept at least the area beneath them clean. "Prince?"

A flash went off behind him. "Sir?"

"Light a lamp if you can find one, would you? It's getting too dark to see."

"Yes, sir."

"And get pictures of all the tabletops and the mantelpiece."

"Fingerprints?"

"I didn't see any. But dust everything anyway. Start with the counter and the cash box."

He heard the sound of an engine, no, two, outside. They paused, idling, and he heard Wy's voice. He went swiftly to the door and in the dusk saw a man on a four-wheeler with two Blazo boxes strapped on behind with bungee cords. He looked to be in his late fifties, early sixties, maybe, a burly man with thick dark hair streaked silver that hung raggedly below his ears, and dark, narrow eyes nearly hidden in a mass of wrinkles that began in the middle of his forehead and cascaded down into laugh lines bracketing both eyes and mouth. He saw Liam over Wy's shoulder, and Liam stepped forward.

"What's going on?" the man said, his smile fading as he took in Liam's uniform. He looked from Liam to Wy, who couldn't meet his eyes and looked ashamed of it. He killed the engine and dismounted. "Where's Opal?"

"Who are you, sir?" Liam said.

"This is Leonard Nunapitchuk," Wy said. "Opal's husband."

Liam removed his hat and took a deep breath. "Mr. Nunapitchuk, there is no easy way to say this. Ms. Chouinard flew in this afternoon to deliver the mail, and she found your wife."

Leonard Nunapitchuk's skin paled beneath its ruddy tan. "Is she hurt? Opal? Opal!" He stepped forward, only to halt when Liam held up a hand.

"I'm afraid she's dead, Mr. Nunapitchuk. I'm very sorry for your loss."

Leonard Nunapitchuk stared at him without comprehension. "Opal is dead?"

"Yes."

"No." Opal's husband shook his head decidedly. "No, she isn't. I was just here, last weekend. We were all here." He waved a hand, and Liam looked beyond him, across the airstrip where the trees parted for a path. The moon had risen as the sun had set and painted a stepstone path of silver across the ripples of Kagati

51

Lake. The breeze paused, and in the momentary lull Liam heard the murmur of voices, punctuated by a laugh.

There was a sudden shaft of light from the open door of the house as Prince lit the large Aladdin lantern sitting on the hutch next to the door, and Liam looked at Leonard Nunapitchuk, who was about five feet four inches tall and whose belly was just barely restrained by a wide, worn leather belt. There was a hunting knife in a stained leather sheath hanging from the belt. He had a rifle, a Remington .30-30, it looked like, hanging over his shoulder.

His clothes, a fatigue jacket over a cotton shirt in faded blue plaid and jeans, were grubby. His boots were shiny with fish scales. He smelled like woodsmoke, sweat and salmon, like Moses did when he came back from Old Man Creek.

It looked like fish camp had been a success and that Leonard wanted to tell his wife all about it. "Opal? Opal, where are you?"

"Sir," Liam said, and something in the single, forceful syllable got through the way nothing else had before.

Realization came hard to Leonard Nunapitchuk's eyes, but it came, followed by shock and the awful need to know, to see, to make sure there hadn't been some dreadful mistake, because of course there must have been some mistake, this couldn't be happening, not to him. Liam had seen the reaction before, and he stepped to one side so that Leonard could go through the door.

Prince looked around from lighting the Coleman lantern hanging from a bracket next to the kitchen door and saw Leonard. "Sir, I—"

Liam held up a hand and she stopped.

Leonard saw Opal in the same moment, and a terrible groan ripped out of his chest. "No," he said. "No, Opal, no." He dropped to his knees. "Opal. My Opal."

He was weeping now, and when he dropped forward to crawl toward her Liam had to restrain him. "I'm sorry, sir. You can't touch her yet."

"She's my wife!"

"I know. I'm sorry."

Nunapitchuk wrapped his arms around his body and rocked back and forth on his knees. "Opal. Why? Why, why why why?"

Liam heard voices, and Wy's voice responding. Before he could turn, Nunapitchuk was on his feet. "The children can't see this, they can't see this." He ran his sleeve across his face and went outside, Liam following.

There were five more people in the yard, two young men no taller or slimmer than their father and their wives, one a young woman who looked like Opal must have thirty years before, with a plump baby perched on her hip doing his best to snag a dragonfly as it buzzed past. His mother caught him just before he took flight after it.

All of them stared at Liam, at Leonard. It was obvious by their shocked faces that Wy had told them of Opal's death. He knew a faint guilt that she should have assumed this burden, but it was very faint, and he adjusted the duck-billed hat with the seal of the Alaska State Troopers on it and stepped forward to put the necessary questions to the bereaved.

Down the shingly scaur he plunged, in search of his Elaine. Elaine the fair, Elaine the lovable, Elaine, the lily maid of his Astolat. She had left him before, his wandering love, but never for long, and she was always glad when he found her again, glad to return to her chamber up a tower to the east.

Long years had they lived there, and would abide together there again soon. He missed her presence during the day and her warmth during the night. She knew so little at first, but he taught her, and taught her well, so that she kept his shield and tended his wounds with skill and love.

He wished that like Lancelot he had a diamond to give his Elaine for her loyalty, her faithfulness. He trusted her as he trusted no other, to tend his hearth, his clothes, his home, to cook his meals, to warm his bed, to stand beside him summer and winter, his companion, his lover, his friend. She surrounded him with grace and beauty.

Yes, a diamond to give.

He quickened his step over a fallen log and ducked beneath a low-hanging branch. A ptarmigan exploded out of the brush, catching him by surprise. He unshouldered his shotgun. Ptarmigan was good eating. Elaine baked them in a butter-wine sauce that turned brown in the oven, crisping the skin of the birds and marinating the flesh with a flavor that was at once sweet and sour. When they had it, Elaine would mix in a little evaporated milk to turn it into a cream sauce, and serve it over flat noodles.

Elaine. Elaine the fair, Elaine the lovable, Elaine, the lily maid of As-

tolat. His lady, his love, his queen. Children together, teenagers together, married the day after high school graduation. There had never been anyone else for him or for her.

They didn't need anyone else, he told her when she had come back from the doctor with the news that they could never have children of their own. They had each other, and their cabin in the wilderness. They ran their trapline in the winter, planted their garden in the summer, lived life the way it ought to be lived, day by day, year by year, seeing the seasons in and out together.

In winter the wolves might howl, but they had stout log walls and a thick door between them and the hungry pack. The temperatures might drop to forty below zero, but they had six cords of wood stacked in a pile beneath its own shelter, and thick parkas and mukluks Elaine had made from furs gathered from their own trapline. They had a cache filled with moose and caribou and ptarmigan and goose and salmon and berries, a root cellar beneath the house filled with carrots and potatoes, and a pantry filled with canned goods, so they'd never go hungry.

In summer, they had fourteen hours of daylight and never wasted a moment of it, working all day, loving all night. He closed his eyes for a moment to revel in the deep delight the thought brought him. Elaine, gazing up at him with serious brown eyes, dark hair falling back from her smooth skin, mouth open a little to catch her breath, her hands resting lightly on his shoulders, her heels digging into the base of his spine, reaching for the sun, the moon and the stars. He gave them all to her, and she gave them back again.

He had promises to keep, and miles to go before he slept. He abandoned the too-heavy jade by the side of the creek, adjusting the lighter pack on his shoulders as he headed south by ways known only to the wild things of forest and stream. What other treasures would he find to lay at her feet?

Elaine, my Elaine. I'm coming home, my lady, my love, my queen. How will you reward me this time, my own, my lady, my love?

FIVE

Nenevok Creek, September 1

Mark couldn't understand why she was so angry. In seven years of marriage, he hadn't known she could get this angry. He'd never known silence could be so loud, either; this one was thunderous, reverberating off the steep sides of the three peaks and tumbling down the mountainsides until it filled the valley down to the very surface of the creek.

One moment she had been in his arms, and the next he was on his ass, his chest still smarting from the foot she had used to push him away. The silence began as she made him corned beef sandwiches with mustard and lettuce, just how he liked them, on bread out of the Dutch oven the night before. Nothing interfered with Mark's appetite, so he wolfed them down with the macaroni salad and the large dill pickle Rebecca produced to go with them. He'd made the effort, holding up his end by carrying his plate to the wash tin on the counter, but when he tried to pull her into his arms again, she had slipped free, sat down and used the bead tray to block any further attempt at embraces.

In seven years of marriage, he had never once been incapable of seducing her into seeing things his way.

Now, clad once again in hip waders, he bent over the creek to wash dirt out of a pan in pursuit of that elusive gleam of color. An eagle cried overhead, and he raised his head to look, shading his eyes against the sun. A rustle of brush warned that some wild thing was nearby, how sharp of teeth or long of claw he had no idea. He ignored it, as he always did. "Come on, honey," he'd said to Rebecca, "we'll leave them alone, they'll leave us alone. There's nothing to be afraid of."

Pity about that bear charging them the first week. It had only been a fake charge, the sow had skidded to a halt fifty feet away, bellowed out a roar of defiance and then turned abruptly on the space of a dime and lit out for the hills like she had been shot from a catapult. They had come to no harm, but the experience had unsettled Rebecca. Well, that and the moose eating all the broccoli and cauliflower out of the garden and then approaching the cabin to nibble at the bark of the logs. "They're eating the house!" she'd said when he had come home that evening.

He had laughed and loved her out of her fear. God, she was beautiful, his wife. He couldn't see her even in jeans and T-shirt without wanting to rip them off and wallow in her, inhaling her, burying himself in her.

He'd never been quite sure how he had managed to win her. Looking like she did, Rebecca had had men lining up three deep wherever she went. He had beat them all to the gate, by god.

He tilted the pan and let the rest of the water drain out. There were a few specks of color, nothing more. He rinsed out the pan and looked upstream. There was an outcropping of large rocks at the first bend that he had been slowly, steadily zeroing in on. If he hadn't run out of summer he would have discovered the big one, the pocket where the heavier gold had settled as it was being washed downstream. No mere dust there, he was sure, but nuggets the size of peanuts, nuggets by the pound, never mind the ounce. One more summer and he would hit pay dirt. Why couldn't she understand that?

Bewilderment was giving way to resentment. She was his wife. She had promised before God and man to love, honor and obey him. He hadn't insisted on the traditional words; she had. In his turn, he had promised to provide for her, to endow her with all his worldly goods. His worldly goods were about to increase in a big way. Under the next rock or around the next bend, the gold beckoned him on, promising wealth and riches beyond his wildest imaginings and, evidently, her comprehension.

Gold. Number 79 on the periodic table. He'd panned his first gold at the Alaska State Fair two years before. He hadn't wanted to go, but Rebecca had beaded some artsy-craftsy thing into a small brass ring and entered into one of the competitions, and she'd dragged him along for the judging. He had wandered off and discovered a long trough with water circulating through it. The water was very dirty.

"Like to try your hand?"

He looked up and saw a man twice his age, half his weight and a foot shorter than he was peering at him through Coke-bottle lenses. "At what?"

The man had handed him a battered gold pan that looked as if it had come across the Chilkoot Pass in 1899, and that was when he'd first realized he'd stopped in front of the Alaska Mining Association booth.

He'd filled the pan with dirt and water and swirled it around. The man showed him how to tilt it so the water ran out and the dirt settled in a half-moon at the bottom. He dipped more water and dirt, swirled out more water and dirt, wetting his sleeves to the elbow, soaking the front of his shirt and jeans, repeating the motion again and again until there, in a few grains of sand, there it was, a single tiny perfect flake of gold, gleaming up at him, beaming up at him.

He'd looked up and the man had grinned at him. "Nothing like it, is there?"

No, he thought now, looking down at the pan in his hands. Nothing.

Fine. He set his jaw. They'd never had a bump in the marriage before, but all marriages had them. They'd ride it out. Anchorage wasn't much of a proving ground, all the modern luxuries, the modern conveniences. Out here, a man was tested.

A woman, too.

His resentment began to fade. Hell, it wasn't her fault she'd never hauled water from the creek, or chopped wood for a fire to keep her warm. It would take time for her to get used to the life, that was all. Maybe he had enough time before the hard frost set in to dig a new hole, move the outhouse closer to the cabin. That'd probably make a big difference.

He looked at the rock upstream, a shard of quartz sparkling at him with a come-hither look in its eye. The sun was well behind one of the mountains by now, and getting to it earlier every day. Not enough daylight left to fetch the pry bar. For a moment he was sorry he hadn't taken on someone to help, someone who might know more about mining than he did, but he dismissed the thought almost at once. At least that was one thing he didn't have to worry about out here, no men to vie for Rebecca's attention. Out here, he had her all to himself. Days hunting gold, nights sleeping with Rebecca. Although they never got all that much sleep. Last night, for example. He shrugged his shoulders, and the marks still stung.

Why couldn't it be enough for her, too?

He put away his equipment in the shed and hung the hip waders to dry. The smell of salmon frying and rice boiling greeted him as he opened the door. He brightened. Good. She must be over her mad. He'd known it wouldn't take long.

He pulled the door closed behind him, and without turning around from the counter, she said, "I don't care what you do, Mark, but I'm flying out of here with Wyanet Chouinard on Monday." She flipped the salmon steaks onto a plate and put it on the table. "Supper's ready. Sit down and eat."

He sat automatically. "But, Rebecca —"

She brought the rice, the soy sauce and the salad, already dressed. "No, Mark," she said, and whatever he had been going to say was stopped dead by the firm decision in her voice. "I have done everything you've asked me to. I quit my job when I didn't want to, I turned over our home to a house sitter I didn't know, I left behind my friends —"

"I sold it," he said, looking at his plate.

"—and family and—what?"

"I sold the house."

Silence. He looked up to see her fork suspended in midair, her blue eyes staring at him unblinking. "Before we left in May, I sold the house."

More silence. Compelled to fill it, he said, "I sold it to Jeff Kline. He always liked it, and you know he'll take good care of it. You don't have to worry about our stuff, I paid a mover to pack it up and put it into storage. We'll have it shipped out here after I add on a couple of rooms to the cabin."

He looked up and her eyes were fixed on his face but she was looking more through him than at him. "Rebecca?" He took her hand. She let it lie in his, limp, lifeless, unresponsive.

"How could you sell it?" she said finally.

He misunderstood. "It was in my name. It was my house before we were married. We never did get it changed over."

"No," she said, her voice coming more strongly. "How *could* you?"

He couldn't quite meet her eyes, couldn't quite face that wounded look. "Just give it a chance, Rebecca, okay? We'll be together and that's all that really matters, isn't it?" He took a deep breath and made the supreme sacrifice. "And maybe we can have that kid you're always bugging me about. Great place to raise kids, isn't it? No drugs on the street corner, no crazy people shooting up the high schools, no television to monitor. You could teach him, home-school him, you know, and I could teach him everything else. You'll like it, Rebecca, you'll—"

She stood up, pulling her hand free.

"Rebecca? Honey?"

Her eyes darted around the room, looking at the thin mattress of the cot they'd slept on for the last three months, the corners of the room filling with darkness five minutes earlier this evening than the evening before, the stained and torn linoleum covering the floor, the battered counter that served as kitchen, laundry and bathroom, the rough, peeling surfaces of the uninsulated logs.

There was a look on her face that he didn't like. "Rebecca, I know it hasn't come as easily to you as it has to me, but—"

She pushed back her chair and walked around him to the door. She flung it wide, and he heard the splash of the neighborhood grizzly as he went into the creek for supper.

Rebecca stood on the doorstep for a long time, but she never stepped outside.

Kagati Lake, September 1

An hour later they had the body bagged and in the plane, and the rolls of film out of the camera and carefully labeled. The prints Prince had lifted were in an envelope, also labeled. The family was gathered around the kitchen table, a fire in the fireplace shared by both kitchen and living room, and all the lanterns in the house lit. Leonard had insisted on cooking everyone a meal, fried salmon steaks, salad from the garden out back and boiled potatoes, also from the garden out back. Simple food, well cooked, it tasted of dust in Liam's mouth and he knew from Wy's expression that she felt the same. Prince cleaned her plate and asked for seconds.

"Who could have done this?" Leonard said for what had to be the ninth or tenth time.

"We don't know yet, sir," Liam replied. "It looks as if your wife was getting ready to open the post office for the day. What time might that have been?"

"She was always early," one of the daughters-in-law volunteered. "She was always at the counter by nine o'clock, catching up on the books, ordering stamps, stuff like that."

"What time do you normally get here?" Liam said to Wy.

Wy pushed away her plate, still full. "Depends which way I fly the route. Sometimes I start here and work south, sometimes I start at Mable Mountain and work north. Today I started at Mable Mountain."

"Anybody know which way you're flying on any given day?"
She shook her head.

"Who else lives in Kagati Lake?"

Leonard answered. "Not that many. This area is just a collection of homesteads, but not the normal kind of homesteads, you know, buying land from the state, proving up with a cabin in seven years and then it's yours. A bunch of gold miners came through around the turn of the century, on their way to the Yukon, and some of them stopped off to do a little panning. They found color, so they staked claims. Some stayed, like my great-grandfather."

Leonard pointed at a row of gold pans lined up on top of the kitchen cupboard that looked as if they had seen long and hard use. "He always said he was a gold miner, but he never did pack out much gold. Other than the one big nugget." He got to his feet. "I'll show you."

The rest of them waited. "What the hell?" they heard him say, and then he reappeared in the kitchen door. For the first time he looked angry. "Is that what this was about? Opal killed over a lousy goddamn gold nugget?"

Not only was the gold nugget missing that had sat on the burlwood table for seventy years, but walrus bookends carved from jade, a hair clasp made of ivory and baleen carved in the shape of a whale, the ivory tusks that had hung from one wall, the collection of Yupik ivory animal charms from the mantelpiece, and a couple of the masks. Leonard pointed out the empty nails on the walls, his face dark with rage. "Somebody must have been ripping us off, and Opal caught him. Son of a bitch!" He rounded on Liam and said fiercely, "You got any idea who did this?"

"No," Liam said.

Leonard glared. "Then what good are you?"

Prince opened her mouth and Liam waved her to silence. "I'll need the names and locations of all your neighbors, Mr. Nunapitchuk."

"Oh bullshit," Leonard said. "Ain't one of them going to do

something like this. We've been living side by next to most of them for years."

"Any of them you don't get along with?"

"No!"

"Dad," one of the sons said. "What about Dusty Moore?"

"Who's he?" Liam said.

Leonard's lips tightened, and the son said, "Dad and Dusty have been mad at each other for ten years, ever since Mom won the postmaster's contract. Dusty wanted it, and he wasn't a good loser."

"He make any threats?"

"He made threats all over the place," Leonard said, "but he wouldn't kill over something like this."

To the son Liam said, "Do you have a map of the area, with the settlements marked?"

"You going to try finding them tonight?"

"No, we have to get your mother's body back to Newenham tonight so we can get it into Anchorage first thing tomorrow morning."

"I can do that, sir," Prince said, and from the expression on her face immediately regretted it. She'd rather be in hot pursuit than ferrying a body.

To Wy Liam said, "You give me a ride back in the morning?"

She hesitated. "What about Tim?"

He'd completely forgotten about Tim, and the reminder made him uncomfortable. "Tim," he said. "Right." He turned to Prince. "Give Bill a call, tell her to tell Moses that he's got baby-sitting duty."

Prince nodded crisply. Natalie Gosuk had never mentioned Wy's name, so Prince had probably not made the connection, Natalie to Tim to Wy. Liam was relieved. Prince was a straight arrow. She wasn't going to take kindly to him helping to flout a court order, and he would just as soon put that evil day off as long as possible.

"Certainly, sir," she said.

"Okay?" he said to Wy.

"Okay." To Prince she said, "Tell Bill to tell Moses to tell Tim I'll be back before noon tomorrow."

Prince nodded.

"About that map," Liam said to the son.

Later, the dinner dishes cleared away, Liam and Wy stepped outside to allow the family to mourn in private. "Poor Leonard," Wy said.

"I would have said, poor Opal."

Wy shook her head. "That's not what I meant. This is the second time in eight years he's lost a member of his family."

"Who else?"

"They had another daughter. Ruby."

"What happened to her?"

"Nobody knows." Wy sighed. "Leonard took all four kids out hunting one fall some years back. They spread out in back of a herd of caribou. Ruby got lost. They never found her."

"Poor Leonard," Liam agreed.

)IX

Rainbow Creek, September 1

Peter Obadiah Cole was widely believed by other Bush rats to be on the run from the law, and that was true.

He was also on the run from Congress, the courts and the White House; in fact, from all branches of government. He was on the run from traffic, in the air, on the ground or out at sea. He was on the run from bad movies, and television commercials, and television reporters with shellacked hair who couldn't pronounce the name of the place they were reporting from. He was on the run from Mormon missionaries knocking at the door wanting to save his soul, from local politicians who made promises to get into office and then made more to get into higher office and never did get around to keeping the first ones.

He was on the run from no-smoking sections in restaurants.

He was on the run from jets taking off around the clock from Anchorage International Airport.

He was on the run from people tossing butts out of the windows of their cars while they waited for the lights to change at Fourth and L.

He was on the run from Jet Skis run by drunks all over Big Lake. He was on the run from people letting their dogs run loose on the Coastal Trail, shitting all over the place and biting little kids and fighting each other every chance they got. He was on the run from the Kmarts and the Wal-Marts and the Fred Meyers and the Eagles and the OfficeMaxes, all the big ugly box stores full of high-priced crap that nobody really needed and paid too much money for anyway.

He was on the run from faxes and e-mail and voice mail. He was most especially on the run from cell phones.

He'd been born in Anchorage, Alaska, in 1949, the only child of parents who worked hard and never said much. His father had been a veteran of the war in the Pacific, and as soon as he was old enough, Peter followed in his footsteps and joined the Marines. He spent three tours in Vietnam, and never would have rotated out if goddamn Nixon hadn't declared peace with honor and brought them all home, with the Cong nipping at their heels all the way.

Nobody spit on him when he came home. He regretted it. You don't train somebody in special weapons and tactics, hone him into a killing machine and then get in his face when he gets off the plane.

Back home in Alaska, work was gearing up on the Trans-Alaska Pipeline and there were Texans and Oklahomans everywhere you looked, most of them welders and drunk welders at that. They traveled in packs, swaggering around town in their cowboy hats and their cowboy boots and their flashy belt buckles and their snapped shirts and their tight jeans and they acted like they owned the world. He was in Chilkoot's one night, back when he still believed in women, and a group of them took exception to him, as one of them put it, "cutting one of the fillies out of our herd." He'd made it out the back door just enough in advance of the sirens pulling up out front, the bouncer giving him an approving thump on the back as he went through. The pipeliners had to be carried out, he read in the newspaper the next day.

He held his animosity in when he went to work on the Slope for Alyeska. Had to, or he wouldn't have lasted long at any of the pump stations, and there was always a line five deep waiting to take the next job that came open. He did a little plumbing, a little electrical work, some carpentry, pretty much anything that needed doing that he could do or teach himself to. He socked the money away, living in his parents' house, empty since his parents had died in a small plane wreck. Pilot was drunk, but what could you expect.

He had a plan. The house was paid off, and he had inherited the property on Rainbow Creek. The lawyer telling him about it was the first Pete knew of its existence. Records showed that his father had bought it back in 1971, no one knew why, not that his father had had any friends Pete could ask. He chartered a plane with the rest of his back pay and flew out to take a look. Rough, rocky, dangerously sloped landing strip, one-room cabin about to fall over, no well, an outhouse. The remains of a sluice box in the creek fifty feet from the front door. A greenhouse with the roof caved in and the glass broken out. There were mountains all around, and a dense thicket of trees, and only the rush of water between the creek banks and the wind in the trees to hear.

It was his, his place on earth, from the moment his foot stepped out of the plane.

He didn't believe the government was coming to get him, like some of the Bush rats did. He didn't think the Trilateral Commission was invading anytime soon, or the United Nations, or NATO or SEATO or OAS or any of the other acronymical organizations regarded with such suspicion by the conspiracy theorists of the world. He hated noise, that was all, only slightly less than he hated stupid people, and it seemed to him that the world was chock full of both.

So he left. One day he looked at his bank account, decided it was enough, quit his job, cashed out his retirement, put the house on the market at the appraised value, and pulled together a load of supplies while he waited for the deal to close.

That had been in 1982. He hadn't left Rainbow Creek since.

He wanted for nothing. He ran a trapline up the creek in winter, pulling in a few mink. It was exercise. In summer, he tended his garden. In fall, he always got his moose. In winter, he hibernated.

Once in a while he got hungry for a woman. If the stack of *Playboy*s next to his bed wouldn't get the job done, all he had to do was slip down to Nenevok Creek with five-finger Mary and watch the miner, paddling through the creek all alone, while his wife sulked up in the cabin. That was women for you. But one glimpse of her was usually all it took.

Tonight he had had trout for dinner, fresh from the creek, rolled in oatmeal and pan-fried in bacon drippings. The last of his bacon, he noted. It cast a cloud over the rest of the meal, because he would soon have to run up the flag on the roof to signal a need for supplies. He wished Bob DeCreft hadn't sold out to that woman pilot. Still, she'd kept the rates low, and she never offered to make conversation. He appreciated the courtesy. Sometimes, instead of landing, she dropped the mail off in the front yard, like today. He appreciated that, too.

She even brought him a box of books once, stuff the Newenham Public Library was throwing out, probably in order to make room for more Jackie Collins. There was a whole collection of Thomas Hardy in the box, a writer previously unknown to him. He was grateful, and the feeling made him uneasy. Next time she dropped off the mail he put a Coors box full of smoked salmon in the back of her plane. Paid in full, was what he was thinking.

She never made a big deal out of it, said the next time she was there, "My boy and I liked the salmon," that was all. Yes, she was tolerable. Knew how to keep her distance. Knew how to leave him his privacy, and that was what he craved more than anything.

He took the single chair from the kitchen table out on the porch and tilted it back against the wall. Coffee warm in the mug cradled in his hands, he looked up and waited for the stars to come back into the night sky. He missed the stars when they were gone in the summer, effaced by the constant sun which lurked above or just below the horizon the day round. When it got dark enough for the stars to come back, it was the signal for all the hunters and the fishermen and the backpackers to head south for the winter. Welcome to Alaska, now go home. Pete thought that made a fine state motto, although it might have made the Department of Tourism a little irritable.

A star winked into existence over the clump of tall spruce at the edge of the yard. Betelgeuse. Or was it Rigel? He could never keep the shoulder and the knee of Orion straight, but that was what star maps were for. He opened the book on his lap to commune with the ancient Greek astronomers who had remade the heavens in the images of their gods.

One great thing about the Alaskan Bush, at least in summer, you never had to make a dry camp. You could go on forever, stream to creek to river, so long as you had water to drink and bathe in.

The trouble with following the water was that other people did, too. You had to be careful how you approached the sound of water rushing between banks. Even here, even in what most people still considered to be Seward's Icebox, the last frontier, the back of beyond, a few found their way to the call of a clear sky and clearer water, where a man could find peace and a way back to the basics. Food in your belly, clothes on your back, a roof over your head, all those things were readily available if you weren't shy of hard work. The rest was gravy.

Still, a little gravy on the potatoes never hurt. The nugget pressed against his heart from where it rested inside the pocket of his jacket. He couldn't wait for Elaine to see it. It wasn't a diamond, but it would do.

He'd walked all day, following one game trail after another. They were there if you took the time to read them: a stalk of fireweed crushed beneath a hoof, the cropped tops of a stand of diamond willow, a section of creek bank falling into the water. A pile of brush and bones. A grouping of small mounds of dried waste dotted with highbush cranberry pits. A knoll where the wild ryegrass was cropped short and the south face pockmarked with smaller holes leading to medium-size holes leading to large holes. The branch of a birch tree, shaken free of leaves where something had run into it, the rest of the tree's leaves still clinging stubbornly to life, unready to give up summer, unwilling to admit the possibility of fall.

It was the same if you listened. The shrill whistle of marmot and ground squirrel, the boarish bay of the grizzly, the call of the moose bull in rut, the cry of the eagle soaring high above.

The encroachment of man was the easiest of all to sense.

Tired from the long day's walk, he had burrowed between the roots of a giant cottonwood, blown over years before and now stripped down to the bare bark. Other, smaller creatures shared the hollow, who had smelled the smoke before he had and whose agitated rustlings had woken him.

He eeled down the bank to drink from and sluice his face in the creek, taking care to stay hidden beneath a willow branch trailing leaves in the slow-moving water. The woodsmoke could have meant any of a number of things; there were four hikers scaling Alayak Mountain to the northwest, a group of Japanese fly fishermen pulling the last trout out of the streams flowing near Outuchiwenet Mountain Lodge to the north, two park rangers putting the campsite at Nuklunek Lake into winter mothballs to the west. And there were the isolated homesteaders and miners, firing up their hearths and stoves in anticipation of shorter days, longer nights and cooler temperatures.

This was one of those. He had smelled this type of fire before, the concentrated smoke from a stove designed to burn wood slowly, giving off the maximum amount of heat to the room and letting as little of it as possible escape up the chimney. He rolled over on his back, parted the leaves with gentle fingers and squinted at the sky. Dark, or near enough. Seven o'clock, maybe seven-thirty, and he still had miles to go before he slept again. He was tired, and stiff from having slept on the ground, and wanting home, and the comforting presence of his fair lady, Elaine, Elaine-fair. He loved the old legends best, of Arthur and Camelot, and Lancelot and the Holy Grail, and Sir Gawain and the Green Knight. Each with his quest. Elaine had told him once that Guinevere was not so noble as the knights in her life, that she was a liar and a deceiver and an adulteress. There was nothing tragic about her end, she deserved to be burned at the stake, not rescued and taken to live out her life in the comfort of a rich woman's nunnery. He'd been angry with her, very angry. That was the first time she had run away, but she was soon back again, and sweetly forgiving.

He followed the smoke to a small clearing with a smaller cabin at the center of it. He could just make out the form of a man seated on a straight-backed chair, tilted on two legs to lean against the logs. He had a book in his lap, and once in a while the bowl of his pipe glowed. The smell of good tobacco drifted across the clearing and into the woods.

The man talked to himself. "Too early for Orion, wait another month. What's that, the Pleiades? Yeah, the Pleiades, the Seven Sisters. What were their names again? Think, Pete, think. Electra, Maia, Taygete, Alcyone, Merope, Celaeno, Sterope." He gave a snort of triumph. "Okay, moving east, great square of Pegasus, Andromeda and the Andromeda galaxy, the only galaxy that can be seen by the naked eye."

Involuntarily he turned over on his back, to follow the man's astronomical lecture. A stick cracked beneath him and a ptarmigan snoozing peacefully four feet away exploded out of the undergrowth.

The man slammed the book shut and shot to his feet. "Who's that? Who's out there?"

SEVEN

Kagati Lake, September 2

"I thought you'd be mad."

She said nothing.

"Actually, I thought you'd be furious."

It was the morning after. The two officers had spent the rest of yesterday, before Prince left with the body, gathering evidence, including a piece of lead Prince dug triumphantly from the log wall next to the fireplace—"How the hell did it get over there?" she wondered out loud. Liam held his peace—and what Liam was sure would prove to be a slug from a twenty-two—a pistol and an automatic. The family, holding together with amazing dignity, helped by compiling a catalogue of missing items. A jade necklace, an ivory hairpiece, a gold nugget the size of a baby's fist if the picture of it could be believed.

Breakfast—bacon, eggs and fried potatoes—had been served promptly at eight a.m. Liam and Wy had escaped immediately afterward and walked down to the dock on the lake together, partly to allow the family some privacy, and partly because it was a relief to be away from their grief. Leonard's grief, especially, because his was compounded by guilt. The reason there had been no rifle in the clips beneath the post office counter was that Leonard had borrowed it to take with them to fish camp. There was a shotgun in the kitchen, mounted in a rack over the door, but she hadn't been able to get to it. "I should have put it behind the counter when I took the rifle," he kept saying. His children gathered around in anguished sympathy. Liam checked to see that the shotgun was where it was supposed to be and then he and Wy slipped outside.

It was another clear day, colder than usual. The outside thermometer had read forty degrees when Liam got up. Birch leaves were falling like rain, golden and brittle. The peaks of Oratia and Alayak and Outuchiwenet were already capped with snow. Their southwestern faces were a collection of reds, ranging in hue from salmon to salmonberry to blood. A faint mist hung over the lake like the ghost of summer past, the warm temperature of the water rebelling against the cooler temperature of fall air.

Liam was sitting on the edge of the dock, feet dangling over the side a foot above the water. Watermarks on the pilings showed that he would have been nearly up to his knees during spring runoff. "I figured you'd want a six-inch strip of my hide before breakfast."

She was sitting next to him, legs dangling next to his, one foot swinging slowly back and forth, sneakered toe pointed with the elegant and unconscious grace of a ballet dancer. Her head was turned away. She seemed to be looking toward the north end of the lake. All he could see of her face was the tip of her ear, revealed by the loose braid that pulled back her dark blond hair. The morning sun picked out gold and bronze and red highlights. It was very pretty, but he'd rather see her expression, have some clue as to what he was dealing with.

He sighed and faced forward. Who understood mothers?

An eagle flew high and slow straight up the center of the lake, heading for home after a summer spent fishing the rivers and streams for salmon. When winter came the eagles would have to work for a living, hunting rabbits and other small mammals, follow the ravens to a downed moose or caribou and share in the pickings, or find a Dumpster. The prospect didn't seem to worry the eagle over Kagati Lake.

Liam watched him until he was out of sight. September meant the mosquitoes were gone. They needed their jackets, though. Everything's a trade-off.

"Thank you," she said.

"Excuse me?"

She turned to face him squarely. "You're an officer of the court, sworn to uphold the constitution, and the judicial system, enforce their powers."

"Yes," he said cautiously.

"If you'd done that, you would have enforced Natalie's writ."

He shifted. The plank surface of the dock was hard and far from clean. It was probably messing up the seat of his uniform pants, and his two tailor-made uniforms had seen hard use over the past summer. "Yeah. Well."

"John Barton will eat your ass if he finds out."

"John Barton eats my ass all the time anyway."

She smiled. "True." She paused. "Liam?"

He stared out at the mist hovering indecisively over the surface of the lake. "Yeah?"

"Thank you." She reached for his chin and pulled his face around. Her eyes stared straight into his. "Thank you."

He almost squirmed. "Yeah. Well."

"He'll be safe with Moses. And you were right, Natalie never lasts long away from the bottle." She gave a faint sigh.

"What?"

Her shoulders moved up and held. "I don't hate her anymore. I feel sorry for her. She can't stay off the sauce, every time she hooks up with a guy he beats on her, and now I've taken away her son."

"She's a drunk and a child abuser," Liam said.

Wy smiled at him, eyes narrowed against the first direct rays of the sun, which was just cresting the V between Alayak and Outuchiwenet. "There's the cop I know."

"I thought you'd be mad at me," he said, a little plaintively.

She grinned. "You say that like you're disappointed."

"Well, I had this great comeback all planned, and then I had a

75

fallback position, and when you demolished that I was going to jump you."

"We could skip directly to three," she suggested.

He looked over his shoulder. "Down, girl. I'm on duty."

She followed his gaze. "Yeah. Those poor people. What do you think happened?"

"The money's gone from the till. There's a bunch of jade and ivory artwork and a gold nugget the size of a red potato missing. She was robbed, she resisted, and something went wrong. She might have known him, but she ran the only post office in miles, so she could also have not known him. You get drifters out here the same way you get them everywhere else. It's just that here you hope the Bush takes them out before they start killing people."

"And usually it does."

"And usually it does," he agreed.

"Not this time."

"No."

"Her family seemed to love her very much."

"Yes."

A brief silence. "Liam. You think you'll find him?"

He pulled his blue ball cap from his head and examined the cloth badge fastened to the crown. A brown bear with all of its teeth bared in a snarl held a badge between his front paws. "Alaska State Troopers," the badge read. In between the "State" and "Troopers" was a circle with the unsetting sun and the Alaska flag set inside it. Eight stars of gold on a field of blue.

"I'll look for him," he said finally. "We dusted for prints, and if we're lucky we'll find some out of the hundreds that postal customers and family members have left behind that match up with some we've got on file. I'll go around to the neighbors, see if any of them saw anything, got hassled by anyone. Of course, the nearest neighbor's four miles away, so chances of that are not good. When I get back to Newenham I'll call around to the other trooper posts in the area, see if they've had anything similar happen." He put his hat back on and pulled it down over his forehead. "I'll look for him."

He got to his feet and reached for her hand and pulled her up next to him. "But unless he kills again, I'm probably not going to find him."

"Not necessarily something you want to hope for."

"No."

She dusted her hands on her jeans and looked at the palms. "Liam."

She looked at him, the rising sun causing her hair to gleam with dark red secrets. Half a smile kicked up one side of his mouth, and her heart turned over. She cleared her throat. "Ford Ranger," she said.

"Uh-huh," he said, smile spreading.

"Wide tires all around."

"Okay."

"Snap-on tool chest in the bed."

"Got it."

"Hot pink paint job."

"Oh man, oh no," he said, his head shaking in disgust, "no way, girl truck trying to look like a boy truck. Paint job's a dead give-away."

In that moment she loved him as much as she ever had. "Liam—" *There are some things I have to tell you,* she wanted to say. *There are things that have to be said.*

"Hold it." His hand touched her arm, and when she raised her head he was looking up. She heard the sound of the engine then. "Prince," he said, and started for the airstrip.

She opened her mouth to call after him, closed it again without saying anything, and followed him up the path.

Old Man Creek, September 2

"You're here because your mother's in Newenham," Moses said bluntly. Moses never said anything any other way. "She wants to see you, spend time with you. I don't think that's a good idea, so I brought you here to keep you out of her way."

Tim paled beneath his summer tan, suddenly looking much younger and more vulnerable.

"She can't last long without a drink. She never does. We'll stay here three, four days, be home in time for the first day of classes. Your math teacher'll still be there when you get back, don't worry."

Bill waited for Tim to wander disconsolately down to the mouth of the creek before she said, "Lower the boom, why don't you."

Moses shrugged. "No point in taking it easy on him. Life won't."

He was right, of course. Bill said no more, refilling her mug from the pot that sat warming itself on the Earth stove at the back of the cabin. She went outside to enjoy the contrast of hot, strong coffee and crisp, cool air. A porch fronted the little cabin, built of deck boards Moses had conned somebody out of a couple of years back. There was a creaky rocking chair, a bottomed-out armchair with square cushions covered in some nubby brown fabric, and a couple of metal folding chairs with no cushions at all. Bill opted for the armchair, propping her feet on the porch railing.

Moses Alakuyak's fish camp sat on the confluence of Old Man Creek and the Nushagak River, about thirty miles upriver from Newenham, around Black Point and about halfway between there and Portage Creek, where Moses kept his skiff when he wasn't at fish camp, and where there was a landing strip. And wouldn't Wy be royally pissed when she discovered that Finn Grant had flown the four of them in.

The camp itself was a modest affair, a cabin with bunks for eight, a propane stove for cooking, a woodstove for heating, and two counters, one inside for cooking and one outside on saw-horses for cleaning fish. There were racks for drying salmon, a smokehouse made out of an old refrigerator for smoking them, a banya for sweats, a tiny dock made of wooden planks fastened to Styrofoam floats anchored to the bank. There was a well and a pump, although the water was brackish and had to be filtered. A clothesline was strung between the house and one of the few trees, an overgrown alder really. There wasn't much between Scandinavian Slough and Bristol Bay that was over three hundred feet above sea level. It was one big swamp south of the Nushagak from here on, and the fish camp was on the leading edge of that swamp. It didn't encourage tree growth.

Moses came out here every summer, to catch and dry and smoke and salt and kipper the salmon that every year made the long journey from the north Pacific Ocean to the upper reaches of the Nushagak and all its tributaries. He didn't eat much of it, she reflected, staring toward the river, instead giving most of it away to family and friends. He had no place to store it, come to that; Moses didn't own a house. Probably he would have said he didn't own the fish camp, either, he was just borrowing it from the Old Man for a time. As near as she could figure, the sum total of Moses' personal belongings amounted to a Nissan longbed pickup, his tai chi uniform and the clothes on his back. He ate — and drank — in her bar. He slept with her.

And he communed in solitude at fish camp. It was a good place for communing. Bill had never seen so much sky before, not in Alaska. She was more used to mountains jostling for position with the sun and the stars and the clouds filling up the spaces in between. Here, there was nothing to interfere with your line of sight, only a dome of pale blue over a flat marsh filled with dwarf alders and stunted willows and fireweed and reeds and ryegrass. The water table was very high here. The river had both split and narrowed by the time it got this far north, although it wasn't really that far north, as it hung a right and then another right east of Newenham before correcting course for north again after the Keefer Cutoff.

It was a place to be valued, a home for hundreds of different species of birds and water-loving mammals. Case in point — an otter poked his or her head above the bank, whistled indignantly, as if to say, I thought you left for the year once already. A small splash and it was off again. Little trickles and tributaries riddled the country in every direction, all winding their way somewhere safe to the Nushagak River, and thence to the sea.

Tim needed a dog, she decided, a dog to drape his arm around when he was sitting on a dock with his feet dangling over the edge. Maybe the dog would make him look less frightened, less forlorn.

The door opened and Moses came out, dressed in his sifu clothes, a black jacket and black pants with the cuffs folded and tied closely at the ankles. He walked down the steps and into the yard, faced north, brought his feet together and his hands up, right fist cupped in left palm, and bowed once, holding it for a long moment.

He straightened, his hands dropped to his sides, he took several long, deep breaths, his knees bent, his arms came up, elbows at his sides, to form two gentle curves before him, and he appeared to go into a trance. Minutes passed, and more minutes, until Bill could see the beginnings of a fine trembling about his thighs and knees, first hinted at by the faint vibration of fabric in his pants. Still he held it, what he called standing post, until the trembling increased into an obvious tremor, and what must have been twenty minutes passed before he sighed, a long, continuous inhalation and exhalation of air, and slowly straightened into an erect posture, only to sink back into it again, and this time from the stance into motion.

She never tired of watching him practice tai chi chuan. In Chinese the name meant "soft boxing," a form of martial arts dating back five thousand years. It focused more on defense, designed to take advantage of an opponent's offensive moves and discourage them, deter them or deflect them.

Moses in motion was grace personified, wholly concentrated on his art, from commencement to conclusion, through movements with prosaic names like Pull Back, Press Forward and Push, to the more exotic movements with names like Step Back and Repulse Monkey, Stork Spreads Its Wings and Retreat to Ride Tiger.

He went through the form three times. Sounds natural to the creek, birds calling and fish jumping and branches creaking in the breeze, seemed muted and distant. One was aware, watching Moses practice his art, of the inherent possibility of mankind. One grieved that, in five thousand years of practice, that potential had yet to be achieved. But for a few precious moments Moses shrugged off the millstones of modern man and reached back in time for the grace and strength and endurance inherent in us all. It was always there, waiting to be tapped. It was only that so few knew to reach for it.

Bill looked around to see that Tim was watching Moses, too.

Moses said, "Come here, boy."

At first it didn't seem that Tim would obey.

Moses waited, without turning, without moving, without repeating himself, facing north, waiting.

Tim approached reluctantly. "What?" He affected a yawn.

"This is called a modified horse stance," Moses said, sinking back into the bent-knee, arm-bent-at-the-elbow position.

"So?"

"So," Moses said, displaying a rare patience, "this is the best exercise to tone your muscles for the practice of tai chi chuan."

Tim opened his mouth to say "Who cares?" caught Bill's eye, and changed it to the less dangerous "So?"

"So do it. Now." Moses stood straight and walked behind Tim, poking his hands into the backs of the boy's knees and manipulating Tim's arms into the raised position, much as someone would operate a marionette. "Not like that, like this. Not straight, curved, and cup your hands. Deeper." He nudged the backs of Tim's knees again. "You're young and healthy, you can go deeper than that."

"Why would I want to?" Tim muttered, just loud enough for Moses to hear.

Surprising everyone in the clearing, Moses laughed. "Oh, you want to, all right, young Gosuk. You were watching me, and you thought what I was doing was way cool." He raised his voice. "Amelia!"

He had to shout her name three times before she came to the door, rumpled clothes and bloodshot eyes and hair askew. She looked hungover because she was.

"Down here," Moses said, pointing next to Tim.

Befuddled, she shuffled down the steps, and stood next to Tim, swaying a little. Tim watched from the corner of one eye. She was pretty, underneath all the bruises, and not that much older than he was. It seemed strange to think of her as married. People seventeen didn't get married, they went to high school. Melanie Choknok, the junior he had a secret crush on, was Amelia's age.

Moses poked and prodded her, too, until she and the boy stood in a parody of Moses' assured stance. "Breathe," he barked. "Feel the air, the breath of life, making a circle around your body, pulling all life to you and in you. Breathe, goddamn it! Bend your knees, deeper, deeper, I said! What are you trying to do, boy, pluck a duck? Give me a respectable tai chi cup on that hand. Yeah, okay, that's close enough for now. You, girl, nobody yelled 'Attention!' Lower your chin. I said lower it, damn it, not fall face forward onto your chest. Bend your knees. Bend them!"

He kept them in one position for half an hour, always carping, always criticizing, grudgingly accepting their stances only as an imitation of the real thing. "Okay. Stand up. Where you going, boy?"

Tim halted. "I thought we were done."

"Who told you to think?" Moses demanded. "Resume your position."

Tim resumed his position. Bill was left to wonder how Moses did it. He was five feet seven inches tall, his features were boringly regular with the merest hint of his Yupik ancestry, he had no dignity to speak of, there was no authority vested in him by the power of the state, in fact no earthly reason for anyone to say "How high?" when he said "Jump!" Tim, who had had a very rough and very nearly fatal childhood in the Yupik village of Ualik and who had been rescued from it by the timely intervention of one Wyanet Chouinard, and who was only now learning how to be an American boy, jumped. Amelia, who had been beaten into a cringing and nearly servile subservience within the space of little more than five months, her obedience was easier to understand.

Still, Moses commanded. There was no other word for it. Maybe it was his eyes, a penetrating gray so light they seemed at times absent of any color at all. Maybe it was the grin, saved from being purely evil by the curl at one corner that invited you to laugh with him. Maybe it was his age, which no one knew but everyone agreed had to be ancient.

He sat on his stool in Bill's and he drank an endless amount of beer, but never got too drunk to talk or make love, the two things most drunks most wanted to do and couldn't. Petitioners for news of the future approached him with the deference normally reserved for royalty, or genocidal maniacs. Should I marry the father of my child, should I quit fishing and go to school, should I move Outside? From time to time he issued proclamations. He had declared Bill's bar to be a cell-phone-free area, reinforced his edict by launching the mayor's cell phone out the front door and into orbit, and no one had murmured so much as a protest. Nobody brought any more cell phones with them when they dropped by for a beer, either.

Half the people in Newenham thought he was crazy. The other half thought he was divine. The whole of the population trod with care in his presence, and most of them listened when he spoke. If and when they didn't, they almost immediately regretted it. If they lived.

She watched him chivvy and chastise Tim and Amelia for two hours, a grouchy little bully even older than she was, and loved him and wished for him immortality, or to live as long as she did, because she had no wish to live without him.

"All right," Moses finally decided, and stepped back.

Amelia, trembling in every limb, tears and sweat running down her bewildered face, folded up where she stood, subsiding to the ground with a thump and a grunt. Tim, more prideful, managed to walk to the porch and more or less fell onto one of the folding chairs.

"Now to the sweat," Moses said. "Come on, come on, move it!"

Amelia began to cry in earnest. With no regard for her distress, Moses took hold by the scruff of her neck and yanked her to her feet. Tim, determined to work the old fart into the ground if it killed him, struggled upright on his own. Both of them tottered around the cabin to the sweat lodge next to the creek, a tiny, enclosed shack, weatherproofed more to keep the steam in than the cold out. There was a woodstove inside, vented through the roof, with a pan of rocks sitting on top and a bucket of water sitting on the floor. Built-in benches wide enough to lie down on provided space for four. Moses stripped both kids down to their underwear and more or less shoved them onto a bench. Tim tried not to look at the lacy little brassiere Amelia was wearing, or at the further bruising the removal of her clothes had revealed. Amelia lay down and closed her eyes, oblivious to his presence.

Moses' head popped around the corner of the cabin. "You coming?"

Bill smiled at him. "A little too crowded at the moment for my taste."

His grin was equal parts understanding and lechery. "Later."

"Later," she agreed.

EIGHT

Nenevok Creek, September 2

The bed shifted as Mark got stealthily to his feet. Clothing rustled as he dressed, the door creaked as it opened and creaked
again as it closed. Rebecca rolled to her back and stared at the
ceiling, at the patched, cracked, stained ceiling of uninsulated
plywood four-by-eights cut haphazardly to fit. The double bed
was shoved into a corner, and the air blew cold through the
chinks. They'd used the down comforter all summer except for
eleven days at the beginning of July.

Now it was September. September 2, four days from a flight
home.

She was going home. There was no doubt of that. She was
going home with or without her husband. She was going back
home, going back to Anchorage, if not to that nice split-level in
the old neighborhood in Spenard with the thirty-year-old
prickly rose bush bending the back fence out of shape and the
thirty-one-year-old birch coating the lawn with leaves. The yard
sloped down in front of the house, and when the four different
varieties of poppies she had planted and so carefully nursed
through their infancies were in bloom it was like something out
of Disney.

It was only a house. She could plant poppies in another front

85

yard. This time she could plant some of those flashy Himalayan Blues. And raspberry bushes, dozens of them, so she could make framboise, and give it away to all her friends at Christmas.

Because she was going home. Mark could stay here, a thousand miles from nowhere, and wash dirt until the creek froze in around his legs if that was what he wanted. To honor and keep, in sickness and in health, forsaking all others, so long as you both shall live. She had believed in those words. She was going home, with or without her husband.

There was enough water left in the kettle on the woodstove to fill the coffeepot. She used some of it to make a single cup of coffee and the rest to take a spit bath. She dressed in jeans and a tank top beneath a short-sleeved T-shirt beneath a long-sleeved flannel shirt. She would have worn long underwear if she'd thought to bring any with her. She hadn't been warm since they had left Anchorage. She wanted electric baseboard heating in her new house, and a thermostat she could crank up to eighty degrees.

She wanted another cup of coffee, but the water was all gone. She put on two pairs of socks and a pair of short leather hiking boots, picked up the plastic five-gallon jerry can and headed for the door. At the last moment, she paused next to the counter and picked up the paring knife, a three-inch blade on the three-and-a-half-inch black plastic handle. Mark made fun of it and tried to get her to use the slim, deadly skinning knife he'd bought for her, in its own leather sheath meant to be threaded onto her hand-tooled leather belt, but she liked the paring knife. It was short and sharp, and it served for cutting up vegetables and trimming bead cord.

There was a stalk of fireweed next to the creek where they got their water. She'd noticed yesterday that the last group of blooms at the very top of the stalk had opened, and she wanted to bring them back to the cabin with her. She was designing a bracelet, a wide cuff with picoted edges and a raised pattern in a floral motif. She had two tubes of size eleven seed beads, one Ruby Rainbow

Matte and one Purple Blue Transparent Matte, hoarded as her reward for sticking out the summer. They were as close to the color of the fireweed blooms as she had in her private stash, and the blooms would make a lovely motif for the bracelet. She would give it to Nina for Christmas. Nina loved reds and purples and hot pinks. Her Volkswagen Beetle was a silvery fuchsia. She'd always gone more conservative with her car colors.

She left the cabin door standing open and trod the path to the stream with soft, carefully placed steps, listening for anything that might be beyond the bushes. She no longer started at every rustle or creak, but neither did she ignore them.

She hoped she wouldn't run into Mark. She hoped he was prospecting up the creek somewhere.

It had been a long, still night. Neither of them had slept, but they hadn't talked, either. Rebecca had said all she was going to say, and Mark was still confident he could change her mind. It was the second of September. Wyanet Chouinard and the Nushagak Air Taxi would come on the sixth of September. Four days, if she counted today. She'd made it through three months. She could make it through four days.

The brush opened up at the creek, where a small slope of reddish dirt fanned into a narrow gravel bank. The rocks were round and flat, and many of them gleamed white and sparkled in the early morning light. Quartz. Quartz and gold were found together, Mark said. She thought of the half dozen tiny vials filled with dust and the one nugget the size and shape of a kidney bean back in the cabin, the fruit of a summer's labor, and shook her head.

She filled the jerry can. The fireweed was still there, still blooming. She used the paring knife to cut the stalk just below the last set of blooms, feeling slightly guilty as she did so. It had been perfect just as it was.

She sat down on the bank with her elbows on her knees and looked at the fireweed. She knew a little about herbs thanks to

Amy Kvasnikof, who worked at Southcentral Foundation in Anchorage and who had come to Pedersen, Barcott, Tsonger, Jefferson and Moonin for help in a divorce case. Rebecca had worked on the case with Pete Pedersen, and she and Amy had become good friends.

Amy was from Nanwalek, what they used to call English Bay, and she had learned about Alaskan herbs at her grandmother's knee. Fireweed leaves could be used to brew tea for indigestion, and dried fireweed root could be ground and mixed into a paste with bear grease and used as an ointment on sores or bug bites. It had its culinary purposes as well; young fireweed made for fine salad greens, and the tea didn't have to be medicinal.

Amy had given Rebecca a book, Eleanor Viereck's *Alaska's Wilderness Medicines*, and Rebecca had brought it with her, thinking she might spend part of the summer looking for the herbs listed there. The book described the herbs in alphabetical order, each with a black-and-white drawing of the plant, and at the back of the book there was a glossary and a couple of lists, one A Therapeutic Use of Alaskan Plants. Under A it had Aphrodisiac — angelica. Under B it had Baby bath — rose leaf tea.

Baby. Babies. Rebecca stared hard across the stream, at the trunk of a cottonwood lying on its side. She wanted babies, at least one, preferably two. She'd always wanted them. She'd talked to Mark about it before they got married, and he had said sure, just not right away. "Let's give ourselves time to play first," he had said, and grinned, leaving no doubt as to what kind of play he meant.

It wasn't as if she had disagreed with him, but this year they had celebrated their seventh anniversary. Rebecca was now thirty-two years old, and she was beginning to have visions of pushing a stroller and a walker at the same time. She'd tried to reopen the discussion with Mark over the Christmas holiday, but at the same time he started to tell her about this defunct gold mine for sale in the Wood River Mountains. He'd always had a hankering to look for gold, he told her, although in seven years of marriage this was the first she'd heard of it. He seemed so excited and so enthusiastic, though, and Rebecca tried so hard to be the good wife. This was obviously something Mark wanted very badly. How could she say no?

Halfway through the summer she began to wonder how much the gold mine was a ruse to avoid the baby talk. Moving out here, in the middle of nowhere, no hospital, no doctor, no pharmacy, how could she have a baby out here? The nearest school was in Newenham; how could she raise a child out here? She wanted to drive her child to soccer practice and ice-skating classes, and to the movies and Baskin-Robbins afterward. She wanted to go to parent-teacher conferences. She wanted to join the PTA. She wanted to shop at Gap for Kids and Gymboree.

Mark knew how she felt. They had talked about all the important things, children (not now, but no more than two later), money (one joint and two separate checking accounts, only one credit card each, both paid off at the end of the month, take care of the upkeep on the house first and the retirement fund second), where to live in Anchorage (Turnagain or Spenard), where to retire (Alaska, not Outside). They'd made separate lists and discussed each item, each taking care to respect the other's viewpoint, reaching accommodation without too much blood on the floor. It wasn't just the sex, which was thrilling, it was also a shared commitment to a long life together and a shared determination to make that life the best it could be. They had been very pleased with themselves, and Rebecca for one had marched up that aisle in the full conviction that she knew exactly and precisely what she was doing and that she had never done anything more right in her life.

He had bought the gold mine without consulting her first, emptying out their joint checking account and explaining it away afterward as "I had to, honey, he had ten other buyers waiting in line. I would have lost the deal if I hadn't jumped on it quick."

"I thought we were going to start a family this year," she had said. "I thought that was why we'd saved all that money."

He had laughed, a quick, excited laugh, and kissed her soundly. "We've got all the time in the world to start a family. We've got time to start a gold mine." His hands wandered. "Besides, we're not done having fun yet."

Like always, her knees had given way beneath the onslaught.

It isn't all his fault, she thought, still staring at the log across the stream, still twisting the fireweed between her fingers. I should have been more forceful. I should have insisted we sit down and talk about it, then and there. But he distracted me. Like he always distracts me.

"You know what's wrong with Mark?"

"What?"

"He's too good in the sack."

Remembering the conversation with Nina at City Market, Rebecca realized just how often Mark had resolved their differences in bed.

It was ironic that here, in this place she feared and despised, in this place to which Mark had seduced her into coming, here she had found the time and the solitude to think, to reflect, to learn to see a different side of their relationship. It shamed her to realize that all he had to do was lay hands on her and she would do anything he wanted.

"Hey!"

Mark's shout jerked her to her feet. She turned. He wasn't there.

"Hey, what the hell do you think you're doing? Get out of there!"

The sound of a shot echoed off the walls of the canyon.

She grabbed for her waist, and only then remembered that she had been so angry at her husband that morning that she had forgotten to strap on the .357 before stepping outside.

For the first time that summer since the bear charged her, she was outside the cabin and unarmed.

Nuklunek Bluff, September 2

The air was very still that morning, probably why the sound of the shot traveled so far.

"Hey," John said. "Did you hear that?"

"Yeah," Teddy said, head cocked. "Warehouse Mountain?"

"Too far. Nenevok Lake, maybe."

"Or maybe the creek."

"The gold mine," John said, and burped.

"Maybe she shot him."

"Maybe he shot her."

They both thought back to their first sight of Rebecca Hanover, and said simultaneously, "Nah."

They stood, listening. There were no further shots.

"A bear, maybe," John said.

Teddy made a face, and pointed in a vague, easterly direction with a half-empty bottle of beer. "You think we should go see?"

John drained his own bottle and set it down with exaggerated care inside the almost empty second case. "Sure," he said, and picked his way carefully to where his rifle stood leaning against a tree trunk.

Teddy watched him go, bleary-eyed. "What about Wy?"

"Why?"

"Wy. Our pickup. Noonish. Round there, anyway. Maybe four. Five?"

John made a regally dismissive gesture with one hand. "Be back in plenty of time."

Teddy, flush with beer, gave no thought to the various areas of dense brush and swampy muskeg between them and the shot they had heard, and agreed without a blink.

Kagati Lake, September 2

"I've got to get home," Wy said. "I'm supposed to ferry a couple of fishermen back from Outuchiwenet Mountain, and I've

91

got a couple of hunters to pick up this afternoon. I'll need to re-fuel before I head out. See you back at the house?"

"Okay." Liam squeezed her hand and let go. Prince pretended not to notice, and continued to pretend not to notice as Liam stood watching Wy climb into her plane, start the engine, taxi and take off to the north. The plane banked left and came back down the strip at two hundred feet and waggled its wings. Liam raised an arm in reply and turned back to Prince. "So nothing else, no similar incidents reported out this way?"

"No, sir."

"No burglaries, robberies, no assaults?"

"And no murders."

"I don't like it," Liam said.

"I don't either, but we don't have a lot to go on," she said. "I sent the prints in with the body. Maybe we'll get lucky." She paused.

"What?"

"You sure about the family?"

"Yes. They were all at fish camp, anyway, all except Opal. She stayed behind to do her duty by the U.S. Postal Service. Come rain, shine, sleet or fish camp, the mail must go through."

"Who checks their mail here, sir?"

"There are about thirty-two people in the immediate vicinity." He caught her eye. "Well, okay, within a day's hike. From the look of things, most of the people with mailboxes here don't make the trip over that often, they let the mail pile up and come in once or twice a month to collect it. She ran a little sundries store, too: over-the-counter medicines, magazines, candy, like that. It would be known, so she'd get the occasional stranger."

"Maybe somebody else saw him."

"Maybe somebody else did," he said.

They borrowed a couple of four-wheelers from Leonard and set off. It took them the rest of the morning and all of the afternoon, following the map Leonard had made for them. Everyone was shocked at Opal's murder. No one had seen anyone strange. Very few had alibis, but then very few had motive, either.

Dusty Moore was a man in his fifties with a much younger Yupik wife and five children under the age of eight, all of whom swore that Dusty had been right there with them every day since coming back from a supply run to Newenham in May. He didn't deny wanting the postmaster job, but in an eerie echo of Leonard's own words said, "Jesus, who would want it this way?"

He escorted them firmly to the edge of his property and left them there.

"Hell," Prince said.

"Hell," Liam agreed. "Well, I guess they can't all be easy."

"If this yo-yo—"

"I know. And chances are we can't do anything unless and until he hits again."

Prince's lips were tight. "I don't like it."

"What do you want to do, Prince? Set out across country? In what direction? We looked everywhere on the Nunapitchuks' homestead for a trail and didn't find squat, except for game trails. We can't follow them all. Maybe we could bring in some dogs, pick up a trail that way. Chances of that are, oh, maybe a trillion to one, and it's even odds they'll track down the local grizzly first, which would be bad for the dogs and worse for us."

He stopped, ashamed of having lost his temper. The Nunapitchuks seemed like nice people: hardworking, self-sufficient, capable, intelligent, everything he admired. He didn't like the thought that he was about to let them down. He sighed. "We won't close the file. The M.E. will be able to tell us about the weapon, and the prints will go into the system. We'll put out a bulletin, circulate it among all the air taxi services in the Bay area in case he tries to fly out and gives himself away. Of course, he'll have to give himself away because we don't have a clue as to what he looks like. He could be a woman for all we know, or a Texas horned toad, or a little green man from Mars." He felt himself getting angry all over again, and took a deep breath and blew it out explosively.

"Canneries," Prince said. "They could pass out copies to their fishermen. In case he tried to hitch a ride downriver."

"Most of the canneries are closed for the winter," Liam said shortly.

"Oh. Right."

"Shit," Liam said.

They thanked Leonard for the loan of the four-wheelers, made vague noises when he asked them what they had discovered, and got the hell out of there.

The Cessna 185 had been in the air less than twenty minutes when the call came in. Liam, as usual preoccupied with holding the plane up in the air by sheer effort of will, didn't hear it until Prince turned up the volume. "This is eight-two Victor November to the distress call, say again?"

A calm, confident female drawl repeated, "This is Alaska Airlines one-three-three calling any small aircraft in the area of Nenevok Creek."

Prince and Liam exchanged glances, and simultaneously looked down at their watches. It was seven minutes past six. "What's the last flight into Anchorage?" Liam said.

Prince keyed the mike while Liam looked up through the windshield, trying to locate the other plane. "Alaska one-three-three, this is Cessna eight-two Victor November. I am twenty minutes out of Kagati Lake on a heading for Newenham. How may I assist you?"

"Eight-two Victor November, this is Alaska one-three-three, I have received a distress call from someone in Nenevok Creek. I repeat, I have intercepted a distress call from Nenevok Creek. The caller did not identify himself."

"Alaska one-three-three, eight-two Victor November, did he identify the problem?"

"Eight-two Victor November, Alaska one-three-three, he said someone had been shot and that they need help now."

Prince looked at Liam, who was already unfolding the map. She watched his forefinger locate Kagati Lake and trace a line south-southeast, until it stopped at Nenevok Creek.

He looked up. Her face was flushed, her eyes were bright and it looked as if her short dark hair was curling into even tighter curls. "Go," he said.

She stood the plane on one wingtip and keyed the mike at the same time. "Alaska Airlines one-three-three, this is Alaska State Trooper Diana Prince on board eight-two Victor November. We'll take it from here. Eight-two Victor November out."

NINE

Nuklunek Bluff, September 2

"Well, hell," Wy said grumpily. "I wasn't that late."

The fishermen at the lodge had been packed and waiting for pickup. She had deposited them in Newenham, refueled and flown straight back to the overgrown strip on the edge of the bluff. She found the camp easily, festooned with tents and a card table and bagged moose and caribou haunches, and congratulated herself on the fact that it was barely half an hour past the time she had said she would be there.

She climbed out and no one was there. She walked to the camp and it appeared deserted. She was confused until she saw the two cases of beer, one empty and the other halfway there.

"Well, hell," she said again, this time with a long, depressed sigh. Her least favorite thing in the world was flying a drunk. They were prone to airsickness, which did the interior of the plane no good at all and her frame of mind even less. John and Teddy were probably out helling around somewhere under the influence, using each other for target practice or some other damn fool thing.

It was odd, though, and unlike them to leave such a big meat stash unprotected. There was enough here to feed both families until the first salmon hit fresh water.

It was also a first-class bear magnet. She rummaged around in the back of the Cessna for the shotgun. She'd wait until a half hour before dark, that was it. If they didn't show, she would leave the meat to the mercy of any wandering critter who happened by, two- or four-legged.

She propped her back against a boulder and closed her eyes against the slanting rays of the lowering sun. The rock radiated heat soaked up during the day, and she felt no need for the jacket in the plane.

She thought of last night. The Nunapitchuks had a small cabin out back of the homestead, one with four bunks they used when family showed up to stay for a while. They had given them sleeping bags and pillows with fresh-smelling cases and left them alone. She loved making love to Liam, in a hard, narrow bunk, in the shower, on the bank of the Nushagak River, it didn't matter, she loved making love to him. She'd read or heard something somewhere, something about when a couple was going through a bad time, the sex helped keep things together until they came out the other end, and that when the relationship was good anyway, it was just the icing on the cake.

That was what it was like with Liam, icing on the cake. She smiled without opening her eyes.

She liked to talk to him, too, about everything and nothing. He kept up most of the time, but sometimes he was way ahead of her, and she liked that too; she didn't think she could live with someone who wasn't as smart as she was. She liked him with Tim, friendly, not pushy, letting Tim get to know him at Tim's own pace. It was important for Tim to learn that all men don't hit.

She liked it that Liam read recreationally. The does-he-read test was the only test she required the men she allowed into her life to pass. She didn't care if they were tall, short, fat, thin, old, young, she didn't care if they were Yupik from Bethel or Hindu from India—or Caucasian from Anchorage—they had to read. She didn't care what they read, they didn't even have to read the same things she did (a good thing because she read fiction, mostly, and Liam read non, mostly), but if they didn't read, they were out.

She'd read out loud to Tim while he lay in the hospital. Half the time she didn't know if he heard her or not. She read to him anyway, books from her childhood like *Little House on the Prairie* and *The Lost Wagon* and *Nancy and Plum* and *Anne of Green Gables* and *The Lion's Paw*. It was make-believe, but it was what Tim needed, and she read them all to him every minute she could spare. The business suffered some that month.

When he came home with her from the hospital, she had already furnished the second bedroom in her house, empty until then. Just the basics, a bed, a nightstand, a reading lamp, a desk with another lamp, some new clothes in the closet, khakis and T-shirts she'd ordered over the Internet from the Gap. There was also a bookshelf she'd filled with books, the Heinlein juveniles, all fourteen of the Oz books, *The Hobbit* and *The Lord of the Rings*, everything by Gary Paulsen. By then he was reading on his own.

He'd stopped for a time earlier this year, when he'd gotten in with a group of kids who had maximum security written all over their futures, but he'd begun easing away from them after Liam's arrival, and he'd broken with them entirely after Kerry and Michael Malone had died. He had respected and admired Michael, who played opposite him on the basketball court, and Wy suspected he had been a little in love with Kerry, a pretty cheerleader.

Liam had handled that with Tim, talking to him honestly about what had happened to the two kids, offering intelligent sympathy without ever once resorting to "Bad things happen to good people."

Liam was good with kids. She'd never seen him with Charlie, the son who had been killed by a drunk driver before he was two, but she'd bet Liam had been great with him, too. He wanted more kids. Well, so did she.

She had to tell him. She could feel something like tears well behind her eyelids and blinked them away.

There was a sudden snapping of twigs and cracking of

branches and she shot to her feet, checking that both barrels were loaded and that the safety was off.

It was only Teddy and John. The smell of beer preceded them into camp by a good twenty feet. "Oh hell," she said, disgusted all over again.

"Let's go," John said shortly, brushing by her to head for a caribou haunch hanging from a tree. Teddy barreled after him. Both of them were pale of face and sweating. Both seemed a lot more sober than she had expected. "How much can we take with us?"

"I thought I was flying you out one at a time," Wy said, standing with the shotgun hanging from the crook of her arm, muzzle down.

He looked at her. "Yeah. Right. Of course. Sorry." He looked at Teddy. "You go in first."

"No, you go in first."

"Goddamn it, Teddy, I said you go in first!"

"And I say you do!"

They went toe to toe, glaring at each other, and it was a moment before Wy, watching stupefied from the sidelines, stepped forward to pull them apart. "Guys. Relax. Toss a coin or something. Whoever gets left behind is only going to get left behind for ninety minutes."

They continued to glare. Teddy Engebretsen and John Kvichak had never been known to raise a hand or even a voice to the other. They stood shoulder to shoulder against all comers, but never against themselves. And now here they were fighting over who should go into town first?

Teddy broke the stalemate eventually. "Okay, John."

Everyone heaved a sigh of relief.

"Good," John said gruffly. "Help me load up." He caught Teddy's eye. "It's okay, Teddy. I'll be all right."

"What's going on?" Wy said.

"Lend me a hand with this line, will you, Wy?" Teddy said.

Old Man Creek, September 2

They ate salmon fresh out of the creek, sticky rice with generous helpings of soy sauce and steamed wild celery, the latter gathered by Amelia, who had finally gotten back out of bed. After dinner they got out the cards and played single-deck pinochle, girls against boys. Bill had to carry Amelia, but Moses told Tim, "Jesus, boy, you think you're some kind of card shark, don't you?" Tim, still sore from the second practice of the day—this one had lasted two hours—trumped Bill's ace of diamonds and shot the moon. Bill sighed and subtracted thirty-three points from their score, which put them at minus ninety-seven. "Another fifty-three points and we can go out the back door," she told Amelia.

Amelia blinked at her. "What am I doing here?" It was the first time she'd spoken all day.

She didn't look good, Bill thought, surveying the girl with a critical eye. Her eyes had deep dark shadows beneath them, the natural warm brown of her skin had turned a pasty kind of yellow in between the big blue and purple bruises, and she kept pulling at her hair.

Bill looked at Moses. "Because you're a damn fool, is why," he said. "Shuffle the goddamn cards."

The girl focused on him as if she were seeing him for the first time. "Uncle."

"Yeah, what of it?"

"Where's my husband? I want my husband."

He looked at her, at the bruises blooming beneath her skin, at the swelling of her eye only now going down. Darren Gearhart had a mean right; short, stiff, packed a lot of power. Amelia wasn't a pygmy but she wasn't his equal in size. Moses remembered Joe Gould, the Newenham ambulance's emergency medical technician, describe a head injury once over a lot of beer at Bill's bar. Joe had just lost a patient to head trauma suffered when a fight at the small-boat harbor led to a fall between boats. "One of the guys told me you could hear the crack all the way up to the harbormaster's office when the guy went in. Like breaking an egg." He went on to explain, with a delivery that became more didactic as the drink in his glass dwindled, that the human brain floated inside the skull like a cork bobbing in the water. When something hit the front of the skull, the brain inside was knocked against the back of the skull, which was why so many blows delivered by fists caused injury to the back of the cerebrum, not the front.

Maybe, Moses thought, maybe I should have run her by the hospital before I packed her onto a plane to get her out here.

He consulted the voices on the subject. They were silent. Figured. Most of the time they wouldn't shut up. Now, when he was actually looking for insight, they wouldn't talk.

"I want my husband," Amelia repeated. Her voice sounded more stubborn than whiny. If that stubborn could be harnessed for her own benefit, she might make it after all.

"No, you don't," Moses told Amelia, and snatched up the cards and began to shuffle them himself.

Later, when both kids were in bed and asleep, Bill and Moses moved to the porch. "What are we going to do with her?" she said.

"Come here, woman," he said. She curled easily into his lap. One of his hands settled naturally on the rise of her hip, the other on the curve of her breast. She sighed a little and wriggled as if to press into both. He gave her a smack on the back. "Be still before I haul you down to the ground and have my way with you."

"You mean you won't if I stay still?"

"I will no matter what you do and you know that perfectly well." He smacked her again, turning it into a caress. "I'm going to keep them isolated and safe for a few days. I'm going to teach them tai chi. I'm going to sweat the evil spirits out of them in the banya."

"It won't be enough for Amelia."

She felt him shrug beneath her cheek. "It's what I can do."

"You told her not to marry him, didn't you?"

"Nope."

"I was there in the bar, I remember."

"I didn't tell her anything. She asked me if she should marry that little prick, and I said her father's name."

"That was all?"

"Yep."

Bill sat up and looked at him. "Maybe you should have tried a little harder."

He stood up, dumping her without ceremony or apology to the selfsame floor he had been giving serious thought to wrestling her to. "How many times do I have to explain it, Bill? How many times do you have to see it? They come to me for all the answers. They think the voices will speak through me and take them by their goddamn little hands and lead them through the goddamn wilderness. It doesn't work like that, even if they do listen, which they most of the time don't."

She picked herself up to wrap her arms around him from behind. "I know."

He anchored her arms against his belly with his own. "They talk at me, all the time they talk at me. They tell me what's going to happen, they tell me flat out. I used to try to tell people what they were saying, but nobody wanted to hear. Nobody does now."

"A prophet has no honor in his own country," she said softly into that firm, erect back.

"Shit," he said. "I can't remember when I didn't hear them. This man will abuse you if you marry him, this boy will leave the village forever if you let him leave once, this girl will die drunk beside the road in winter, this man will fall off his boat and drown next summer. At first I thought everyone heard them. When I was ten my Auntie Christine took me to a shaman in New Stoyahuk to ask him to drive the evil spirits from my brain. He told her he could do nothing, that the spirits chose through whom to speak and nothing we could say or do would change that. When

I was thirteen she sent me to the Alaska Psychiatric Institute. They said I was delusional but functional and sent me home. That's when I started drinking. When I was seventeen, I got Auntie Christine to sign me into the Air Force. I got posted to the Far East, where I learned to do form. First thing that helped."

She'd heard bits and pieces of the story, but never before the story from beginning to end. "I stayed there, traveled all over the world, looking for answers in some of the goddamnedest places. Cassandra was cursed with telling the truth and never being believed. I remember the first time I heard that story, I was happy. I wasn't alone, at least not in myth.

"Then one day, I was about forty-eight, I guess, I went back to Hong Kong to see my sifu, and he told me if I hadn't found the answers I was looking for that maybe I was looking for them in the wrong places." He turned around and linked his hands behind her waist. "He was right. Whatever this is, it belongs here, at home, so I came home." He grinned at her, only a slightly less lecherous grin than before. "And you were my reward."

She searched his face with uncharacteristically solemn eyes. "What?" he said.

She adjusted his collar. "Why are you telling me this now?"

"I don't know." He was silent for a moment. "Yes I do," he said finally. He jerked his head toward the cabin door. "I was looking at her this evening, wondering how bad hurt she is, wondering if maybe I shouldn't have taken her by the emergency room before I hauled her out here." He shifted his shoulders. "I asked the voices."

"And?"

"And they didn't say."

She digested this. "Couldn't say? Wouldn't say?"

"I don't know." He fidgeted.

"Is this the first time this has happened?"

He thought, and shook his head. "No. But it doesn't happen all that goddamn often, I can tell you that."

"You wish they'd leave you alone, and you get nervous when they do."

He glared at her. "I do not get nervous."

"And when you get nervous," she went on inexorably, "you talk too much."

"Well, excuuuuuuse me," he said, insulted. "I didn't know I was boring you."

She kissed him before he could pull away, putting everything she had into it. His pique was instantly forgotten, his response was immediate and enthusiastic. When they came up for air, breathing hard, he said, "That's one thing those goddamn voices haven't interfered with."

"What?"

"Us."

She grinned. "Right." She kissed him again, hands roaming, seeking, finding.

"Gulp," he said. "Good thing I'm hanging on to something, I'd probably be on my ass about now."

"That you would, little man."

They moved to the dock and undressed, savoring the slow shedding of clothes, the slow revelation of flesh, the slow kindling and then culmination of desire. The great thing about being old, Bill thought dreamily, was that you never had to be in a hurry. There was time to linger, time to taste, touch, feel, listen. The hitch in the breath, the murmured laughter, the bittersweet flavor of the drop of sweat that rolled into the hollow of the throat, the quick, shifting arch of the hips, the sly reach of a fingertip, the firm thrust of flesh, and then the well-remembered but always new sensation of falling off the world in a blaze of white-hot glory.

Later they cuddled beneath a sleeping bag Bill fetched from the cabin and watched the moon rise into the sky, taking its time. The flat landscape was drenched with a warm yellow light, and stars began to flicker into being. "Moses?"

"What?" he said, half asleep.

"How's it going to turn out for them? The kids?"

She felt him come fully awake. "Don't ask," he said. "Don't ask me that. You know better."

She swallowed. "Bad for both of them? Both, Moses?"

He was silent for a moment. "The voices aren't always right, Bill. Sometimes people actually see the freight train coming and get off the tracks before it hits them."

She could hear the tension and the near-despair in his voice, and she let it go, but her heart ached for the two kids in the cabin, and for the man in her arms.

Nenevok Creek, September 2

Fifteen minutes after they had received the call from Alaska Airlines one-three-three, Prince put the Cessna down gently on the dirt airstrip between the three hulking mountains and Liam cold breathe again. They followed the path and found the body sprawled half in and half out of the creek, facedown.

It was a man, mid-thirties, hit in the chest at point-blank range with a shotgun. Liam pulled him out of the water but there was nothing he could do; the man was cold and rigor had already set in. The body flopped on its back like a starfish. The blue eyes stared blankly at the sky. Liam tried to close them. They wouldn't.

He yelled for Prince and she came running up the path, weapon drawn. He waved it away. "He's long gone."

They stood looking down at the dead man. "Same guy, you think?"

Liam hid an involuntary smile at the hopeful note in her voice. Prince had had a taste of the headlines on their last case. She'd love another one that put her there, and it was axiomatic in the law enforcement community that multiple murders, serial or mass, got all the best press. "Opal wasn't killed with a shotgun," he reminded her. "Did you find the cabin?"

"Yeah, come see."

It was one room, and crowded with the belongings of two people, one obviously female. "Look," Prince said, pointing at the counter. The remains of a meal sat there, two bowls of a clear broth with vegetables and chunks of chicken floating in it. "There is coffee in the pot," Prince said.

"Hot or cold?"

"Lukewarm."

The bed had been made at some point, and then someone had used the bedspread for a nap—or something more. The comforter was half on the floor and the pillows were dented.

A card table had been set up in the corner closest to the stove. Two Coleman lanterns hung from hooks over the table, and light from one of the four windows shone on it. A ray of sunshine picked up a gold sparkle, a glowing purple, and Liam walked over to find heaps of beads in sizes ranging from a cherry tomato to a grain of sand, shapes ranging from round to flat to oblong to square and everything in between, in colors reaching across the spectrum. One squat, cylindrical glass bead had faceted sides that looked blue until you held it up to the light, when it turned green. A flat, rectangular bead with rounded ends was a yellowish green that looked hideous until Liam saw it worked into a woven shape with other beads. A spill of smaller red beads had fallen to the floor in a splatter of glittering iridescence, ending in a half-empty tube, its plastic cap having rolled beneath the dining table. The beads were arranged in trays and dishes and tiny Ziploc bags. There were spools of thread in varying thicknesses, packets of needles, a coil of silver wire. There was even a miniature anvil with a matching hammer.

"A craftsman," he said. "Did you find any ID?"

She nodded, and held out a driver's license. Liam looked at the picture and whistled. "We definitely need to cherchez la femme." He held out a driver's license in his turn. "Mark Hanover," he said.

"Rebecca Hanover," Prince said. "Chances are, he was the miner, she's the beader." Prince pointed at the table. "Think our guy surprised them?"

"I don't know." Liam stepped outside the door and yelled at the top of his voice. "Rebecca! Rebecca Hanover! It's safe to come out! I'm Liam Campbell, a state trooper! It's safe to come out now!"

He called again at five-minute intervals for fifteen minutes, receiving no answer.

The two troopers followed all the trails they could find, one of which ended at another part of the creek in a narrow stretch of small, smooth rocks, many of them quartz. A flash of color caught Liam's eye, and he stooped to pick up a stalk of fireweed, neatly severed beneath the last blooms. Three feet away he found a paring knife with a black plastic handle. The flowers were wilting now. He looked for footprints but the gravel wasn't giving up any answers, and the mud on the path had dried hard.

In the meantime, Prince had fetched a body bag from the plane. "There's a wheelbarrow next to the cabin."

They loaded Mark Hanover onto the wheelbarrow. Rigor, helped no doubt by the temperature of the creek, kept the body rigid and inflexible. It kept catching on the limbs of bushes and trees on the side of the path and sliding across the edges of the barrow. Prince was swearing under her breath by the time they reached the plane, and it wasn't easy loading him into the plane either.

"You shoot," Liam said. "I'll draw and bag."

"Okay," she said, removing her cap to wipe her brow.

She used up two rolls of thirty-six-exposure film, he filled four pages with drawings and distances. Prince dusted the cabin for prints, something both of them felt was a futile gesture.

"What do you think?" she said, standing in front of the cabin when they had finished. The sun had disappeared behind one of the mountains, all warmth vanishing with it.

Liam had a map of southwest Alaska he'd found in the cabin. He looked at the distance between Kagati Lake and Nenevok Creek. "Nunapitchuk was shot yesterday morning. Our best guess for Hanover is sometime today. That creek water's going to play hell with a time of death." She nodded. "Nunapitchuk was shot, we think, with a small-bore handgun, probably a twenty-two. Hanover was shot with a shotgun. Nunapitchuk was alone, Hanover wasn't."

Dana Stabenow

"On the other hand," Prince said, "we have two people shot, maybe within twenty-four hours of each other. Both were shot at point-blank range. No shell casings at either site. It's the same part of Alaska, although the sites are forty miles apart over some very rough territory, territory even an experienced backwoodsman would be hard pressed to cover in that time."

Liam nodded. "And where is Rebecca?"

"Good question," Prince said. "Should one of us stay here and keep yelling for her?"

In answer, Liam yelled, "Rebecca! Rebecca Hanover! This is Liam Campbell, of the Alaska State Troopers! It's okay to come out! You're safe now! We're at the cabin, come on out of the woods!"

There was still no answer.

"Maybe she's running," Prince said.

"Maybe," Liam said, frowning down at the fireweed he still held in his hand.

"Maybe she's running from us."

His chest rose and fell on a sigh. "Maybe," he said.

They waited for an hour, calling her name at intervals, but Rebecca Hanover never came out of the woods.

TEN

Newenham, September 2

In the end, it took three trips in the Cessna to get all of Teddy and John's catch home, and it was with sore muscles and a feeling of relief that Wy saw them off in John's truck. They were still jumpy and irritable, and they still wouldn't acknowledge it, let alone say why. It was one of their most successful hunts ever; they should have been over the moon. Instead, they were short-tempered and nervous, starting every time a plane landed or a vehicle went by.

Wy shook her head. The evidence, specifically a case and a half of empties, indicated the strong possibility of a hangover. At any rate, it was not her problem. She cleaned out the Cessna, tied it down, piled into her own truck and headed for home, wondering if Liam had beat her there. She chastised herself for being glad that Tim was at fish camp with Moses.

The old man's truck hit a pothole and launched itself a foot in the air, and she realized she was driving a good twenty miles above the speed limit through the heart of Newenham. She hit the brakes, slowing to a more sedate twenty-five, and made herself pull into the parking lot at NC. They needed half-and-half, and her friend Olga had called this morning and told her that the recent NC shipment of Red Delicious apples was good. The Fruit

Hotline, they called it; whenever NC or Eagle got in good fresh produce, phones started ringing all over town and all the way up to Icky, the village on the edge of One Lake forty miles up the road. Wy loved a crisp, juicy apple.

She hated shopping, though. Her idea of shopping heaven was a phone, a credit card and an Eddie Bauer catalogue. Unfortunately for her, NC had yet to accept phone orders. She forced herself to get a cart and walk the aisles in search of specials, too, and even found a few. She counted the items in the cart, came in at one over the limit for the express lane and scrupulously lined up in another, behind a short teddy bear of a man with a stunning brunette on his arm. They were stocking up on Bugles and Corn Nuts, and from the bags in the cart had already paid a visit to the liquor store next door in search of the best Newenham had to offer in the way of merlots. Ah, the food of love.

The brunette nuzzled the teddy bear's ear, and the teddy bear laughed and let his hand, until then resting casually around her waist, slip as casually down to her ass in a brief and, Wy was sure he thought, surreptitious caress. Somebody get these two a motel room, fast, she thought.

At that moment the teddy bear looked around, and Wy gaped at him. "Jim? Jim Wiley?"

The teddy bear revealed himself to be a moon-faced man in his mid-forties with button eyes, plump cheeks and a full head of white hair that looked fresh off the pillow of a very comfortable bed. "Do I know you?" he said.

"No," Wy said, "but I've seen pictures of you swilling beer in college, in company with a certain state trooper of our mutual acquaintance."

The button eyes widened, and a smile spread across the moon face that creased the plump cheeks. He looked like a teddy bear from the front, too, soft, cuddly and eminently huggable. "Wyanet Chouinard?"

"Hi, Jim."

They shook hands. Wy felt the dampness on her palms and

hoped he didn't. This was Liam's best friend since college. This was the one person other than the two of them who knew exactly and precisely how long Wy and Liam had known each other, and how well. He'd been Liam's college roommate. He'd been best man at Liam's wedding. He had stood godfather to Liam's son, Charlie. He had a history with Liam that far surpassed her own. His opinion probably counted more with Liam than hers did simply by virtue of that long history. "Liam didn't tell me that you were coming to town," she said, trying hard to keep the uneasiness out of her voice.

"Liam doesn't know," Jim said. He brought the brunette forward. "This is Bridget, a friend of mine from Ireland. Bridget, this is Wyanet Chouinard."

"How nice to meet you, Wyanet, and what a lovely name. Does it mean something special, now?"

"It's Lakota Sioux," Wy said, "and, before you ask, I'm not. Call me Wy." Bridget had a soft, lilting accent that stressed the penultimate word in every sentence. She sounded to Wy's inexperienced ears as if she had just stepped down from the frame of *The Quiet Man,* one of Wy's favorite movies. "So, you're visiting Alaska?"

Bridget looked at Jim and smiled. "I'm visiting Jim."

"Ah. Oh. Well. Where are you staying?"

"With you," Jim said, and grinned.

It was an impish grin, cheerful and attractive, but there was something in his eyes, a considering look, that kept Wy from succumbing. "Good," she said, summoning a return grin that she hoped didn't look as forced as it felt. She would have loved to have shown him the door, but Liam's friendship and Bush hospitality forbade it. "My son is out of town for the Labor Day weekend, so Bridget can have his room." She didn't say where Jim could sleep, deciding they could figure it out on their own. "Have you got a car?"

They nodded. "Okay, let's pay for our groceries and you can follow me home."

Luckily she'd set a moose roast out to thaw that morning, and it was a big one. She let Jim open and pour the wine while she got busy behind the counter, and Bridget and Jim took their glasses out on the deck and exclaimed over the view of the wide expanse of Nushagak River opening up on the limitless vista of Bristol Bay. An eagle was obliging enough to fly by at just that moment, and three ravens were even more obliging: they launched themselves from where they'd been skulking in the branches of a white spruce tree and started harassing him. The eagle flapped grimly on, ignoring the three black devils as they swooped and dove and k-kkk-raked at him.

Bridget came back in from the deck, glowing. "How amazing that you live in a house where eagles fly by the front windows, Wy!"

"It's not bad," Wy admitted, measuring white wine, raspberry vinegar, sugar and minced green onions into a saucepan. She turned the gas on low beneath it and rolled the roast over again in a marinade made of olive oil, garlic powder and crushed thyme. The thermometer in the oven read three-fifty, and she put in the roast. "I don't know when Liam will be back. He didn't leave a message on the machine, so it's best if we just cook dinner and act like he'll be home on time."

"A cop's life doesn't run by the clock," Jim intoned, raising a glass. "Let's hear it for the chef."

Wy raised her glass in turn. "Only for tonight. The rule is whoever gets home first has to cook. I'm later than he is most of the time."

Bridget had been watching the preparations with an inquisitive eye. "And you said that this was moose meat, then?"

"Yeah, honey, like the big bruiser we saw that morning in my backyard," Jim said. "Chowing down on my mountain ash."

Bridget was properly horrified, and Wy and Jim exchanged a grin before they remembered that they were rivals for Liam's affection. "If he'd beat me home, he would have sliced the roast into steaks, shaken them in his very own special flour mixture and fried them in an inch of peanut oil."

"Why peanut oil?"

"You can get it hotter at higher temperatures without burning. Liam fries everything. If he could figure out a way to do it, he'd fry peanut butter."

The two women laughed. Jim, putting on a puzzled expression, said, "And your point is?"

At eight o'clock the phone rang. "Hey, flygirl, you crash any planes lately?"

Wy grinned, a wide grin of pure pleasure. "Hey, Jo. Driven any politicians to suicide lately?"

"Give me time. Labor Day's coming up."

"You are one hell of a reporter, I'll say that for you," Wy said, one eye on the sauce.

"Smart-ass. I was thinking about coming down."

"Oh yeah?" Wy said. "Were you thinking you might have a place to stay?"

"Smart-ass," Jo repeated. She hesitated.

It wasn't like Jo to hesitate. Wy turned the heat under the sauce down and took the portable phone around the corner and into the hallway. "What's wrong, Jo?"

"Nothing's wrong," Jo said irritably.

Wy frowned at the wall. "You sound funny."

Jo huffed out an aggravated breath. "There's someone I want you to meet."

Wy blinked. "Someone you want me to meet."

"That's what I said."

Now that she was listening for it, Wy could hear the self-consciousness and maybe even a little embarrassment in Jo's voice. Tongue in cheek, she said, "Would this someone by any chance be, ah"—she paused delicately—"male?"

"Kiss my ass," Jo said, varying a theme.

Wy grinned at the opposite wall, and waited.

"Yeah, all right, it's a guy."

"And you want me to meet him."

"Yeah. So?"

"Have you taken him home yet, or am I the first test?"

"Fuck you, Chouinard."

"I love you, too, Dunaway," Wy purred. "By all means, put this paragon on the first available plane, and get on after him." Voices came from the living room. How nice. Liam could have his ex-college roomie and main squeeze to stay, and she could have hers. One big, very full, deliriously happy house. "You'll have to sleep on the couch."

"That's where I slept last time," Jo said.

"Yeah, but this time it's a full house. Tim's up the river with Moses, and I'd let you have his room, but there's somebody already in it."

"Who? Liam?"

"Nope. One of your favorite people. Jim Wiley."

There was a long silence. Unlike Wy, Jo had actually met Jim Wiley. They both lived in Anchorage, not that big a town, and they were both involved in the information-gathering business, more or less. Her paper occasionally employed his services to track down subjects in cyberspace, something they both preferred to keep quiet. "Oh."

"And friend," added Wy.

"Oh." Jo rallied. "Where from this time, Sri Lanka? Peru? Pago Pago?"

"Ireland."

"Figures." Another pause. "So, you need backup."

Wy peered around the corner to see Jim murmuring sweet nothings in Bridget's ear. "It couldn't hurt."

"See you tomorrow." Click.

She walked around the corner and hung up the phone. "It's going to be a full house."

"I thought it already was," Jim said.

"Jo's coming down for the Labor Day weekend." She watched with interest as his eyes narrowed and his jaw set. Wy didn't know what had happened between the two of them because Jo refused absolutely to discuss it. Other than inventing new and better invective to describe Mr. Wiley, his progenitors and his character. Well, this certainly promised to be one of the more interesting three-day weekends of the year. She smiled to herself, and added innocently, "You remember my friend Jo Dunaway, don't you?"

He reached for his wine and drained it with one gulp. "Sure. Jo Dunaway. Pudgy blonde. Nosy reporter type. I've had to work with her a couple of times. Definitely not a fun date." He put his arms around Bridget and said brightly, "Now where were we before we were so rudely interrupted?"

Wy hid a grin and went back to the sauce. It would be nice for Jim to have another moving target at which to aim over the weekend.

It would be nice for her not to be the only target he was aiming at.

At eight-thirty the roast was ready to come out of the oven, the potatoes were done, the salad was dressed with balsamic vinegar and olive oil. Bridget and Jim set the table while Wy stepped the sauce. *"Beurre à montre la sauce,"* she said. In answer to Bridget's quizzical look, she added, "My friend Jo and I backpacked across Europe the year we graduated from college. In Paris we took a cooking class. Madame Claudine was delighted when she heard where we were from, and she made up this sauce for us to use on game. It's dead easy, it just takes forever. You reduce the initial ingredients to a couple of tablespoons, and then use butter to step the sauce. *Beurre à montre la sauce.*" She held out the spoon to Bridget first.

"That is simply heavenly," Bridget said.

"Okay, you get to eat," Wy said, and everyone laughed again.

The door opened as they were sitting down and Liam walked in. "Sit, sit," he said. "Jim, what the hell are you doing here?"

"Come to make your life a living hell," Jim retorted. "You've had it too easy way too long. This is Bridget, a friend who is visiting from Ireland."

"Bridget." Liam shook hands with Bridget, and put a hand on

Wy's shoulder. When she looked up he leaned down to kiss her. It flustered her, this casual demonstration of their relationship, and he knew it and grinned. "Yum, moose roast. No, keep eating, I'll wash up and be with you in five."

When he reappeared, attired in jeans and a T-shirt, he took the seat across from Wy and filled a plate, ladling on the sauce with a lavish hand. "My favorite. My girl, I think I'll keep her."

It was all so domestic that Wy expected the theme for *The Waltons* to begin playing at any moment. She sniffed around the edges of the feeling, decided she could live with it, and joined in the general conversation. Jim was explaining how Bridget and he were both ham radio operators and how they'd met on the air a few months before.

A few months? Wy thought. You're a fast worker, Jim Wiley. As if he could read her mind, Liam winked at her.

Bridget was a computer programmer for a software manufacturer—"We make the buttons work when you click on them"—and she had some amusing stories about people with new systems calling for help. "The first thing you tell them is, Check to see if it's plugged in. You'd be amazed at how offended they get, and how frequently they don't have the machine plugged in."

Liam told them about his week, beginning with the killing of the postmistress in Kagati Lake.

Bridget seemed more interested in how he got to Kagati Lake than in what he found there. "Well, it's not exactly the garda, now is it." She caught Wy's glance. "The garda are our local police," she explained. "They get around on foot, or in cars."

"Not planes," Liam said.

"Not planes," Bridget agreed.

"I should move to Ireland," Liam said ruefully, and in response to Bridget's raised eyebrow said, "I hate to fly. We had to stop off at Nenevok Creek on the way back to Newenham. You should see the strip into that place." He shuddered, a gesture not wholly feigned.

"Why Nenevok Creek?" Wy said, thinking of Rebecca Hanover counting down to Labor Day and liberation.

"Alaska Airlines picked up a Mayday from there and relayed it to us."

Wy put down her fork. "A Mayday from Nenevok Creek? Is that the Hanovers?"

"You know them?"

"I flew them in in May, and I've been doing supply runs in there all summer."

Liam considered. "How well did you know them?"

Wy raised her shoulders in a slight shrug. "Not personally, it was business—wait a minute." She stared hard at Liam. "Why are we speaking in the past tense?"

He grimaced. "I'm sorry, Wy. Mark Hanover is dead."

"How?"

"One shot, point-blank, from a shotgun."

"Who did it?"

"We don't know."

"Where's Rebecca?"

"We don't know that, either."

She was still for a moment. Jim and Bridget sat silent, listening. "Who made the distress call?"

"That's what's weird," Liam said. "We don't know. Alaska Airlines one-three-three intercepted a Mayday from somebody who said they were at Nenevok Creek, that someone had been shot, and that they needed help. They didn't identify themselves, and when we got there, all we found was Hanover's body."

"And no Rebecca," Wy said.

"No. It could be that she saw it happen, that she ran for her life, and that she was too afraid to come out. We'll go back in the morning, do a search of the area, see if we can't pick up her trail."

"You think it could be the same guy who shot Opal?" Wy said, echoing Prince's words.

"The postmistress in Kagati Lake," Liam explained to Jim and

Bridget. "She was killed the day before." In answer to Wy's question he shook his head. "It's possible, but I don't think so. That's a long way to travel in a pretty short time. Guy'd have to be part mountain goat and part moose."

"He doesn't have to be traveling on foot," Jim said. "Too early for snowmobiles, but maybe a four-wheeler?"

Liam shook his head again. "True, but the terrain is up and down a lot of mountains and over and around a lot of creeks and rivers between Kagati and Nenevok. It'd probably take him just as long to walk as ride. Plus, a different weapon was used the second time, too, although there's no law says he has to use the same one twice."

He paused. "Wy, you said you felt sorry for Rebecca Hanover. Why?"

Wy made a face. "From what I could see, her husband had the gold bug bad. She was the one who met the plane because he was always hip deep in the creek, washing that dirt. She seemed lonely." Wy thought for a moment and added, "She seemed bored."

"Did she ever seem resentful?" Liam suggested. "Angry, maybe?"

"No," Wy said. "Like I said. Lonely. She looked tired every time I saw her, too, like she wasn't used to doing without Chugach Electric." She speared her last bite of moose with her fork and smeared up the last of the sauce, cooling now and a little congealed but still delicious.

The fork paused halfway to her mouth. "Wait a minute," she said, a sick feeling beginning in the pit of her stomach. "Nenevok Creek?"

Liam looked at her, alert to the sense of strain in her voice. "Yeah. Nenevok Creek, or rather the airstrip about halfway between Nenevok Lake and Nuklunek Bluff. Why?"

She put down the fork, rose to her feet and walked over to the wall map, tracing the same route Liam had the day before. She located the creek without difficulty, and estimated the distance between the airstrip at Nenevok Creek and the airstrip on Nuk-lunek Bluff at a little less than ten air miles. For someone hiking the same distance, say going from the bluff to the creek, he could follow a relatively easy slope down the bluff, wade through about a mile of swamp, the most difficult portion of the route, and then pick up the creek and follow it the rest of the way. The airstrip was right on the creek, and the gold mining camp was a two-minute walk from the airstrip. It wouldn't have been a particularly difficult hike, especially if the hiker was someone who knew the area.

Someone, say, like John Kvichak. Or Teddy Engebretsen.

Wy thought back to the last trip she had made into Nuklunek that afternoon. John Kvichak had waited with the last of the moose meat, and had helped load it into the Cessna with swift efficiency. Wy couldn't remember a time when John hadn't had a smile and a joke ready to share. This afternoon, he'd been silent and serious. He had also been in a hurry, so much so that he'd dropped his pack when he went to put it into the airplane. The zipper of the flap pocket had been open, and out had spilled a copy of *Riders of the Purple Sage,* a spoon smeared with peanut butter, and a cell phone.

"Wy?"

She turned and looked at Liam. "Can a cell phone on the ground raise a jet airplane at twenty thousand feet?"

The three people at the table exchanged glances.

"They're always after making you turn the things off before they take off," Bridget said.

"Depends on what channel they're both on," Jim said. "If the communications man on the jet was channel-surfing and the guy on the ground was broadcasting steadily, probably. It'd be mostly a matter of chance, I think."

"There was that guy hunting caribou in Mulchatna," Liam said.

Jim snapped his fingers. "Right, I remember that story."

"Yeah," said Liam, "he ground-looped it and an Alaska Airlines jet going to Gambell picked up his Mayday. It was in the paper."

She was so beautiful, in her own way as beautiful as Elaine, so rounded and so feminine. She was frightened at first, of course, but as soon as she realized she had no choice, she calmed right down.

Women were like that. They were a lot smarter than most men gave them credit for, they knew how to survive. They were the weaker sex, certainly, but that didn't mean they were any less intelligent. She knew the instant she looked into his eyes what survival would entail.

He had nothing but contempt for her husband. The cabin was poorly built, there wasn't enough food to last more than a month, the man hadn't done any hunting to take up the slack when the food ran out. A poor provider.

And she didn't weep when she saw her husband's body. Her eyes were fixed on him. Poor little woman, she needed rescuing. Lucky for her he happened along.

Or was it? Was it instead part of God's holy plan? She was a gift to him as much as he was to her; could one argue with any conviction that such things were the product of simple fate? No, it could not be so. She was a gift, and he would guard her and treasure her accordingly.

He told her that he was hungry. She cooked for him, noodles with green onions sliced into them at the last moment before serving and a few drops of sesame oil added, a dish new to him but which he liked very much. He said he was thirsty. She made him coffee, good coffee, too, the best he had had in many years.

She fussed a little when it came time to take off her clothes, but that was only due to the natural modesty of women.

She lay still beneath him, like Elaine, Elaine-fair, and kept her eyes closed, the way Elaine had at first. Her skin was so soft to the touch. He told her to open her eyes. They were so large, the pupils expanded almost to the edge of the blue irises. Her breath came in soft expulsions of air that touched his face in quick pants. Her hands lay at her sides until he told her to place them on his back. It was fine, so very fine, to be held within those arms again.

She was weak and he was strong. It was his duty to protect her, it was her duty to submit. Where he led, she would follow. Their roles had been laid down by God and the Church many years ago.

At last, at last, Elaine had come back to him.

ELEVEN

"Far as I know, they slept the night through," Mamie said. "I wasn't surprised, since they both smelled like they fell off the back of a beer truck when you hauled them in last night. And if you don't mind, it's about my bedtime now."

"Why did you switch to the night shift?" Prince asked.

"It's almost time for school to start. This way I'll be awake in the morning to see the kids off."

Mamie Hagemeister was a short, very well-fleshed woman with bad skin and short, thin, fine brown hair that stood on end from its own self-generated static electricity. With her round, protuberant brown eyes, she looked like a long-haired koala plugged into a wall socket. She was also the single mother of five children ranging in age from three to ten, which explained her constantly harried air.

She was the officer in charge of the local jail, one of the four officers belonging to the perpetually shorthanded local police department Liam had met. "Any chance of seeing Raymo or Berg today?"

She paused for a precious moment in her headlong flight. "I don't think so. Roger's still in Anchorage at that damn trial, and I just dispatched Cliff down to the harbor."

"What's happening at the harbor?"

She shrugged. "Who knows? Somebody called and said Jeff Saltz was cutting his boat in half with a chain saw."

She said it nonchalantly, like cutting boats in half with chain saws was an everyday occurrence in the Newenham small-boat harbor. "I asked the guy," Mamie said, impatient to be gone, "I said to him, is he carving up anything besides his boat? Like a person? Guy said no. I said to the guy, then why do you need the cops?"

"Why did he?"

"The guy with the chain saw's boat was tied to the boat belonging to the guy who called. Anyway, I told Cliff and Cliff went down to see what he could do."

"Mamie?" A voice came up the corridor.

"You hush up, Lorne, I'm trying to get off shift here." She jerked her chin in the voice's direction. "Lorne Rapp. Roger brought him in at three-thirty for beating up on his family. Drunk and disorderly, and he tried, I say he tried, to assault an officer."

"I trust he didn't get away with it," Liam murmured.

Mamie gave the trooper an indignant look. "Not on my shift he didn't. He's got a lump on his head the size of Gibraltar to remind him not to if he ever gets the yen again. The nerve!"

Any woman who could single-handedly raise five children and still string words together in a coherent sentence commanded Liam's respect and admiration, and he held the door for Mamie on her way out.

"We want to talk to Engebretsen and Kvichak," he told Nick Potts, a skinny young man who barely looked old enough to vote. Nick was working day shift. Nick didn't look like he could punch his way out of a paper bag, let alone keep order among the Newenham criminal element. He knew this, and compensated by trying to grow a mustache, which after two months still looked like something applied with a number 2 pencil. "You want the interview room?"

"Please," Liam said. Prince smiled at the young man, who blushed hotly and dropped his keys.

❦   ❦   ❦

The interview room was a narrow rectangle with one barred window, a table and four chairs. Liam and Prince sat on one side, Teddy and John on the other.

Teddy and John still smelled faintly of beer, but after a night in jail they were stone-cold sober. John was tight-lipped and angry, Teddy terrified. "You never charged us with anything," John said. "You never even told us why you were locking us up."

"Legally, I've got twenty-four hours to charge you with anything," Liam said soothingly, "and as for telling you why I was locking you up, I was afraid if I left you at home you'd get drunker and I wouldn't be able to talk to you at all."

"We didn't do anything," Teddy said.

"Shut up, Teddy," John said.

"But we didn't do anything," Teddy repeated.

"Let them tell us all about it," John said. "Don't you say a word unless I say so. Cops always twist everything you say to make it fit how they want. Don't say a word, okay?" He glared at Liam and Prince.

Prince waited long enough to see that Liam was giving her the lead, and opened the folder in front of her.

"You've got a history with us, gentlemen."

Teddy shifted in his chair. John stilled him with a glance.

"Most of it regarding the Nuklunek Bluff, which you seem to regard as your personal, private property."

John snorted. "Ain't no such thing as private property out here."

As if she hadn't heard him, Prince said, "You've been questioned regarding several incidents involving campers and hunters in the area, resulting in, at minimum, destruction of private property and, at most, the threat of bodily harm."

"Yeah, well, shit happens in the Bush. If you don't know how to handle yourself, stay the hell out."

Prince closed the file and folded her hands on top of it. She looked at John, ignoring Teddy. "You hunt the Nuklunek Bluff every year, don't you, John?"

"What of it?"

"Why there, in particular?"

"Because we always get our moose there, why else?"

"Did pretty well this year, too, according to Wy Chouinard. She said you packed out three planeloads of meat." Prince smiled suddenly, a wide, warm smile. It was infectious; John, thrown off balance, nearly smiled back. "Good news for the family."

"Yeah, well. Fishing hasn't been all that great, last couple of years. People gotta eat."

Prince nodded sympathetically. "So you were out there, what, ten days?"

"Yeah, we—what the hell is this? You've talked to Wy, you've probably seen her log, you probably know perfectly well how long we were out there."

Prince's smile vanished. "It's important to confirm what we already know, John. So, while you were out there, did you run across anyone else? Any other hunters?"

"No," he said.

Teddy squirmed.

"Did you hear or see anything unusual? Anything out of the ordinary? Anything you thought was odd?"

"No, why should we?"

Prince frowned down at the file. "Do you have a cell phone, John?"

A brief pause. "Why?"

Prince pulled out an evidence bag, the cell phone sealed inside clearly visible. She put it on the table, in the exact center so that it was the focus of four pairs of eyes. John's were fierce, Teddy's alarmed, Prince's inquiring, Liam's uninterested. "Because we found this in your backpack when we searched your house."

"Oh." Nonplussed for a moment, John fired up immediately. "What business you got going through my house?"

"We had a warrant, John," Prince said, almost apologetically. "We had probable cause."

Teddy whimpered. John nudged him in the ribs with an ungentle elbow. "What's probable cause?"

Prince's smile vanished. Like any cop, she didn't care for the jailhouse lawyer. "Probable cause, John, is when we've got a couple of yo-yos hunting ten miles from where we find a man who caught a load of buckshot in the chest. Probable cause is when both yo-yos have a long record of harassing other visitors to the area. Probable cause is when both these yo-yos are packing rifles to hunt moose and caribou, and shotguns to hunt ptarmigan. Probable cause is when we find the dead guy was killed with a shotgun." Prince sat back and folded her arms across her chest. "Probable cause is when we respond to a call for help from someone who isn't there when we arrive, a Mayday that was picked up by Alaska Airlines and which call, we are reliably informed, was routed through the local cell phone signal repeater with an ID number that traces back to your phone."

Not bad, Liam thought, not bad at all. We'll make a trooper out of you yet, little lady. He had to suppress a grin at Prince's likely reaction should she ever be made privy to that thought.

Teddy broke first, as Liam had told Prince he would. Normally they would have interrogated the two men separately, but Liam was worried about Rebecca Hanover, and he wanted to break the two men as quickly as possible. "We hit them both at once with everything we've got. John will bluster, Teddy will buckle."

Teddy buckled. "We didn't do it," he said, as tears began to leak down his cheeks. "We didn't shoot that man."

"What man?"

"The man in the creek."

"Teddy—" John said, but his heart wasn't in it.

"We heard shots—" Teddy said, tears flowing faster.

"One shot," John said, and flushed.

"—and John said we should go look. We knew Gregg Saltz'd sold his mine to some guy from Anchorage. We even sneaked over to take a look when we first flew in, but they weren't doing nothing except wash dirt. Nice-looking wife, though," he said wistfully. Prince handed him a Kleenex and he blew his nose with a comprehensive blast.

There was a short silence. Prince looked at John. "Goddamn it," he said more in sorrow than in anger. "I love you, man, but you just can't keep your mouth shut."

"I'm sorry," a miserable Teddy told him. "I'm sorry," he said to Prince.

"What are you sorry for, Teddy?" Prince said.

He stared at her with wide eyes. John said hotly, "He's not sorry for killing that guy." Everyone looked at him and he flushed again. "That's not what I meant. We didn't shoot that guy. We heard a shot and we went to go see, that's all! We found the body, and I knew what the cops would think. We made the call on my phone and got the hell out of there, that's all."

"About what time was this?"

"Hell, I don't know. We were done hunting, kind of relaxing until Wy got there."

Translation: They'd opened the beer.

Patiently, Prince led John and Teddy through their last day at hunting camp in hopes of creating a timeline. It wasn't easy since neither man wore a watch. They'd risen at sunrise, heard the shot "a little later," done a forced march of a little over nine miles in "maybe an hour, maybe two," found the body, known they were in trouble, yelled for help and been back at camp in time to be picked up by Wy.

"About how long from the time you heard the shots to the time you arrived at the mine?" Prince said.

John and Teddy exchanged glances and shrugged. "Maybe two hours. Maybe more."

"And you found the body in the creek?"

"Yeah." Teddy paled. "He was dead."

"How could you tell?"

He stared at her. "He was facedown in the creek, man. His chest was blown away. His heart wasn't beating."

"How could you tell that his chest was blown away if he was facedown in the creek?"

"We turned him over," Teddy said, and John groaned.

"You moved the body," Prince said.

"Yeah." Teddy looked from Prince to John, and appealed to Liam. "I mean, he was facedown in the creek. We couldn't leave him like that."

Prince penciled a note.

Liam spoke for the first time, his deep voice slow and authoritative, and both men jumped. "Where was the woman? The wife of the dead man? Rebecca Hanover?"

"We didn't see her," Teddy said. "Is that her name? Rebecca? That's kind of pretty."

"She wasn't anywhere around," John said. "We yelled for her, but she didn't show."

"Did you look in the cabin?"

"Yes."

"Did you look around the grounds?"

"Man, we just wanted out of there. We made sure the guy was dead, we looked for her, we yelled for her, we made the call, we left. That's it."

Prince was all but wagging her tail when they walked into the post. "I got the shotguns on the first flight into Anchorage. I called the Crime Lab to be expecting them. I'm betting the shot pattern from Teddy's shotgun matches the one the M.E. finds on Hanover's chest."

"Teddy, huh?" Liam said. "Why Teddy?"

"Because he's the nervous one," she said promptly. "I can see him popping off without thinking. Plus, he had an eye on the wife."

"Yeah," Liam said, "but why'd they make the call?"

Prince stared. "What?"

"Why did they make the call?" Liam repeated. "If they killed him, why call for help? Why draw attention to their crime?"

After an uncertain moment, she suggested, "Maybe the shooting sobered them up. Maybe they figured if they called for help, we wouldn't be liking them for the shooting."

"Maybe," Liam said equably. "But in that case, where's the wife?"

"They've got the weapons," Prince said, unconvinced. "They've got a history of doing this kind of thing."

"They've got a history of harassment and destruction of private property," Liam corrected her, "not to mention chasing off Dagfinn Grant's customers' moose. They've never shot anyone."

"Teddy Engebretsen shot out the jukebox at Bill's in May," Prince said.

"Shooting a jukebox is one thing," Liam said. "Shooting a person is another thing entirely."

"They were drunk," Prince reminded him.

"Yeah," Liam said, a little grimly. "They were that."

Prince went off to interview the Kvichak and Engebretsen families, to see if Teddy or John had confessed to anything in the four hours between their return and their arrest. Liam called the house to see if Wy was home. After five rings Jim picked up, out of breath. Liam grinned out the window. The morning fog would have burned off by ten, and the sun, he well knew, would be beating down on the deck in front of Wy's living room. "Having a nice morning?" he inquired solicitously.

"Up yours, Campbell," Jim said. In the background Liam could hear Bridget chuckling.

"Wy there?"

"No. I'm hanging up now."

"Hold on. You said you had something to tell me."

A brief pause. "Yeah, but not right now."

"Okay," Liam said. There was something in the tone of Jim's

voice that warned him he wasn't going to like it, whatever it was. "It sounds like it can keep."

"Not indefinitely," Jim said, and hung up.

Liam drove out to the airport, and was lucky enough to see 68 Kilo coming in on final. It was a runway paint job, smooth as silk, and Liam, safely on the ground, could admire the skill and the professionalism and be proud that his woman was so good at her job.

He thought of his wife, put in a coma by a drunken driver, from which she had never woken. He had enjoyed married life. He liked snuggling beneath the covers every night with the same woman. He liked drinking coffee with her the next morning and talking about what the day would bring. He liked coming home to eat dinner with her, catching up on what had gone right and wrong with the day. He'd liked long, lazy weekends on the couch, reading and watching television and eating popcorn and making love.

There hadn't been as much of that last as he would have liked, given the responsibilities of his job, but Jenny had never complained. Jennifer. Jenny with the light brown hair. Jenny-fair, their high school French teacher had called her, and fair she had been. He still missed her, would always miss her. They'd been best friends all through middle school and high school, and when they came back from their respective colleges it had seemed as natural as breathing to marry. There had been no highs and no lows in his relationship with Jenny, no uncertainty, no anxiety.

Unlike his relationship with Wy. With Wy, it was either mountaintop or abyss. But then he hadn't known there were mountains to scale or an abyss to plumb during his marriage to Jenny.

He missed his friend more than he did his wife, and he missed his son more than either of them. He wondered if he should be ashamed of that fact. He wondered if Jenny would understand.

The Cessna stopped ten feet away. Practically before the prop had slowed, the passenger door opened and a man bailed out.

131

"Bailed" was the right word; he managed to miss the step on the strut entirely and hit the ground walking, rapidly, in the opposite direction.

Liam had exited planes in just that manner himself on one or two occasions, and he sympathized. "Rough flight?" he said to Wy as she walked toward him.

She shook her head and smiled. "That was Mr. Frederick Glanville of the Internal Revenue Service. He went out to Kokwok to perform an audit."

Liam began to grin. "Let me guess. He'd never flown in a small plane before."

"Nothing smaller than the 737 that got him to Newenham, would be my guess," Wy said, nodding. "Plus, Stanley Sacaloff was waiting for him on the other end."

Liam started to laugh. "He was auditing Stanley Sacaloff?"

"That was his plan. He was pretty tight-lipped when I picked him up this morning, so I don't know how successful the audit was."

"Pretty successful," Liam pointed out, "if Stanley let him walk away from it." He slid a hand around her neck and kissed her. It started out to be a quick greeting and evolved into something more.

She pulled back with a flush in her cheeks. "Remember the uniform," she said, trying for casual and not succeeding very well.

"The hell with the uniform."

She stepped out of reach and tried to frown. "Behave. What are you doing out here, anyway?"

His hands dropped and his smile faded. "I need a ride."

"Sure. Where to?"

"Nenevok Creek."

"Oh." She was silent for a moment. "Did you talk to John and Teddy this morning?"

"Yes. They said all they did was find the body."

"They didn't see Rebecca?"

"They say not."

"She could have been scared. Running from the real killer. Maybe the same person who killed Opal Nunapitchuk."

"Maybe."

"You don't sound convinced."

"I'm not," he said. "I know you've known them forever. I know you don't think they could kill anyone. But Wy, you've flown me out to incidents before. You know anyone can do anything, given the right motivation. They were on the scene. They had the weapon. They were drunk. And they have a history of harassing people in the area."

"But not killing them," she said quickly, repeating his own argument back to him.

"But not killing them," he agreed. "Anyway, alive or dead, we've got to find the wife. If she's alive, she's got to be terrified, maybe lost. I've already talked to Search and Rescue out at Chinook Air Force Base. They've been quartering the area since dawn."

"Anything?"

"Nothing, no sign of her, no smoke or flares. No signal of any kind." He didn't know how wilderness-savvy Rebecca Hanover was going to be, but even a beader from Anchorage ought to be able to follow a creek downstream. Trouble was, the killer would very probably be right behind her. If he wasn't locked up in the Newenham jail.

"Any sign she returned to the creek?"

"No smoke from the stack, and she didn't come out to wave when the plane went over. They told me they made enough noise to make sure she would hear them."

No more bodies, Wy thought, I don't want to find any more bodies. "Do you think she's dead?"

"That would be the most logical assumption," he admitted.

"But?"

He gave a frustrated shake of his head. "I don't know, but I don't like the smell of this. Something about the mine site is itch-ing at me. Something important I saw that didn't register. I want to go back and find out what it is. Are you available?"

She smiled then, a long, slow, incite-to-riot smile. "I'm always available. I'm just not easy."

"You're telling me."

TWELVE

Wood River Mountains, September 3

She was so tired.

Tired and numb to anything but putting one foot down after the other.

That morning there had been planes flying overhead, and he had kept them both in the rough shelter of spruce boughs he had built the night before. He wouldn't allow a fire, and she was as cold as she was tired. He had insisted she put on every article of clothing she had, and still she was cold, shivering, teeth chattering, she couldn't seem to stop them.

It didn't matter, because none of it seemed real, not from the moment she had heard the shots and come running down the path from the creek to see him standing over Mark's body.

Mark, already dead. Mark, to whom she would now never be able to say she was sorry.

Somewhere deep inside, the pain and the grief stirred once, stilled again. To feel pain, to feel grief, one must think, and she would not allow thought.

She would not think of how he had stood looking at her as seconds passed, then minutes, as she did nothing, said nothing. No protest, no scream for help, she hadn't tried to run, nothing. He'd told her he was hungry, and she'd made him the lunch she had planned for Mark. He'd admired her beadwork, and she'd said thank you. He'd told her to take her clothes off, and she had. He'd told her to lie down on the bed, and she did. He had raped her, and she had endured it, motionless, unprotesting, her husband's body cooling in the creek not fifty feet from where they lay.

She didn't know where they were, except that they were in the mountains, tall ones. He seemed to know where he was going, and she was aware enough to see the sun rise in the east and to see that they were traveling in a southeasterly direction.

They had seen grizzlies feeding on salmon in the creeks they crossed. They had seen moose standing in still ponds, up to their shoulders in water and with their heads submerged as they rooted for forage. They had seen rabbits beginning to shed their brown summer coats and replace them with winter white. They had seen no other people.

He carried a backpack, and they ate food cold from cans. They couldn't risk a fire, he said, not now that they were so close to home. When they got home, he said, he would build her a fire in the stove and she would be warm again. He'd missed her, he said, he'd had no one to cook for him, to clean for him, to put the buttons back on his shirts, to help him tan the hides of the mink and the marten and the beaver he trapped during the winter, to help him dress and butcher the caribou he shot in the fall, to plant the garden in spring. He smiled at her, his odd light-colored eyes serene with happiness.

He waited for an hour after the sound of the plane engines died away before he crawled out of the shelter. He stood at the opening for a long time, listening. She stared at the backs of his knees.

He turned and bent down to hold out his hand to help her to her feet. She came out clumsily, her hair catching on a spruce branch, a lost bead, red as a drop of fresh blood, spilling from her pocket. He brushed the twigs from her jacket and jeans, plucked a spider from her collar, adjusted the straps of her knapsack. He stood looking down at her, smiling. "I've been looking for you everywhere," he said, "and now I've found you." He traced her cheek with a finger and smiled. "And now we can go home."

She shouldn't have run off, he had told her reproachfully during the night. She was safest with him, he would protect her, watch over her, and their children. She almost came alive at that, but then he spread her legs and raped her again, and again she went numb.

It was all happening to someone else, anyway. She, Rebecca Hanover, had a husband and a home and a job. She, Rebecca Hanover, lived in Anchorage, and went ice-skating on Westchester Lagoon during the winter, and bicycling on the Coastal Trail in the summer, and took beading lessons at Color Creek Studio, and had coffee with Nina on Saturday mornings at City Market. She, Rebecca Hanover, did not hike through the backwoods, cold and tired and hungry and terrified. She, Rebecca Hanover, was not raped in those woods by a stranger who had murdered her husband.

So of course none of this could be happening to her. It was a dream, a bad one, from which she would soon wake up, warm and safe in her own bed.

All she had to do was wait.

Old Man Creek, September 3

The second morning began the same way the first had, with tai chi and a sweat. Afterward, Moses put Tim and Amelia in the skiff and took them down to his favorite fishing hole.

Bill sat on the front porch with a lap full of files that needed closing after the latest spurt of infractions during the most recent fishing period. She regarded the thick pile with some disfavor, wondering if perhaps she wouldn't rather be hip deep in fish gurry after all.

Bill was in the business of justice, not retaliation, and she evaluated every case brought before her with the same care and attention. The problem was, the fishermen against whom fish and game trooper Charlene Taylor swore out complaints kept saying the same things, over and over again, until they sounded like a sixth grader excusing the loss of his homework. The engine broke. The trooper didn't give us the signal. My clock stopped. The bilge pump went out. The engine broke. The mechanic got seasick. The net got caught in the prop. The engine broke.

So far Bill had heard every excuse except "My dog ate it," and it was difficult to summon up the necessary compassion to temper the letter of the law and still enforce it. Her problem was she had no tolerance for fools, and after sitting on an average of three hundred such cases every summer, along about August most of the fishers looked pretty foolish.

First file, Gary Samidia, fishing over the line, two-thousand-dollar fine, four points on his fishing license. Another four and he wouldn't fish next year. Eric Redden, nets in the water before the period started. It was his second time before her that summer and the third time in two years, and she was tired of smelling his unwashed self in her courtroom, which was very small and lacked ventilation. Three thousand dollars, five hundred suspended, and six points. Silas Wood, spotted from the air with his nets in the water a good hour after the period on Friday before last. He'd pled a burst hydraulic line, and had held up a length of tubing that he swore was the guilty party. Silas, Silas, Silas, you dumb son of a bitch, if you take all the fish before they hit the creeks, there won't be any left alive to spawn and send chilluns back out to sea.

Still, Silas had lost his wife two years before and was now the sole support of seven children, all under twelve years of age. One thousand, seven hundred fifty suspended, no points, and forty-five hours of community service. Bill had already talked to the high school principal. Silas would serve out his sentence in the computer lab there, proctoring the fall semester's students during the day and at night receiving some tutoring in the finer arts of data entry. Mayor Jim Earl was chivvying the town council into hiring another clerk for City Hall, and Bill was pretty sure he would succeed.

She put aside the stack of fishing violations with relief and made herself a cup of coffee. By the time she came back out on the porch, Moses had returned with the two kids and a boatload of fish, and they were unloading down at the dock. She stood watching for a few moments, sipping at her mug. Tim liked cleaning fish and he was good at it, the tip of the knife inserted in the anus, the quick slit up the belly, the efficient scooping out of guts. Amelia was equally efficient, if a little slower. Lack of practice, probably. She hadn't been out to her family's fish camp this summer. Her husband wanted her home. Probably to use as a punching bag.

Bill sighed and sat back down, setting the mug on the railing and picking up a single legal file sitting separate from the others.

It was the record of a presumptive death hearing, the results of which the parents of the deceased were challenging. A young man, one of a youth group affiliated with a Presbyterian church out of Akron, Ohio, who had come to Alaska for a lesson in wilderness experience, had gone hiking with three friends on a glacier in the Wood River Mountains. The young man had gone for water and disappeared, and after four days Liam Campbell had called off the search and requested a hearing on the presumptive death of the young man.

At the hearing, he had displayed photographs of the area, photographs of the pot lying on its side next to a sluggish stream of meltoff, a map with distances penciled in showing a narrow, easily overlooked and seemingly bottomless crevasse a few feet away from which Liam reported the sound of a lot of water running hard, and SAR's report of lowering a fiber-optic cable down the crevasse and finding no body. The trooper's best guess was that the boy had gone for water, slipped and fallen into the crevasse, and immediately been caught up in the subglacial river. The location of the boy's disappearance was near the mouth of the glacier, and the force of the subsurface meltoff swift and strong, but given the slow rate at which glaciers melted, it would be a long time before the body could be recovered, if ever. With luck the glacier would calve quickly and in ten or fifteen years one of the slabs that fell from its face would yield up the body of the lost boy.

The parents had flown up from Akron, and they fought Bill's finding of death by misadventure every step of the way. They reported quarrels between the hikers, a grudge held against their son by another of the hikers, whose girlfriend their son had taken, and even floated the idea that the instructor had harbored feelings of animosity and possibly homicide toward the boy because of some disagreement over grades back in McKinley High School.

Bill understood; it was difficult to accept the fact that your golden boy had tripped over his own feet and fallen headfirst into a glacier, never to be seen again. There was no sense in that kind of death. Better foul play, a murder, an event that would give them someone to blame, to punish.

Presumptive death hearings were Bill's least favorite duty. When a fisher was lost at sea, when a climber died on Denali, when a plane was lost in the Bush, and when the bodies of the fishers and the climbers and the fliers were unrecoverable, a presumptive death hearing was held. Most of the time the procedure gave the families some closure, the insurance companies the go-ahead to pay off policies and the lawyers permission to file for probate.

Sometimes, though, the families could not or would not accept the inevitable.

Like Lyle Montgomery. The first of the month, every month, he called, looking for his daughter. He didn't weep anymore during his phone calls. Bill couldn't decide if it was worse now than when he had. You wanted to do your best for the families and especially the parents. You wanted to give them a way to put their missing children to rest and a chance to get on with their lives. Some accepted your help. Some did not.

They'd never found Ruby Nunapitchuk, either, lost on a hunting trip eight years before. Opal and Leonard had handled their loss better than Lyle Montgomery had his, though. Probably helped that they lived in the Bush, and knew the risks inherent in a Bush lifestyle. Probably also helped that they'd had three other children, and grandchildren shortly thereafter.

A hand grabbed her hair and pulled her out of her melancholy reverie. She saw daylight for approximately one second before it was blotted out by Moses' grin. He kissed her, completely and thoroughly, and as always she felt the world go a little fuzzy around the edges, as if everything else went out of focus when he stepped into the frame.

He pulled back, inspected her and seemed satisfied. "You looked sad."

"Do I now?"

"No," he said smugly, and she had to laugh.

He took the file from her hand and tossed it behind him without noticing where it fell. "You can either work on your trip to New Orleans, or you can help us get the fish into brine. Your choice."

Her smile was sweet. "I don't do fish."

"Bourbon Street it is," he said, and kissed her again before swaggering back down into the yard. "Get a move on, you lazy little shits, before I boot your behinds up around your ears! We've got form to do before lunch!"

Nenevok Creek, September 3

They were on a short final into Nenevok Creek to scratch Liam's itch when the throttle cable on the Cessna broke.

They'd had to go around at the last moment, about ten feet off the deck and fifty feet off the end of the airstrip, when a bull moose wandered out of the trees. He looked up at them, startled, and then lunged across the strip and into the brush on the opposite side, at the same time Wy grabbed for the throttle and shoved it all the way in.

141

Liam, sitting in the right seat and cursing steadily and color-fully, didn't notice anything else wrong at first. It helped that he had his eyes screwed shut. He opened them when he heard her voice over the headset.

"Oh, shit."

Of all the words in the world that someone who is deathly afraid of flying can hear in the air, "Oh, shit" are the two you least want to hear, and the two most productive of sheer terror. "What!"

"Shut up!" she yelled back. "I'm busy!"

Of all the words in the world that someone who is deathly afraid of flying can hear in the air, "Shut up, I'm busy" are the four you least want to hear, ranking right down there one notch above "Oh shit." He didn't shut up, although he did try to remain calm. He gulped, trying to get his heart out of his throat and back down in his chest where it belonged. "Wy, what's wrong?"

"The throttle cable broke when I put on power to go around," she said. She seemed very calm, lips pressed together in a prim line, face set. She was wearing sunglasses, so he couldn't see her eyes.

It had finally happened, his worst fear: the plane had broken while they were in the air. "I love you, Wy," he said, and bravely prepared to meet his death.

"Give it a rest, Campbell," she said, irritated. "All I have to do is fly the plane. We'll be fine." She glanced at him and saw the fear writ large upon his countenance for all to see, but it was only her in the cockpit with him, and only she could get him down in one piece. He needed reassurance, but she didn't have time to give him any.

Maybe she could talk him down.

She began to speak, keeping her voice steady, her tone casual. "I felt the cable go when I went full ahead to get altitude for the go-around. It's stuck in the full-throttle position, all the juice, full-ahead go. We need low power to land, not full power."

The plane's engine seemed louder and fiercer at this moment

than any Liam had heard before. The Cessna was at a hundred feet and in a shallow right turn, Nenevok Creek, the tops of the spruce and birch and a small but rugged outcropping of rock passing in rapid succession beneath the right wheel. The single wheel of the landing gear visible to him was shuddering beneath the vibrations of the RPMs, and to Liam's fascinated eye looked as if it were ready to launch out on its own.

Over the headset Wy's voice came, unruffled, no hint of panic, a throttle cable could have broken in flight every day of her flying career for all the emotion she put into the words. "I'm going to pull the carb heat, that will slow us down some." Her hands moved to another control. "Now I'm going to trim the nose down, to keep from climbing. That will slow us down some more."

It did seem like they were slowing down. It took a long time to get on the other side of that rock outcropping, which seemed more threatening the longer Liam looked at it. "I love you, Wy," he repeated.

"Now I'm going to lean the mixture. That cuts the gas going into the engine, slows it down even more."

What if the engine quit completely? It took everything in him not to ask the question out loud. He could no longer watch the ground rush up at them and lowered his gaze to the control panel. The first thing to meet his appalled eyes was the altimeter. Fifty feet. Thirty. The tail of the Cessna came up. Twenty.

"Okay," Wy said serenely, "we're looking good. Now I'm going to pull the mixture all the way out. That means that the engine will be getting all air and no fuel, and that means that—" Wy's hands went to a knob and pulled it all the way out.

The engine died.

There was no sound but the rush of air past the plane. The prop slowed and then came to a stop, the blades straight up and down in front of the windshield.

They touched down easily, smoothly, connecting solidly on all three wheels all at the same time, as if they'd done it a thousand times before and, praise be, would live to do it a thousand times again.

The plane rolled to a stop well before the end of the strip, plenty of room to spare.

The two in it sat for a moment, silent, staring forward.

Wy moved first, removing her headset and tossing it on top of the dash. She took a deep breath and turned to smile at Liam. "That's what we call a deadstick landing. No power. All up to lift and gravity."

His mouth was so dry he couldn't speak, could only nod to let her know he had heard.

They got out of the plane, moving with exaggerated care, as if the return to of terra firma was still a tentative thing.

A loud squawking caw came from the top of a nearby spruce tree, and Liam squinted up to see the raven sitting in its very top. It squawked again and launched suddenly, sailing over their heads on shiny black wings. It swooped and dived, climbed and banked, did snap rolls and Immelmanns in an aerial exhibition of consummate grace and power that mocked the rigid form of their own craft.

Liam watched with a kind of numb incomprehension, Wy with envy. "God, to fly like that," she said. "It's all we want when we take to the air, to master it, to make it our own. And we never even come close."

She looked at Liam, still mute. She looked at the Cessna, planted placidly on its gear. "We were never in that much danger, Liam," she said gently. "Yeah, the throttle cable broke, but there's a way to handle it. There's a way to handle pretty much everything in the air, as long as you don't get excited. Bob DeCreft used to say, no matter what happens, don't panic, just fly the airplane." She took another deep, careful breath. "He was a good teacher, old Bob."

Finally Liam found his voice. "Yeah. He sure was. Wy?"
"What?"

"I love you."

It was her turn to look shaken.

"I love you, Wy," he said again.

"Liam," she said with obvious difficulty, "we have to talk."

THIRTEEN

Newenham, September 3

Diana Prince had never wanted to be anything but what she was: an Alaska state trooper. Her great-grandfather had been with the New York City police, her grandfather had worked for J. Edgar Hoover at the FBI, and both parents were thirty-year detectives with the Anchorage Police Department who shared three citations for valor. Her brother and only sibling had disgraced the family twice over, first by becoming an attorney and second by going to work for the ACLU, so upon Diana's shoulders rested the honor of the present generation of Princes, and her parents and grandparents had made sure she knew it.

Her father, a gruff man with eyes that could bore holes right through you, had sat her down at the kitchen table her senior year in high school and had interrogated her as to her reasons for becoming a trooper. "It's in the blood," she'd said, but he hadn't let her get away with that. It might have been partly family tradition, but it was also the reading of *The Klondike Rush*, which in part recounted the activities of Samuel Benton Steele, the Canadian Mountie whose forces had kept the peace during the Klondike Gold Rush.

Her father looked at her mother and said, "So. It's the hat," referring to the round-crowned, flat-brimmed hat that made all state troopers look like Dudley Do-Right.

Well, maybe it was, again only partly, but it was mostly because Diana had a strong sense of right and wrong, an even
stronger sense of duty, and a liking for authority. She stumbled
her way to an explanation of these feelings which omitted her
main reason, which was that she had no wish to stand in her parents' shadows, cast long in the Anchorage P.D., and which must
have satisfied her parents because her father then pointed out all
the disadvantages that came with the job—the horrible hours, the
daily stress of dealing with the lowest level of the gene pool, the
alienation from the general population, the ever-present risk of
injury, even death—and he had asked, no, he had demanded that
she think it over before she made her final decision. This included, he decreed, four years at college, for which he and her
mother would pay so long as she pulled down grades of B or better and elected a discipline that would be useful for promotion.
"It's better to be boss," he said. "A degree will get you there."

She came home from the University of Washington with a
B.A. in criminal justice, and filled out her application for the
trooper academy the next day.

The academy was notoriously picky in its selection of recruits,
thanks to the state's munificent endowment of troopers' salaries,
but they took one look at Diana's sex, citizenship and degree and
snapped her up. She graduated at the top of her class, and at the
graduation ceremony recited the short, simple oath of the Alaska
State Troopers with the absolute conviction that she was going to
be the best trooper who ever was, with the highest conviction
rate and the lowest percentage of citizen complaints in the history
of the service. She would serve, she would protect, and before
long, she knew in her secret heart, she would be running the
joint.

Her first assignment after her probationary period had been
Newenham, where she'd arrived a little over two months before.
Newenham, in spite of it being a seven-step pay increase because
of its Bush location, was not first pick on anyone's list. The sergeant in charge before Corporal Campbell had been that unusual

individual, a careless trooper: careless of the law, careless of the safety and security of his community and, most unforgivably, careless of the reputation of the service. He had been loathed from Togiak to Igiugik, he had been despised by fellow and superior officers alike, and if he hadn't been a former governor's brother-in-law, he would never have lasted as long as he did. As it was, he'd only been transferred, taking his problems with him to Eagle River, where at least he would be answerable to an on-the-scene authority other than himself, and where everyone prayed he wouldn't screw up for the next year, after which he became eligible for retirement.

Into this mess stepped Liam Campbell, recently broken in rank and transferred in disgrace because of an error in judgment that had left five people dead in Denali Park. The way Prince heard it, it hadn't been Campbell's fault, but he'd been the sergeant in charge of the post and the buck stopped on his desk. Up to then, his record had been exemplary. He'd been John Dillinger Barton's golden boy, and the smart money had him moving up the chain of command high and fast.

Instead, he got Newenham, a fishing community of two thousand at the end of an hour's ride by 737, on the edge of Bristol Bay, which had once seen the largest runs of salmon in the world, where fortunes had been made in the set of one net. Now, the salmon were returning in ever-dwindling numbers, incomes were falling, and alcohol consumption was on the rise. There were foreign vessels docking now and then for supplies, there was tension between the white and Native communities, there was tension between all Alaskans and the state and federal governments. It was a community ripe with possibilities. Diana had taken a long, hard look at Liam's record, made a few discreet inquiries and had liked what she had learned. She sensed an opportunity to pile up numbers in the "Cases Closed" column and expressed a preference for a duty assignment in Newenham, knowing full well she would get it by default.

When she and Liam were done with it, Newenham would be first on everybody's list.

All of which explained why she was on the phone to the Crime Lab in Anchorage that day three times before noon. Tired of talking to her, the receptionist finally gave her the direct line to the ballistics lab. An anonymous tech was brusque and uncommunicative. She called again in an hour and he hung up on her.

She called the medical examiner, one Dr. Hans Brilleaux, known less than affectionately to the law enforcement community as Brillo, for his Brillo-pad hair, a black, wiry nest that looked like it could provide houseroom for a flock of swallows. It smelled like it, too.

Brillo was less than enthusiastic. "I've got four stiffs ahead of yours," he said in answer to her query, and then he hung up on her, which seemed to be the day's universal response.

She drummed her fingers impatiently on the desk. Until the autopsy came in, she would have nothing comparing the pattern of buckshot to the patterns Teddy and John's shotguns had presumably produced for the Crime Lab, so she went down to Bill's for a fat pill. Dottie and Paul Takak were dispensing comfort in the form of bacon cheeseburgers and fountain Cokes. Dottie, a Yupik elder and a pillar of the local Native community, sat in back of the bar, arms folded, and refused to serve any Yupik customers alcohol. In the kitchen, Paul put ketchup on every burger, whether you wanted it or not. Sighing inwardly, Diana opened up her burger to scrape the layer of red sauce away. Life in Newenham went to hell with Bill and Moses both gone.

This thought had the effect of drawing her up short. She was thinking about Newenham as if it were home, instead of a stepping stone. This would never do.

She wiped her mouth and turned to survey the bar in search of miscreants. Evan Gray, one of three local drug dealers, held court in a back booth. He saw her looking at him and sent her an impudent grin. He was a tall, good-looking devil, and he knew it.

Two months before Diana had sat in that same booth with Colonel Charles Bradley Campbell of the United States Air Force, and, coincidentally, Corporal Liam Campbell's father. The two men didn't get along. She smiled to herself. It wasn't that Charles was incapable of getting along with anyone, as she had extensive personal knowledge that he could.

Across the room, Evan Gray mistook the smile and excused himself to the plump little brunette sitting within the curve of his arm. She pouted as he sauntered to the bar and ordered another round for his booth. He smiled at Diana. "Hey, beautiful."

"Hey, handsome," she replied.

Gratified, he said, "Join us for a drink when you get off duty?"

She smiled at him. "Not in this lifetime, Evan."

He laughed. "Haven't you heard? Marijuana is legal in the state again."

"Haven't you heard?" she countered. "Only for medicinal purposes."

He shook his head, smile in place. "There's a lot of sick people out there," he said sadly. "Somebody's got to help them."

"Yeah, Evan, you're a real humanitarian."

Her tone stung, just a little, and his eyes dropped to her mouth. "You don't know what you're missing."

"Three to five, with time off for good behavior?" she suggested.

It surprised a laugh out of him.

Dottie slapped his drinks down on the bar. "Eighteen-fifty."

He tossed her a twenty. She glared, but she kept the tip.

"See you around, officer," he said as he left.

"Yes, you will," Diana said.

Dottie was glaring at her now. Diana toasted her with the last of her Coke. "Keep your friends close, Dottie, and your enemies closer."

Dottie's glare did not lessen. "Sleeping with the enemy is about as close as you can get."

Diana Prince had been in Newenham less than two months, but two months was plenty of time to learn that it was never wise to attempt to match wits with the bartender at Bill's, whoever she happened to be that day. Meekly, the trooper paid her tab and returned to the post.

Waiting on the doorstep was Natalie Gosuk. "Ms. Gosuk," Prince said, and held the door for the woman. She took off her hat and settled in behind the desk. "How may I help you?"

In the custom of the country, Gosuk kept her eyes and her voice low in response. "I want to see my son."

"Yes," Prince agreed, "so you said when you were in here yesterday. You still have the court order?"

Natalie displayed it.

"Is the foster parent denying you access?" Natalie looked confused, and Prince elaborated. "Won't she let you see him?"

"She is not there. He is not there."

Prince looked up and said sharply, "Do you mean she has taken him somewhere else? Have they moved? Left town?"

Natalie looked confused again, and Prince remembered the class in Native relations taught at the academy, which had stressed patience and courtesy when dealing with Alaskan citizens who spoke English as a second language. This was a Yupik woman, the product of a culture where a woman seldom raised her voice, where a problem was always resolved within the family. The fact that Natalie Gosuk, alone, was looking for help from a state trooper spoke volumes about how seriously she regarded her complaint. "Let's start over, Ms. Gosuk," she said. "Please. Have a seat."

After a moment's hesitation, Gosuk sat on the extreme edge of one of the two armchairs across the desk. Prince pulled an incident report from the file. "As I understand it, your son was placed with foster parents."

"A woman."

"Here in town."

"Yes."

"What is her name?"

"The woman who flies."

"I beg your pardon?"

"The woman who flies," Natalie Gosuk repeated.

Diana Prince looked up from the form. "Do you mean Wyanet Chouinard?"

A nod.

"Your son is living with Wyanet Chouinard."

Another nod.

Prince thought back to the morning before, to Natalie Gosuk's first appearance at the post, of Liam's subsequent distracted air, and identified the child in question for the first time. "You're Tim's mother."

A third nod.

"One moment, please." Diana looked up Gosuk, Timothy, on the computer, and her initial irritation at Liam not telling her the truth about Natalie Gosuk abated a little. "Ms. Gosuk, Tim was removed from your custody nearly two years ago."

"I'm sober now," Gosuk said, still staring at the floor. "I want to see my son." She raised her eyes for the first time and held up the court order. "The judge says I can. She says the woman who flies must let me see him."

Prince looked at the court order. "Did you go to the house?"

"Yes."

"And did Ms. Chouinard refuse you entry? Would she not let you in?"

"The woman who flies is not there."

"And your son is not in the house?"

"They say no."

"Who says no?"

Gosuk gave an infinitesimal shrug. "The people who are there. I don't know them."

Prince looked at the clock. One-thirty. Of course the woman who flies was not there, she was at present providing air transportation for one Corporal Liam Campbell to Nenevok Creek. How very convenient. "Have you tried the airport?"

"I have no car."

"How about a cab?"

"I have no money."

Prince thought again of Liam's description of Tim when Chouinard flew him out of Ualik, the bleeding wounds, the broken bones, the doctor's warning that the boy might not regain his hearing in one ear, mercifully proved wrong by time and care. There is a difference between the letter of the law and the spirit of the law, Campbell had said. Natalie Gosuk had the might of the law on her side, and the court order in hand to prove it. Moreover, she was Tim's mother.

On the other hand, babies should not be, should never be, hit. According to the official report, even one as sloppily filled out as this one by Sergeant Corcoran, the woman sitting in front of her had hit her baby. Repeatedly. Over a period of many years. She was also a drunk. Because she was sober now didn't mean she would be tomorrow, or even tonight. Whatever genetic, societal, geographical, historical or financial pressures had combined to make this happen did not matter, only the result and the way Prince dealt with the result.

And then there was the boy. Liam Campbell said he had no wish to see his mother. He had rights, too.

Diana Prince was a trooper. She had sworn to uphold the constitutions of the United States and the state of Alaska. She held out her hand for the court order. "We'll serve it this evening," she said, "when everyone comes home."

Newenham, September 3

"Hi," Jim Wiley said without enthusiasm.

"Hi, yourself," said Jo Dunaway, with even less.

"Hounded any bereaved fathers lately?"

"Ha ha," Jo said, very carefully.

"I'm supposed to tell you to make yourself at home," Jim said, waving a hand, "so make yourself at home. There's beer in the fridge. We've got Tim's room. You get the couch."

"So I've been told." She tried hard to keep the edge from her voice, but Luke Prior looked at her with his eyebrows raised.

They were very nice eyebrows, to go with his very nice eyes, and it was only a bonus that he was at least ten inches taller and twenty pounds lighter than Jim Wiley. "Luke, this is Jim Wiley. Jim, this is Luke Prior."

The two men sized each other up. One looked like a surly teddy bear. The other looked like a Greek god. "Good to meet you, Jim," Luke said, extending a hand.

"Yeah, sure," Jim said, clasping it briefly. There was a noise at the door onto the deck and he looked around. "Oh, and this is Bridget from Ireland. Luke Prior."

Bridget smiled and came forward with her hand extended. "It's Bridget Callahan, Luke."

Luke's very nice eyes had widened upon catching sight of Bridget, and he took her hand and bent his head over it in appreciation of her manifest charms. "I'm delighted to meet you, Bridget."

The two of them were surveyed with varying degrees of mixed feeling by the other two people in the room. On one hand, Luke was poaching on Jim's preserve. On the other hand, he was meanly delighted that Jo's honey couldn't keep his hands off other women. Jo, who on the now rapidly fading chance he might be a keeper had brought Luke to Newenham so Wy could vet him for her, felt much the same.

Jo remembered first that they were guests in this home and avoided open warfare by opening the refrigerator and peering inside. "Where's Wy? You want something to drink, Luke?"

"Actually, I'm starving," Luke said. "Anything in there to eat?"

"There's leftover roast from last night," Bridget said, bustling around the counter and all but elbowing Jo out of the way, who, truth be told, was no help in the kitchen and happy to step aside.

Jo rescued a couple of Coronas and handed one to Luke. She followed Jim out onto the deck, perched on the edge of the bluff that fell fifty feet to the bank of the river below. The sun was shining but there was a nip in the air that brought color to her cheeks, and a sharp breeze that ruffled her short blond curls. Clouds were forming low on the southeastern horizon, dark with purpose. Storm coming, she thought. Beneath the clouds the Nushagak flowed gray with silt into Bristol Bay, swiftly, as if in a hurry to finish the business of summer before winter set in and froze it into a winter highway for snow machines.

Jim wasted no time in going on the attack. "What's Luke do?"

"He's a business consultant."

Jo could hear Jim as if he'd spoken the words out loud. *Now there's a perfect title for somebody who's never held down a real job.* She said "Where's Wy? You didn't say."

"I didn't get a chance, and flying, where else?"

"Flying where, and with whom?"

He sneered at the *whom* and made sure she saw it. "To Nenevok Creek, with Liam," he said, and was irritated when Jo snapped to attention.

"That the guy they found shot on his gold claim?"

"Jesus," Jim muttered, "don't you ever stop being a reporter?"

"No," she shot back, "don't you ever stop being an asshole?"

A murmur of voices was heard from the kitchen, a low laugh from Bridget. Jim looked over his shoulder, and Jo turned to see that Luke was helping Bridget make sandwiches. "They're getting along," Jim said.

"Aren't they, though," Jo said, staring at him.

"What?" he said.

"I didn't break that story, Jim," she said in a level voice.

"Yeah, right," he said.

"I didn't break that story, Jim."

"Save it, Jo. You've made a career out of breaking stories, the nastier the better. I understand; this was a particularly juicy one, young trooper on the fast track up, loses both wife and son in one tragic accident, goes off the deep end, falls asleep on the job and five people wind up dead in Denali. How could you resist?"

The louder his voice got, the softer she spoke. "I didn't break that story, Jim."

"Bullshit. It came out under your byline."

She put the beer down. "You know the three rules Edna

Buchanan gives a cub reporter? One, never trust an editor. Two, never trust an editor. Three, never trust an editor."

He wanted to say, Who the hell is Edna Buchanan? but he couldn't bring himself to be that petty. "So you're saying it's all your editor's fault."

"No. I'm saying, Never trust an editor. I did, so, in fact, it was my fault."

He was acutely aware that she had not apologized, and understood that she had no intention of doing so. "So, what're you looking for, peace?"

"That's pushing it, given our history. How about a truce, for the duration of our visit? Wy's my best friend, Liam's yours, we're sharing their hospitality. They probably won't invite us back if we leave blood on the floor."

"Probably not."

Something in the tone of his voice alerted her. "What?"

He met her eyes, his stern expression sitting oddly on his usually happy-go-lucky face. "Is she going to tell him?"

Her face went very still. "Tell him what?"

He snorted. "Yeah, right." he went to the door, and said curtly over his shoulder, "If she doesn't, I will."

"Jim."

His name cracked like a whip, and he turned around, ready to do battle, all thoughts of truce gone.

"You don't know everything there is to tell. Sometimes it's better just to keep your mouth shut. It isn't our business, after all."

"The hell it isn't."

"The hell it is," she fired back. "You're not in love with Wy."

"Liam is, and anything to do with Liam is my business."

"His love life isn't," she said. "And he would be the first to tell you so."

He really hated it when she was right. He really hated it when he was wrong about anything, but he really, really hated it when he was wrong and Jo Dunaway was right.

She interpreted his expression correctly, and very carefully refrained from any retaliatory expression of triumph. "So, you'll sit on it."

"I'll sit on it," he said grudgingly, and added with a glare, "Not forever. But for now."

It was the best she could do. The rest was up to Wy. "All right."

"Hey," Luke said from the doorway. "Luncheon is served. Anybody hungry?"

Sunshine Valley, September 3

Home, he was home again, and Elaine had come home with him, was with him, again. That first night was like heaven on earth, renewing her acquaintance with the snug little cabin tucked away at the head of the creek. Hand-hewn logs, sanded to a smooth finish inside and gleaming warmly from years of lovingly applied polish. A high-peaked roof with a loft beneath twin skylights, a large, square bed piled high with soft sheets and a down comforter. A stove with a stained glass door, behind which a banked fire glowed. Two chairs drawn up at either side, hand-hewn like the rest of the furniture from the same logs that built the house, sanded smooth and piled high with cushions in nubby fabrics and muted colors. The simple dining table, a slab of wood lathed and sanded to show the grain of the wood swooping and swirling across the perfectly flat surface, so level a marble dropped upon it would roll to a stop before it fell off the edge.

Outside, a thick stand of spruce and cottonwood crowded the eaves, so that fifty, even twenty feet away the logs, unfinished, unoiled and allowed to fade to a silvery gray, shimmered and shifted between the restless boughs like an illusion, an oasis trembling at the edge of a subarctic dream. From the air, the cabin, nestled between two overlapping ridges in the eastern foothills of the Wood River Mountains, was virtually invisible.

It was a beautiful home, in a beautiful place. How could she not love it? How could she not wish to stay here forever, with him? She'd run away, but he had brought her back, and she had fallen in love with the place again, *with him again. He'd had to be firm, of course. She was only a woman after all, gentler, weaker, in need of protection and guidance, but that was what he was for, what men were for, and the strength of a man was measured by his ability to forgive, by his tolerance, his patience.*

He smiled at her. "We will live here together, forever."

She looked at him with wide eyes and was silent, as he had taught her. The silence of the wilderness was a sacred thing, and not to be violated with impunity. The silence called to him in ways no one could comprehend, not even Elaine the fair.

FOURTEEN

Newenham, September 4

Trooper Diana Prince walked into the post at precisely 8:00 a.m. The phone rang at precisely 8:01. "Hey, Princess Di."

She leaned back in her chair and smiled. "Hey, Nick."

"Have I told you lately I love you?"

"Let me check my watch."

He laughed, a low, rich, husky sound, and as sensibly and methodically as Prince had chosen her duty assignment, she did find occasion to regret it now and then, just the tiniest bit. Usually whenever she was on the phone with Nick Schatz, the head ballistics man at the Crime Lab. He'd lectured her class on the fine art of telling which bullet came from which rifle. It remained her favorite week out of the sixteen, although she'd come perilously close to losing her head-of-class standing due to lack of sleep.

"So when you coming to visit me in Anchorage?" he said.

"You still married?"

"Yep."

"Then I'd better keep my distance."

"Come on, Diana. You know you want to."

"I don't always give myself everything I want."

"How about what you need?"

The purr of that deep, sexy voice was almost irresistible. Almost. "Sitka was one thing, Nick. Your wife was a thousand miles away. In Anchorage, she might as well be in the next room."

A brief silence. "What if I came to Newenham?"

She sat up. What was this? "Do you think that's a good idea?"

"Maybe the best idea I've had all day."

"And it's only five after eight," she said dryly. He laughed again, and she said, "Why did you call? Other than to whip me into a frenzy of sexual frustration."

"Well, that was my first priority, but as it happens I also have news of an interesting professional nature to relate."

"Relate away."

"Those two shotguns you sent me yesterday?"

"Yeah?"

There was a smile in his voice that told her he heard the excitement in her tone. "The Winchester produced a splatter pattern pretty near identical to the pattern on the body you sent Brillo Pad the day before."

"Yes," she said, with emphasis.

"God, you're just so sexy when you're in hot pursuit."

"Is it a positive match?"

"Could I swear in court that the Winchester you sent me is the weapon that killed Mark Hanover? Not without a shell casing, and you didn't recover one from the scene, did you?"

"No."

He sighed. "Then all I can say absolutely is that the shot that killed Mark Hanover came from a Winchester Field Model, probably a 16339."

"Great."

"Yeah, I know, there's only about ten thousand of those floating around the Bush. Good duck guns. And they're relatively cheap, I don't think any one of the Field Models goes for over four, five hundred dollars. Hell, they're all over Anchorage, too, people buy them for home defense every day. Quicker than calling the cops."

"Ha ha."

"Try to find me a shell casing."

"There wasn't one, Nick. We searched the area thoroughly."

"We, that'd be you and Trooper Liam Campbell."

She smiled at the opposite wall. "Yep."

Another brief pause. "Good trooper, I hear, until that mess in Denali. He'll do well in Newenham. Take the hoodoo off that post, Barton says."

"Yep."

"Good-looking guy, too. Pity about his wife and kid."

"Yep."

"Bitch," he said without rancor.

She laughed. "Thanks, Nick. Talk to you soon."

As she hung up the phone, the door opened and Jo Dunaway walked inside with three other people. Before Prince had a chance to stiffen into official press-repulsing mode, Jo said, "Wy and Liam didn't make it home last night."

Old Man Creek, September 4

Tim's first year in Newenham had been fine. He stayed home mostly, except for school. He'd always liked to read, but his birth mother (he'd quickly learned the jargon of the adopted child, especially anything that might hurt his birth mother if she ever came to know of it) had never seen the need. "Go out and play," she'd said, pulling the book from his hands and shoving his coat at him. Of course, that was usually when his Uncle Simeon (or his uncle Curtis or his uncle Jeff) had come over and he was more than happy to leave the house.

The trouble was, he didn't have a lot of places to go. It was a small village, to which his mother had come with her man thirteen years before. Her man had lived long enough to father a child and then been killed three months later when his snow machine had plunged through an open lead on the Nushagak River.

He'd gone up the river to Bright's Point, where there was a liquor store. This was the return trip. It happened all the time.

Back at Ualik, his grandmother washed her hands of Tim's unwed mother, and when his grandmother washed her hands of someone, the whole village did, too. Tim was born after twenty-nine hours of hard labor, his mother alone in the shack that was all the worldly goods his father had left her.

His first memory was of being curled up on the cot jammed into one corner of the shack, trembling behind a length of worn chintz suspended from a string tied between two nails, as the shack jolted from the force of blows being struck, bodies falling, people screaming. His mother and his Uncle Simeon. Or maybe it was Uncle Felix, or one of his other uncles, it was a long time ago and he couldn't say for sure. There was a loud, smacking sound and another jarring thump that shook his bed, and silence. He gathered all his courage together and peered around the edge of his makeshift curtain. His uncle was lying stretched out full length on the floor, his head next to the honey bucket. The honey bucket was a tin pail with a sharp rim. It was overturned and the contents spilled across the floor, the piss and shit mingled with the spreading red pool beneath his uncle's head.

He didn't remember more than that, but that much he remembered in clear and vivid detail.

He couldn't remember a time when his mother hadn't drunk. At first it wasn't so bad, an uncle would bring over a bottle and they'd drink it and then his mother would order him behind his curtain. But slowly it became more than an evening bottle, soon it became an afternoon bottle, then a morning bottle, then it was the first thing she reached for when she woke up.

The first time she hit him was when he didn't get out of her way fast enough. The second time she hit him was for getting out of her way before she could hit him. Pretty soon his uncles picked up on it and joined in.

He developed habits of compulsive neatness. When he made his tea he never spilled so much as a grain of sugar, he never dribbled water from the teakettle in pouring, he disposed of the tea bag as soon as it was out of the mug, he never let his mug sit on the counter after it was empty. He made his bed with perfect corners, the edges of the tattered blankets neatly aligned. He folded his clothes into one Blazo box, kept his toys and books in another, the books on one side with their spines out, the toys on the other, biggest one on the bottom, littlest one on the top.

He washed the dishes every night and put them away. He swept the floor every morning before he went to school. He kept the top of the oilstove scrubbed clean. He lined the cans up in the cupboard according to size.

It didn't matter. She hit him anyway.

After a while he started hiding under the sagging porch, even in winter, but when she found him she dragged him out and hit him for that, too.

When he was ten he made his first friend, an older girl who tutored him when he fell behind in class. Her name was Christine, and she had dark eyes and a merry smile. She was going to be a teacher, Christine told him, so she was practicing on him.

As soon as she got to know of it, the old woman, his grandmother, had tried to get Christine to stop tutoring him. He wasn't worth it, she declared, this bastard son too stupid to learn what every other student could in school, this bastard son of an unwed daughter who didn't even have the decency to move to Newenham, or Anchorage, even, somewhere far away where she could bring her decent, hardworking, God-fearing family no shame. Christine had heard the old woman out with an expression of polite attention fastened firmly to her face, and had tutored Tim anyway, staying after school to instruct him patiently in the mysteries of geography and history. They spoke English in the morning and Yupik in the afternoon at school, and you had to speak both fluently before they'd let you graduate. English was easy, his mother never spoke anything else and wouldn't let him, either, not around her house. "It's bad enough you got a brown skin in a white world, kid," she'd said. "Don't talk like you got a brown skin, too."

Christine had taught him Yupik. But then she had gone away, one day she was there, the next she was not. Tim figured the old woman had gotten her way after all, and he retreated once again into solitude.

One day soon afterward his mother had been very drunk and the hitting had been very bad. Uncle Simeon had done other things to him, too. The counselor in the hospital had tried to get him to talk about them, but he wouldn't. He never would, not ever.

Besides, that was all done now. He was with his true mother. Wyanet Chouinard had flown into Ualik that day when the hitting had been very bad, and when she had flown out again she had taken him with her. She had visited him in the hospital, she'd come every night and talked to him and read to him and brought him presents, and when he was well enough, she had taken him home. She had asked him if he wanted to live with her always and his throat had been so choked that he hadn't been able to speak, to say, to shout, to scream out the word "YES!"

He had thought he'd died and gone to heaven.

Newenham wasn't heaven, though, and getting used to the differences between Ualik and Newenham was a long and difficult process. Ualik, his birthplace, was a village of two hundred, Newenham a city of two thousand. Newenham had cable, and two grocery stories, and nine churches and two bars. Ualik had one satellite dish that acted as a conduit for the state-run channel, no churches and a bootlegger. Ualik was Yupik. Newenham was mostly white.

He tried so hard to fit into this new world, afraid that if he didn't he'd be shipped back to Ualik. For a while he had thought fitting in meant wearing the baggiest jeans, smoking the most cigarettes, saying "fuck" between every other word and hanging with Eric Walker and his gang. He'd been lucky there; his mom, his adopted mom, had been watching too closely for him to follow Eric and Vasily into McLaughlin. He shivered. Liam had taken him down to the place in the woods and shown him Rudy's body, what Eric and Vasily had done to it. It had looked like something out of the movies.

It had looked like something from the other side of the curtain in Ualik.

Now here he was at Old Man Creek. Old Man Creek sure wasn't Ualik, and sure wasn't Newenham, either. The old man, Moses, was sober for a change, although that wasn't necessarily an improvement. Drunk, he was one tough bastard. Sober, he was a fiend from hell.

They'd been standing post for twenty minutes and Tim was afraid he was about to disgrace himself by falling flat on his face. Moses had gone up on the porch, where he'd pulled Bill to her feet, sat down in her place and pulled her into his lap. Man, those two were always hugging and kissing and patting each other's asses—and other things, too, he was sure. Bill Billington had to be sixty years old, Moses had to be a hundred, old enough to act like respectable elders, for god's sake. The chair creaked and all by itself Tim's head turned to behold Moses and Bill in a liplock that involved more than just their lips. He forgot himself and stared. They were worse than his mom and Liam. At least Liam pretended to sleep in that camper, and Mom pretended to let him.

Bill gave Moses a last kiss and pulled back to see Tim staring. She had the audacity to grin at him. Moses put back his head and howled.

Tim's head snapped around to eyes front. He stared hard at the red lengths of salmon drying on racks and hoped his face wasn't as red as the salmon.

Next to him, Amelia moaned, a quiet little moan, as if she'd had practice in hiding it.

"Keep breathing," he said in a low voice. "Keep breathing, steady, in and out, in and out."

"My legs don't stand up straight anymore," she whispered.

"Mine, neither," he whispered back. "We'll be walking bow-legged by the time that old man is done with us."

She was silent for a moment. "Like cowboys."

He bit back a laugh. "Yeah. Like in the movies." He felt her shoulders shake. "Like John Wayne."

Moses, walking light-footedly up behind them, pounced, buffeting first one and then the other with rough but not brutal slaps about the head. "I see talking don't help your standing post none, boys and girls. Let's see if a little form will keep you quiet."

He took them through the form three times, going from commencement to conclusion slowly, steadily, progressing inexorably from one movement to the next and the next, grinning evilly at Tim when he became completely lost between the second and third Fair ladies, barking his disapproval when Amelia nearly fell during Turn Round and Kick Horizontally.

It's not fair, Tim wanted to say, you've been doing this for a hundred years, we've been doing it for a couple of days, you can't expect us to be perfect this soon.

At the end of the third conclusion, when Tim was sure in his gut that Moses was going to go for a fourth form, the old man straightened up all the way to his five-foot-seven-inch height and brought his right fist in front of his face, snugging it into his left palm. Tim and Amelia mimicked him. The three bowed.

"I suppose that's enough for now," Moses said grudgingly, " 'Course the two of you got about as much style as a rhinoceros at the ballet. Dismissed until this afternoon. Go on, take a dip in the river. There's a backwater about a hundred feet up the bank, shallow and still pretty warm. Go on, git!"

They got.

It was a nice little pond, snugged into the curve of a short, smooth ridge of glacial silt and rimmed with tall reeds. Tim stripped down to his underwear and fell in face first. He surfaced to see Amelia standing on the edge, uncertain. "What?"

She blushed. "I don't have a bathing suit."

"Just do like me and keep your underwear on."

She hesitated.

"It's real nice," he said. "Warm, and the bottom's sandy."

"Okay," she said.

He tried not to look as she undressed, but as with Moses and Bill, he couldn't help sneaking a peek or two. Her breasts were bigger than they'd seemed under her shirt, and she wore bikini panties he'd only ever seen on magazine models. Her bruises were fading, faint shadows on smooth skin.

She was up to her waist when she saw him looking at them. She didn't blush this time.

"Your husband do that?" he said.

She nodded.

"You going back to him?"

She stood where she was, fingertips making circles in the water. On the opposite side of the pond, a lone brant honked at them and then was silent. "I don't know. He's my husband."

"He shouldn't hurt you," he said, and he was filled with a sudden and welcome anger. "Nobody should hurt anybody."

She looked at him then. "Somebody hurt you, too."

"My mother." He swallowed, and said as much as he could. "My uncles."

She nodded, understanding without words.

"Nobody should hurt anybody," he repeated, and he turned and dived, as if the water could wash away all the bad memories.

They paddled around the pool, quietly at first, until he accidentally splashed her and, after a moment's surprise, she retaliated. The battle was on, and before it was over a good third of the pool had wound up on the bank. It was an hour before they came out, giggling and shoving like a couple of kids.

With her wet hair sleeked back from her face and her skin flushed and damp, she looked like she was barely old enough for the sixth grade. He finished dressing first and tapped her on the shoulder. "Tag, you're it!"

"No fair!" she yelled, and charged after him.

They chased each other down the path, laughing, startling

ducks out of the brush at the side of the river and an otter family into the water. She tagged him and surged ahead, and he pounded after her, skidding around a corner and running into her full tilt where she'd stopped abruptly at the end of the path. They both crashed to the ground at the edge of the trees.

"Shh," she said, putting her hand over his mouth when he would have yelled.

He looked up and saw.

Bill and Moses. On the porch. Without any clothes on. Bill was on top, her hair a silver curtain around Moses' face. His hands were on her hips, muscles flexing in his arms as they moved together. They were so caught up in each other they didn't hear anything else.

Tim's jaw dropped and he turned to Amelia. Whatever he had been about to say was halted by the look on her face.

She held one finger to her lips and crept backward, one noiseless movement at a time. Tim followed. She halted in a clearing, out of earshot of the cabin.

He stood still, hands dangling, awed, confused, aroused.

"Is that how it's supposed to be?" she said, her face bright with wonder.

He told the truth. "I don't know." Liam had come into his mother's life only five months before. He'd caught them a few times in an embrace that was more than a kiss, but nothing like this.

"She was really liking it." Her voice rose to a squeak. "She was on *top*."

"Yeah," he said, because he didn't know what else to say. He couldn't get the picture out of his mind, the man and the woman doing the nasty, only it hadn't looked nasty, or sounded nasty. It had looked—well, he didn't know how it had looked. All he knew was that it was nothing like what he had grown up hearing from the other side of the curtain. His body stirred. "Yeah," he said again, his voice husky.

She looked at him, suddenly aware.

They reached for each other at the same time. He was almost

169

as tall as she was, and glad for it. She smelled good. She felt good. She tasted better than good, although their teeth kept bumping. He was afraid of hurting her, and she was afraid of being hurt. She looked a little like Christine, which helped him, and he was younger and smaller than she was, which helped her.

In the end, she stared up at him in amazement. "It doesn't have to hurt," she said.

He shifted on his elbows, careful not to let his whole weight lie on her, mindful of her bruises. "I guess not."

She moved experimentally. "There's something else, though."

"Yeah," he said, closing his eyes and adjusting his body to match with hers.

"Tim?"

He opened his eyes. "What?"

"Did you—?"

"Yeah," he said, reddening.

"Was it—did it feel good?"

He tucked his hot face into the curve between her shoulder and her neck. "Yes. I think so. I don't know."

She was silent for a moment. "Tim?"

"What?"

"Could we do it again?"

FIFTEEN

Sunshine Valley, September 4

He rose with the sun and built up the fire in the stove. There was a pump handle on the edge of the sink. He saw her looking down from the loft as he filled the kettle. "The well's right under the house," he said. "Long as we've got a fire in the stove, the pipes won't freeze in winter. Fresh water all year round, and you don't have to go down to the creek to get it."

She murmured something, something humble, acquiescent, admiring. It seemed to be enough; he nodded, satisfied, and put the kettle on the stove. He smiled up at her. "Elaine the fair," he said softly.

She had already learned to be afraid of that tone of his voice, and her body went very still beneath the covers.

"You'll make us some breakfast, won't you, Elaine? You're such a good cook, I can hardly wait to taste those pancakes of yours again." He went to the door. "I'll be back shortly," he said, and went out the door, closing it behind him.

She rose, scrambling into her clothes, buttoning her shirt up to the last button beneath her chin, cinching her belt in to the last possible notch. She could barely stand to look at the bed they had shared, but she knew enough to make it.

She climbed down the ladder and went to the little kitchen, all hardwood cabinets and counter, the same wood from which the furniture and the cabin itself was made. There was a Coleman stove on the counter, very similar to the one she had cooked on for Mark, and the sight of it should have moved her to tears.

The door, the only door into the cabin, a meticulously finished slab of wood allowed to retain its natural color, remained shut and mute.

She located the ingredients and the frying pan, and mixed pancake dough. There was no syrup, but there was brown sugar and maple flavoring and water, so she made some. She found a cone filter and a carafe and filters and coffee. All she had to do was wait for the kettle to boil.

The minutes ticked by, one by one, and still he hadn't come back. She looked at the door, looked away.

She found stoneware plates in a pretty Delft pattern and set the table. There was a full set of stainless steel flatware in a drawer, pristine and polished. She used paper towels for napkins, folded into perfect little triangles.

Something tapped at the window, and she looked up to see a spruce bough scrape at the glass. It was a tiny window, with four panes, barely big enough for a dog to climb through. Bears, she thought numbly.

The shadow of the bough shifted on the glass and she saw a faint smear of something. She found a bottle of Windex and washed it off. She washed the other window in the opposite wall, too.

The door had no window.

She swept the floor, depositing the dirt carefully in the plastic trash can. She dusted the shelf. It held three books, a collection of Shakespeare, the Bible, and *Idylls of the King*.

A small wooden box stood next to the Tennyson, a light layer of dust covering its hand-carved lid. She was clumsy and knocked the box to the floor, scattering its contents. A shaft of pure terror speared through her. She waited for the footsteps to sound. For the door to push open.

After a moment the racing of her heart slowed and she managed to kneel down and collect the items and put them back in the box. A cheap Claddagh ring, a wide silver bracelet that looked Southwestern, a plain gold wedding band. Five pairs of earrings. Two crosses on chains, one gold, one silver. A choker of crystals strung between tiny silver spacers.

Carefully she put them back into the box. Her hands were trembling. It took her three tries to get the lid back on, and she nearly dropped the box again when she tried to put it back on the shelf.

The shelf stood against the wall next to the door.

Taking up Windex and cloth again, she dusted the door handle, a handle shaped like a vine with leaves, with a latch beneath. She pressed down on it a little too hard. There was a click. The door opened.

A light breeze fanned her face. Sunlight dappled the floor. A bird called. Leaves rustled.

She reached out a hand, touched the door. Like everything else in the cabin, it was very well crafted. It swung silently outward.

She took a step forward, another, and the next thing she knew she was outside. No one shouted at her. No one grabbed her. No one hit her. No one forced her down, tore at her jeans, spread her legs and pushed painfully inside her. No one smiled his crazy smile at her afterward, patted her cheek in a travesty of affection and concern and said, "There, there. You'll learn. It'll take time, but you'll learn. You've been gone so long, I understand, it's like a new place to you. You used to love it. You'll love it again."

Her heart beat rapidly high up in her throat. She took another step forward, another and then another.

A branch caught her cheek, the sore spot high up where he'd hit her the night before when she'd tried to pull away from him, and only then did she realize how quickly she was moving, walking, shifting into a kind of stumbling run. She had no idea where she was going, which direction was best, the trees and the cliffs behind them were so close, so overwhelming. There might be bears, but she kept going.

She stumbled out into a tiny, circular clearing. Late flowers were blooming, fireweed, wild roses, even a few poppies, orange and red and yellow. They grew up around the stumps of trees cut off at knee level.

Except they weren't trees, or stumps. She took a step closer to the nearest one. One side had been planed smooth for an inscription.

"Elaine," she read. "Elaine the Fair, Elaine the Lovable, Elaine, the Lily Maid of Astolat." The letters were carved into the wood with the same care and craftsmanship demonstrated in the construction of the cabin and all its contents.

She didn't want to, she didn't think she could force herself to move, but her feet stepped forward on their own. The next stump was also planed smooth, also carved, also read "Elaine the Fair, Elaine the Lovable, Elaine, the Lily Maid of Astolat."

One stump after another, all planed, all carved. "Elaine the Fair." "Elaine the Lovable." "Elaine, the Lily Maid of Astolat." "Elaine."

Elaine. Elaine. Elaine.

You'll make us some breakfast, won't you, Elaine?

But her name wasn't Elaine.

She counted slowly, lips forming soundless numbers. One, two, three. Four. Five, six, seven, eight.

You're such a good cook, I can hardly wait to taste those pancakes of yours again.

But she'd never cooked for him before.

There, at the edge of the clearing, so faded it was almost invisible, nine. Ten, eleven.

Twelve. A gleaming new piece of wood with the dirt tamped around it still fresh and free from moss and lichen.

"Elaine."

I'll be back shortly.

She spun around.

He stood at the opposite edge of the clearing, fifty feet away.

He shook his head sorrowfully. "I told you not to go outside. Didn't I tell you that?"

She couldn't speak.

"I told you you could do anything you wanted, anything at all, so long as you kept on the inside of the door."

Her tongue felt swollen in her mouth.

He sighed. "What am I going to do with you?"

He sounded for all the world like an overindulgent parent faced with the dilemma of a spoiled child.

"Come here," he said.

He had almost reached her when she realized she was still holding the bottle of Windex. She raised it and squirted him in the face. He yelled and clawed at his eyes.

She turned and ran.

Nenevok Creek, September 4

The Cessna touched down smoothly, jolting only a very little on the gravel surface of the airstrip, and rolled to a halt just short of the Cub parked at the end. Liam was standing to one side. Prince cut the engine and opened the door. "Good to see you're all right."

"Good to be all right."

"What happened?" This as Wy came down the path.

"Throttle cable broke on approach."

"Jesus," Prince said. "That's a new one on me."

"Me, too."

Trooper poise was quickly replaced by pilot curiosity. "What'd you do?"

"Pulled the carb heat, trimmed the nose. Cut the engine on final."

"A deadstick landing."

"Yeah." Wy said it laconically, like she did deadstick landings every day and twice on Sundays.

"Impressive," Prince said, trying not to sound grudging. Nothing that exciting had ever happened to her in the air. "So, you spent the night up at the cabin."

Something fizzled in the air between Liam and Wy, some emotion to which Prince was not privy. It seemed there had been trouble in paradise the night before. It wasn't anything she was going to get into if she could help it. "I can take you both out in the Cessna."

"I'll stay with my plane," Wy said.

"Like hell," Liam said.

"You can't," Prince said.

"Why not?" Wy said to Prince.

"You've got a problem back in Newenham."

"What?"

"You know that boy you adopted?"

Wy's eyes widened and she came the rest of the way down the path in four quick strides. "Is Tim all right? Has something happened to him?"

"Far as I know he's fine. His mother isn't."

Wy's lips tightened. "I'm his mother."

"His birth mother, then," Prince said. "She's got a court order allowing her to see him. Limited, supervised visitation. She can't be alone with him, but she can see him." She looked at Liam. He met her eyes without expression. She looked back at Wy. "For the moment, the boy is out of town. Up at a fish camp on the Nushagak, I hear tell from the friends you've got staying at your house."

Wy nodded. "Yes," she said through suddenly stiff lips.

Prince looked at Liam. "You find anything more out here?"

Liam shook his head. "I don't know." He put his hand in his pocket and pulled out a Ziploc bag.

Prince took it and held it up to the light. It held half a dozen round green beads. "So?"

"They're jade, I think," he said.

"So?" she repeated.

"So a bunch of jade was stolen from the post office on Kagati Lake. A clock, animal carvings, bookends."

"A necklace?"

"They didn't say, and I didn't know enough to ask."

Prince thought it over. "There were a bunch of beads inside the cabin, weren't there?"

"Yeah."

"And some stuff, some bracelets, barrettes, like that, made out of beads."

"Yes."

"So this could have been part of Rebecca Hanover's supply."

"Could have been."

"Something to tell you, too," she said.

"What?"

"The Crime Lab called. The splatter pattern on Kvichak's Winchester matches the splatter pattern on Mark Hanover's chest."

She handed back the plastic bag, and he pocketed it. "That's that, then."

"Looks like."

"No shell casings, though, no other real physical evidence."

"No. No sign of the wife?"

"No." He sighed. "We followed everything that even remotely resembles a trail for at least a mile this time. We yelled every hour for her all night. No answer. Nothing."

"Did you look for a grave?"

Wy looked at Liam, away.

"Yeah," he said. "We looked for a grave."

Prince thought. "How about the creek?"

He pulled his cap from his head and whacked it against his leg. "I followed it downstream as far as I could. It's too low this time of year for anything the size of a body to float down it."

"Pretty big lake it ends in."

"Yeah. We should do a flyover on the way back, just in case SAR missed her."

"Always supposing she's a floater. She could have got wedged in a downed tree, something like that."

"Yeah." He put his cap back on. "We're going to need confessions if we want to clear this case."

"Yes. And we'd better get a move on if we want to get back to Newenham today. Storm coming in. Big low moving up out of the Bering. The Weather Service has small-craft advisories out. They're talking an early freeze, maybe even snow."

Liam looked at the sky. The morning had started out sunny, but a bank of clouds, thick and low, was creeping up on the sun. There was a bite in the stiff little breeze whipping across the airstrip, too. Still, "Snow before Labor Day?"

She shrugged. "Hey. It's Alaska. Worse, it's Bristol Bay."

Wy nosed the Cub into the prevailing wind and tied it down against her return with a new throttle cable. The Cessna was in the air ten minutes later, and Prince got on the radio to let the world know that Liam and Wy were found and well. Neither of the rescuees looked especially happy about it, but their friends took up the slack. "So, home again, home again, jiggety-jig," she said, hanging up the mike.

"Just step on it," Liam said. From the back seat Wy said nothing.

"Stepping on it," Prince said, and did.

Newenham, September 4

Jim, who like most ham operators knew somebody everywhere he went, had rustled up a truck, a Chevy Scottsdale, brown and tan but mostly rust, with brand-new outside rearview mirrors and tires, and a Jesus fish eating a Darwin fish glued to the tailgate.

Jo pointed at the decal. "Do you suppose the Christians know that that decal only shows Darwin in action? Bigger fish eats littler fish?"

"I don't think Christians waste much time thinking," Jim said, climbing in behind the wheel.

"I beg to differ," Bridget said tartly. "We Christians are thinking all the time. Mostly we're thinking sad thoughts about our non-Christian brothers and sisters who are going straight to hell when they die."

Luke laughed.

So did Jim. "My mistake."

Honors about even, the journey to Bill's was accomplished in dignified silence. "Little nip in the air," Jim said, holding the door for Bridget. He looked toward the southwest. "Storm coming in, looks like."

Bridget tucked her arm in his. "Good day for a hot toddy next to a roaring fireplace."

The south and west horizon were filling up with a rapidly advancing wall of dark clouds. "Hope they don't get caught out in that," Jo said.

"Looks nasty," Luke agreed. His hand was warm on her shoulder. She saw Jim looking at it and the hand became somehow heavier.

One-thirty on a Saturday afternoon, and it was after fishing season and before hunting season really began. Just enough reason for the party to get started early, and it had. Kelly McCormick and Larry Jacobson had drawn up chairs next to a booth filled with three giggling young women. Jim Earl, the mayor of Newenham, and four of the five sitting members of the town council were deciding city business at another. The jukebox was playing "Fruitcakes," and although no one was skating naked through the crosswalk—yet—Jimmy Buffet would have felt right at home.

They grabbed the last booth and settled in, only to have Dottie bellow from behind the bar, "You want something, get your butts up here and get it! Not you," she said to Molly Shuravaloff.

"But Dottie—"

"Don't you 'but Dottie' me, girl, you're lucky I let you step inside the door. You ought to be home being a comfort to your mother in her old age."

"She's forty-seven, Dottie!"

"Whatever."

Molly sulked back to her booth, where Mac McCormick put an arm around her waist and offered her a surreptitious sip from his beer.

They conferred, and Luke and Bridget went up to the bar to order, returning with hot buttered rums all around. Luke sipped and closed his eyes. "God, what's in this?"

Jo tasted and choked at the resultant wave of heat that seemed to envelop her sinuses. "Besides a fifth of rum?"

"Brown sugar," Jim said.

"And powdered sugar," Bridget said.

"Ice cream?" Luke said.

Jo, still gasping for air, croaked, "Butter. And rum. A whole lot of rum."

The second sip went down better and faster than the first, and when Dottie shouted that their burgers were ready, it was time for a refill. By then everyone had a pleasant glow, marred only somewhat when a burly man came in the door and saw them. He whipped off gold-framed aviator sunglasses to reveal dark, frowning eyes in a blunt-featured face. Tiny blood vessels turned his nose and his cheeks a deep, angry red. His hands were big-knuckled and scarred, dangling at the end of arms too bulky with muscle to hang straight. He shouldered his way across the floor with an impatient, slightly bowlegged stride, taking no notice of the lesser mortals in his path. He looked, on approach, like a cross between George Patton and King Kong, with a luxuriant mustache that sported evidence of past meals.

Jo saw him first. "Finn," she said.

He looked at Jim from beneath the brim of a cap advertising the Reno Air Show. "Your people still up?"

"And you are?" Jim said.

"Finn Grant," Jo told him, and to Finn said, "They're on their way home."

"Storm coming in," he said to Jim. "I don't want to have to run no patrol out after pilots who don't know how to come in out of the rain."

"Finn is a member of the Civil Air Patrol," Jo told Luke and Bridget. "He's made a career out of not finding people who have gotten themselves lost in the Bush."

Finn's face darkened to the color of the clouds in the sky outside. "Fuck you, Dunaway," he said, and stamped to the bar.

Jim looked at Jo. "My, my, you just endear yourself to everyone who comes down the pike, don't you? What did you do, break the story that his girlfriend is sleeping with his uncle?"

Jo fluttered her eyelashes. "You do say the sweetest things, Mr. Wiley, suh."

The aroma wafting up from the cheeseburgers became too much to resist and they tucked in. Plates polished clean down to the shine, a third toddy seemed like something even Jim and Jo could agree on, and Luke went to fetch them. Bridget said, "What was Mr. Finn so upset about, Jo? Is Jim right? Did you write a story about him?"

Jo, in that state of well-being that always follows the ingestion of equal amounts of alcohol, salt and deep-fryer fat, said with an expansive wave, "Finn Grant's the name, losing clients is his game."

Jim had to grin. Luke returned with the drinks and Bridget demanded further explanation. Jo fortified herself with a sip, burning her tongue in the process, and launched into what was one of her favorite stories. "Dagfinn Grant is a pilot, the owner and operator of a nice little air taxi service right here in Newenham. He's quite the businessman: a member of the Anchorage Chamber of Commerce and the Rotary Club, an old hunting buddy of ex-governor Hickfield, and he's been a guide since Alaska was a territory.

"Anyway, he makes his living flying people in and out of the Bush. He takes them into the Four Lakes for fishing and the foothills of the Alaska Range for hunting. He flies them up to the Togiak Peaks for that rough-neck climbing people do, you know, the ones who actually enjoy hanging from a ridge by their fingernails while they dangle over a one-thousand-foot abyss."

"Or say they do," Luke said, grinning.

"Or say they do," Jo agreed, grinning back. Luke's handsome face had begun to take on a rum-enhanced allure that made her think of the couch in Wy's living room with increasing anticipation. "In all fairness, it must be said that old Finn makes a pretty good living out of the air taxi business, so much so that he has to buy additional planes and hire on more pilots. Pretty soon he's running things more from the ground than he is the air. Until one day . . ."

"What?" Luke said.

"Don't encourage her," Jim said.

Bridget looked from Jo to Jim and back again.

"One day," Jo said, "not long ago, Finn was sitting in his office, all by his lonesome. I just want to point out," she added parenthetically, "that he was by himself. Nobody else around."

"Nobody else to blame, we got it," Jim said.

"Hush up," Bridget told him. "Go on, Jo."

"The phone rang. It was one Eric Silverthorne, who was calling on behalf of himself and his brother Rodney, and their wives Stella and Anna, respectively. They had just gotten off the jet from Anchorage and they wanted to go caribou hunting north of the Togiak Peaks. His name had been given them as a recommendation by the ticket agent at the Alaska Airlines terminal; could he oblige?"

Jo drank some more of that lovely toddy. She had a full stomach from the burger, a warm glow from the rum, Wy was safe and on her way home, the threat of Jim Wiley's disclosures were on hold, Luke's face was becoming increasingly beautiful across the table, and she was truly on vacation for the first time in three years, no story to research and write, no crime scenes to inspect, no politicians pulling in illegal campaign contributions, nothing at all to do, in fact, except enjoy herself. She was practically dizzy with delight, and she was definitely off the chain.

"As I said, Mr. Dagfinn Grant was all by his lonesome when his phone rang because all of his planes were in the air and all of his pilots were with them. He didn't have a plane available to transport a hunting party of four and all their luggage. He scurried around and managed to rustle up an old Cessna Skywagon belonging to a friend, which always surprised me because it is my understanding that Finn Grant has no friends. The Silverthornes arrive and aren't kept waiting more than two, three hours before Finn is ready to launch.

"So he takes them up to the Togiak Peaks, and manages to wedge the Skywagon into that little gravel strip west of Weary River, unloads passengers and crew, and leaves them, with the understanding that he's supposed to pick them up in ten days."

The toddy had developed a fine, heady bouquet and she inhaled it with abandon.

"What happened?"

She opened her eyes and smiled across at Luke. "He forgot them," she said simply.

He stared at her.

"What are you meaning, he forgot them?" Bridget said.

"I mean just that, the tenth day rolled around and he forgot to go get them."

Luke and Bridget stared at her, mouths open. Jim, having read this story on the front page of the *News,* stared into his mug. Better than looking at Jo, whose green eyes were bright with unabashed glee, whose dark blond hair seemed to be curling into tighter knots, whose face was glowing with the joy of storytelling. That's who she was, really, he thought, just somebody sitting around a fire late at night, hoping to get a few coins in her bowl before everyone fell asleep.

And, he had to admit, albeit reluctantly, that she was damn good at it.

"Well?" Luke demanded. "When did he remember?"

"He didn't," Jo said, and the glow faded a little. "Eight days after he was supposed to pick them up, old Julie Baldessario, a homesteader on Weary River, looked up from salting his silver catch to see Eric, Rodney and Anna stagger out from the brush.

He almost shot them, until they managed to convince him all they wanted was a ride out. They were filthy, Anna had a broken arm, Rodney had a broken leg, and a grizzly had bit Eric's ear clean off."

"Wait a minute," Bridget said. "What about—what was her name? The other woman?"

"Stella?" Jo drained her mug. "They waited three days, they said, until their food ran out, and then they started hiking out. Three days into the hike, they woke up and Stella was gone. The troopers went back in, the Civil Air Patrol, Search and Rescue. They quartered the area, back and forth, up and down. They never found her."

"Anybody suspect the husband?"

Jo shook her head. "They asked, of course, but Eric and Stella Silverthorne, to all outward appearances, had a solid marriage. Good reputation in the community, financially stable, two kids, twelve and fourteen. No reason to suspect the husband. It looks like she just wandered off."

"Uuiliriq," a voice said, and everyone looked up to see Molly Shuravaloff peering over the top of the booth. "Little Hairy Man," she added, blinking bleary eyes. Mac had been sharing more of his beer.

"Who's he?" Jim said.

"Nobody knows," she said. "He lives up in the mountains. He comes down to steal people, little kids mostly. Parents say never to play outside after dark, or Uuiliriq will get you."

Another head popped up next to hers, round-faced, dark hair and eyes, smooth olive skin, so like Molly she could have been her sister. "Don't talk about the Hairy Man, you know it only scares you. Come on, Darrell wants to dance."

The heads disappeared.

Luke looked over his shoulder at Finn. The big man was still standing at the bar, surrounded by a group that was mostly men. As they watched, he bought another round. "When was this?"

"Five years ago this month."

"And he's already back in business?"

Jo snorted a laugh and shook her head. "He was never out."

"What!"

"He's best buddies with Walter William Hickfield, former governor of the great state of Alaska. Hickfield pulled some strings. Plus he's known to be the softest touch around for a free fly-in fishing trip. Long as you're a judge, state court or higher, of course." She drank. "You know how it works."

"Doesn't it bother you?"

Jo managed a smile, a shrug. "It's just a story. I write them, the paper prints them, and I move on to the next."

Luke stared at her.

"She got it on the front page of the *News* for five days running," Jim said.

Jo looked at him, surprised.

"Let's have another toddy," he said.

SIXTEEN

Newenham, September 5

Liam started the recorder and gave the date and the time. "Present are myself, Corporal Liam Campbell of the Alaska State Troopers, Trooper Diana Prince, and suspects John Kvichak and Teddy Engebretsen."

The wind howled outside and the window shuddered in its frame, leaking cold air into the tiny gray room. The four of them sat crowded around the single rectangular table. It was dark outside due to the low overcast, and light flickered from the single fluorescent tube overhead, the second tube having burned out long ago. The room smelled of stale cigarette smoke and fear, an odor part ammonia, part fresh sweat. The lies told behind the door echoed off the hard surfaces of the wall and the ceiling, muttering dully beneath the scratching of the branches against the glass. *I didn't do it, officer. I only had one beer. I never hit her, she's a lying bitch. Nobody told me my license was suspended, I don't know what you're talking about. The door was open; I just went in to make sure everything was all right. I was just borrowing that truck. I loved that girl like she was my own daughter. I could never hurt him, he was my best friend. I was over at my mom's, at the bar, down on my boat, on the river, out hunting, in Anchorage, Outside.*

The room, with all its odors and echoes, had a pronounced effect on the people who were questioned there. Once Liam had come upon Mamie Hagemeister, the police station clerk, prepared to clean the interview room. He had himself removed mop and bucket from her hands and poured the hot soapy water in the nearest toilet. If he had his way, the room would never be cleaned, the walls never repainted, the ill-fitting window never replaced. The light fixture would always be kept to one bulb, and that bulb ready to give out at any moment. The chairs would never acquire cushions, the table would forever retain its scarred and unlovely surface.

"Kvichak has asked for a lawyer," Prince said tentatively, as if referring to a subject in questionable taste.

"Yes, he has," Liam said cordially, "and we'll see that he gets one. Just as soon as Anchorage can rustle one up."

"What happened to Brian Keogh?"

"Our judicial district's most recent public defender? Came in on the plane before yours? That Brian Keogh?"

"That would be the one," Prince acknowledged. "What happened to him?"

"He quit. Said he couldn't face another winter in the Bush. He was posted in Kotzebue before here," he added, in answer to Prince's interrogatory lift of eyebrow. "Says he's had enough ice not in a glass. He was offered a job as house counsel for some international import firm and he snapped it up. So Newenham is once more without a public defender." Liam's voice did not indicate massive sorrow at this turn of events. "And with this storm coming on, it'll probably be a while before we get a temp."

The two troopers sat across the table from Engebretsen and Kvichak now, Prince erect and all business, Liam sitting back with his long legs sprawled at an angle, looking out the window as if he weren't even listening, in fact as if he were about to doze off. In the three hours since starting that tape, he had yet to say one word.

"I'm thirsty," Engebretsen said. "Come on, gimme something to drink."

"In a minute," Prince said, the crease in her blue uniform sleeve as crisp as it had been when she walked in, her tie as impeccably knotted. Her black curls formed a tight cap against her skull, her blue eyes were hard and merciless, her mouth held in a stern, uncompromising line. She looked like a cop from the bone out, and she sounded like one, too. "Let's go over it one more time. You say—"

"Shit, man," Kvichak said, exploding onto his feet. His chair slammed against the wall and turned over. Engebretsen jumped and looked as if he was about to burst into tears.

Prince rose to face him, eye to eye. Liam didn't move, didn't turn from the window. "We've told you the goddamn story about six different times this morning, how many times you want us to tell it?"

"Until you get it right."

"Shit! You want us to say we killed that man! Well, we didn't, and nothing you can say or do is going to make us say we did! I want a lawyer!" He leaned across the table and shouted directly at Liam. "I want a goddamn lawyer!"

Liam didn't turn his head. Prince stared without changing expression. "Sit down." The two words were uttered in a soft, unthreatening voice, but they were a command. Kvichak picked up his chair, slammed it down on the floor and sat down hard. It must have hurt his tailbone, but it didn't affect his glare.

Prince sat opposite him and looked down at her notepad. "Now. You were hunting, you say."

Engebretsen, so verbal during the arrest and at the beginning of the interview, had withdrawn into silence and the occasional whimper. Kvichak was a one-man monument to fury; he spat out sentences as if they were being fed into the breech of an automatic rifle. "Yeah. We were hunting. We were hunting up on Nuk Bluff, like we do every September of our lives, like we have every single year since we could hold a rifle by ourselves. We were up there for ten days, we limited out in caribou, moose, geese, spruce hens and ptarmigan. We gutted and skinned and packed everything back to camp, so we didn't violate no wanton waste law. We didn't shoot the day Chouinard flew us in, so we didn't violate the fly-and-shoot-same-day rule." Again, he spoke directly to Liam. "We didn't see nobody and we didn't hear nobody, and we sure as hell didn't kill nobody."

Liam didn't stir.

"You can't always say you haven't seen anybody, can you, John?"

Engebretsen gave a low moan.

"Sometimes we do,"John said truculently. "What of it?"

"Sometimes you see them, and sometimes you talk to them, and sometimes you do more than that."

"I don't know what you're talking about."

Prince consulted a file. "September 12, 1998, Todd and Sharon Koch of Anchorage were paddling a canoe from the Two Lake campsite to the Four Lake Ranger Station when two men matching your descriptions appeared on the beach and started shooting at them."

Engebretsen whimpered.

"Got nothing to do with us," Kvichak growled. "We were home by the twelfth."

"So your sister Barbara said," Prince agreed. "And your brother-in-law Rob, and your nieces Karen, Sarah and Patricia, and your nephews John, Patrick and Tom. I'm sure your mother would have said so, too, only she was in the hospital in Anchorage on the twelfth."

"You can't prove a goddamn thing."

"You're right," Prince said, nodding. "We can't, and we couldn't. Same way we couldn't when a bunch of hikers up Utah Canyon got their camp trashed."

Engebretsen drew in a long, shaky breath. Kvichak shot him a warning glance. "Yeah, Corcoran asked us about that, but we were on the other side of the bluff from Utah."

"Of course you were," Prince said.

"I wanna go to the bathroom," Engebretsen said.

"In a minute," Prince said.

Engebretsen plucked up his courage. "You're always saying 'in a minute.' How come not now?"

She smiled at him, a thin-lipped, humorless stretch of the lips. "Because we're not done talking, Teddy."

He slumped back in his chair.

"For crissake," Kvichak said angrily, "let the poor bastard go to the john, why dontcha?"

She turned the smile on him. "In a minute."

"Fuck you!"

Liam turned his head and said, "John, your Winchester shotgun was the one used to kill Mark Hanover. Crime Lab called, and they say there's no doubt."

Kvichak stared at him, his face white and shocked, whether at the sound of Liam's first words in three hours or at the words themselves.

Liam rose to his feet. "Let's get some lunch," he said to Prince, and led the way out of the interview room. Prince had to hustle to get behind him before the door closed.

They stood in the hallway. "Shh," Liam said with one upraised finger.

An outburst of shouting came from behind the door, and Liam smiled.

"Sir, I—"

"They were thirsty, they were hungry, they did need to pee. Now they're scared. Let's let them be scared for a while."

Prince chewed her lip. "How much longer can we hold them without charging them?"

"Another twelve hours."

"The local magistrate would pick now to head up the creek."

"All to our advantage. If Bill were here, she'd probably sign off on a warrant, but she'd let them out on bail." He saw Prince's look. "Hey, John Kvichak's brother-in-law's the biggest bum unhung. John's the sole support of his sister's family and his mother. Teddy Engebretsen's dad is eighty-two, and he lives with Teddy. Neither one of them is a flight risk. Besides, where would they go?"

"Anywhere in the Bush?"

"It's coming on winter, they'd either starve or freeze."

They went to Eagle and cruised the deli counter, Liam settling on deep-fried chicken and Prince on a ham and cheese sandwich. They journeyed back to the post, ate their lunch without haste, called the Anchorage D.A. with information about a sex offender recently paroled, which parole he had immediately broken, big surprise.

At fifteen past one, they presented themselves back at the jail. At sixteen past one, they walked into the interview room. Engebretsen looked up and said, "I want to talk."

"Teddy—" Kvichak said.

"No," Engebretsen said with unaccustomed firmness. "Let's just tell them the truth, Johnny. One more time. Either they'll believe us or they won't—"

"They won't. Cops never know the truth when they hear it."

"Either they'll believe us or they won't," Engebretsen repeated, his voice wavering a little. "Either way, I'm talking."

"Shit." Kvichak folded his arms and glowered. "I ain't having nothing to do with it."

"Fine," Engebretsen said. "I'll tell."

Prince looked at Liam with undisguised admiration.

They'd heard the shot from their camp on the bluff, Engebretsen said. "It was our last day, you know, we'd limited out on everything, we butchered everything out, put it in game sacks, we were just waiting on Wy." He glanced sideways at Kvichak. "So we opened the beer."

"How long was it before you heard the shots?" Prince said.

"Man, I don't know," Engebretsen said. "We opened the beer early. I think I was on my third. I mean, we just didn't need to be sober anymore, so we weren't trying to be. Hell, we'd been drinking most of the night, if it comes to that. I don't know, nine o'clock, maybe? Maybe earlier."

Liam looked at Kvichak. Kvichak held his eyes for a long moment. "Oh hell," he said, slumping. "It was about eight-thirty, and before you say anything, yeah, we were already half in the bag."

"It was the first shots we'd heard that didn't come from our guns, you know?" Engebretsen said. "We hadn't even heard any planes, and the nearest cabin is that crotchety old Italian at Warehouse Mountain, and that's twenty miles away. Then we remembered that mining claim on Nenevok, and we thought maybe they were in trouble? Like one of them fired a warning shot for help, you know?"

"Tell me something, Teddy," Prince said, gazing at the earnest face sitting across from her. "Did you ever meet the miner on Nenevok?"

Engebretsen flushed and glanced at Kvichak, who folded his arms across his chest again. "Not really. Well, kind of."

"Which? Not really, or kind of?"

"Crissake," Kvichak said. "Wy dropped off supplies at Nenevok when she was bringing us into the bluff."

"And you met Mark Hanover, the miner."

Again the two men exchanged a glance. "Didn't meet the miner, he didn't come to the plane," Kvichak said finally. "The wife was there, though."

Prince gave a thoughtful nod, and glanced at Liam to see a muscle working in his jaw like a nervous tic. "The wife," she said. "Rebecca Hanover."

Engebretsen, forgetting for the moment where he was and who was listening, gave a long, blissful sigh. "Oh yeahhhh."

"Hear tell she was pretty," Prince observed in a neutral voice.

Engebretsen gave her an incredulous look. "Pretty! She wasn't just pretty. She was—she was—" He struggled for suitable words. "She was flat fucking drop-dead gorgeous," he said finally, with a touch of awe. "I never seen nobody so pretty outside of a movie. And built, wow!" A low, reverent whistle accompanied the words.

It is a maxim of the law enforcement profession that jails aren't filled with smart people. Nevertheless, this might be just about the dumbest person on the face of the earth sitting across from her now. "So, on that last morning of your hunt, you got tanked, you heard shots, you thought fired from the direction of the mine on Nenevok Creek, you remembered meeting a gorgeous woman there, and you decided to investigate."

"I told you," Kvichak said, more in sorrow than in anger. "I told you, Teddy, I told you they'd never believe nothing we said."

"No," Engebretsen said, becoming frightened again. "I mean yes. I mean, we hiked over, took us, hell, took us forever, and we were sober as judges by the time we got there."

"Uh-huh," Prince said. "When you got to the mine, what did you find?"

Engebretsen leaned forward. "There was a man, facedown in the creek."

"You pulled him out."

"Well, yeah, we didn't know if he was dead or not. I got my feet wet. Ten days I kept them dry, and the last day I have to go get them wet."

"So, Mark Hanover was dead when you found him."

Kvichak slammed his hands down flat on the table. In the ensuing silence, he leaned forward and he met Liam's eyes with a flat, unwinking stare. "Yes. Mark Hanover or whoever he was was dead when we got there. We heard the shot right after we got up. It took us two hours plus to get from the bluff to the Nenevok. We found his body in the creek. We pulled him out to see if he was dead. He was. We yelled for his wife. She didn't come out of the woods. I yelled for help on the cell phone."

"And then Johnny made us leave," Engebretsen said. "He said you'd nail us for doing it." He paused, and added defiantly, "And he was right."

There was a brief silence. For a moment, for just a moment, Prince allowed herself to be impressed by their sincerity.

Liam stood up. "Interview terminated, two-thirty p.m." He turned off the recorder and looked at Kvichak. "Crime Lab says yours was the gun, John."

Kvichak stared back. "The Crime Lab is wrong."

"Wasn't a bad bluff," Prince said on the way back to the post. "I would have believed him, but the lab doesn't lie." She thought of Nick, and had to erase the grin that came out of nowhere.

"Have you ever been forced to bushwhack your way across muskeg?"

Prince was thrown off track. "I beg your pardon?"

"Have you ever been forced to bushwhack your way across muskeg," Liam repeated. "I have. It's slow going."

She digested this. "Come on. They've got it all, means, motive, opportunity. They've even got a history of pulling this kind of stuff, going back years."

"They've never killed anybody before."

"They shot at two people last year," she retorted.

"They didn't hit anybody, though," he said thoughtfully. "You notice? Just the canoe. You see that drawing Corcoran did, showing where the bullet holes were? One amidships, directly between the two thwarts where the two people were sitting. The second in the stern. Both just at the waterline."

"So?"

"So, they both limited out this year."

She pulled into the space in front of the post and turned to stare at him. "And?"

"And I'd like to know how good they are with those rifles."

He called Charlene Taylor. "Johnny and Teddy?" she said. "They're hell on the moose and the caribou, but I can't see them killing anybody."

"Do you know what kind of shots they are?"

"First class," she said promptly. Charlene was Liam's alter ego in Newenham, the fish and game side of the troopers. It was her unenviable lot to enforce, or try to enforce, the state fish and game laws, which she did by four-wheeler, Zodiac and Cessna 206. Wet your line too early, shoot your bear too late, take the rack on your moose and leave the meat, and Charlene was there, a smile on her face and a summons in her hand. "I've checked out their camp a time or two, up on the bluff. Always go for a head or a shoulder shot, and they always get it, too. Probably has something to do with needing the meat to feed their families. Trophy hunters'll go for the gut every time."

Liam heard the disgust in her voice but refused to be sidetracked. "You ever have to haul them in, Teddy or John?"

"I probably could have, a time or two," she admitted. "Maybe even should have. But I didn't. They don't take more than their families can eat in a winter, and if they hold over the hunting season by a couple of hours, I'm not going to notice."

"Thanks, Charlene."

He hung up the phone. Prince had her arms folded and was staring at him. "Please tell me you don't think they're telling the truth."

He put his cap back on. By way of answering, he said, "Let's check out Teddy's hunting boots."

Teddy's dad suffered from Alzheimer's. One of John Kvichak's nieces, a tall, cool, blond drink of water named Karen, was staying with him while Teddy, she informed Liam in icy tones, was in jail. She examined Liam and Prince from behind oversize glasses that somehow lent an extra air of contempt to her expression, and produced Teddy's boots.

They were leather, and laced up over the ankles. They were also damp right through.

"This doesn't prove anything," Prince said.

"No," Liam said. "Let's go back to the office and make some calls to Anchorage."

They reached Rebecca Hanover's best friend, Nina Stewart, on their fourth call. She was upset and yelling by the end of the call, but what she unconsciously let slip along the way about the Hanovers' summer on Nenevok Creek had even Prince raising an eyebrow afterward. "Well," she said.

"Well," Liam said.

"A reluctant miner."

"Her husband was the miner," Liam said. "Seems Becky wasn't all that thrilled at the prospect of moiling for gold."

"Can't argue with her there," Prince said. "You ever panned gold?" Liam shook his head. "My folks took me out to the Crow Creek mine when I was kid. I was soaked to the skin with mud up to my eyebrows by the time I was done. Never did find any gold."

Liam grunted.

"If I was dainty little Rebecca Hanover, used to a comfy suburban lifestyle, shopping at Nordie's and dining at Sack's, all supported by my husband's North Slope engineering job, I might be a bit peeved if he quit that job, sold my home and moved me out into the Bush."

"She had a job, too," Liam said mildly.

"Uh-huh. Do you think she did it?"

"We'll have to find her to answer that question."

"The boys still look good to me."

"They look pretty good to me, too," Liam admitted.

Prince looked out the window. It wasn't even six o'clock and the sky was black. "If it's her, and she's on the run, at least she's not getting away easy."

"More than that," Liam said. At her inquiring look he added, "This storm is keeping the magistrate up the creek. Plus, if our boys do insist on a lawyer, it'll take a public defender with a stronger stomach than I've got to put his ass in the air until it blows out or through."

"Meaning?"

"Meaning we've got time. Time to hang on to the boys while we wait for Rebecca Hanover to show up."

Prince was skeptical. "You think she will?"

"If she isn't dead already, yes."

"The Bush is a big place."

"Yeah, but it's amazing how often people wander out of it. Let's go talk to the boys again."

SEVENTEEN

Old Man Creek, September 5

The wind howled around the little shack. The walls creaked, but they were well caulked and Moses had built up the fire in the woodstove so that it was toasty warm.

"Do you think the roof will hold?" Bill said, eyeing it, a collection of water-stained bits and pieces of three different grades of plywood, Sheetrock and one-by-twelves, neatly trimmed and fitted together like a patchwork quilt. Softened by the golden light of four gas lanterns, it looked like a work of art instead of a creation of convenience.

"The walls will go before the roof does," Moses said quite cheerfully, and grinned his evil grin when his three guests exchanged apprehensive glances. "Okay," he said. "Mr. Plum, in the library, with the pipe wrench."

He won, for the second time that evening, and Bill threw down her cards in disgust and eyed him in a frustrated way.

Moses worked his eyebrows. "Sorry, little girl," he purred, "not in front of the children."

After they finished picking up all the pieces, they retired Clue in favor of Monopoly. Moses won that game, too. In desperation, Tim suggested crazy eights, and aided and abetted by Bill and Amelia, who by this point didn't care who won so long as it wasn't Moses, he won handily.

They celebrated with mugs of hot cocoa. Bill leaned her back against Moses' chest, his legs curled around her, her head on his shoulder. Amelia sat on her bunk, hanging over the edge as Tim showed her a card trick that involved a story of ace islands with diamonds buried on them, jacks coming to dig the diamonds up, kings coming to drive the jacks away and the queens bringing their hearts. "Then a big windstorm comes and blows them all away," Tim said, stacking the cards and cutting them repeatedly. "Here." He offered the stack to Amelia. "Go ahead, cut them."

She did so, a puzzled expression on her face, trying to work out the trick.

Tim dealt the cards out again in piles facedown. One by one he turned the piles over, with all the diamonds in one pile, all the jacks in another, all the hearts in another, and so on.

Amelia was impressed. "How did you do that?"

Tim did his best to keep his face impassive, but a delighted grin kept leaking out around the edges. "I can never tell. I took the oath."

Amelia giggled, and Moses nudged Bill. "They're getting along all right."

She cast him an amused glance over her shoulder. For a man who could read the future with devastating and occasionally horrific accuracy, he could be remarkably obtuse about the now.

"What?" he said.

She shook her head and snuggled against him, smiling to herself when she felt him react. Too bad, so sad, old man, she thought, and looked across the room at Tim and Amelia. Tim looked like a kid with a brand-new toy. He cast quick, sidelong glances at Amelia when he thought she wasn't looking, he blushed when she caught him, he took every opportunity of brushing against her, a finger touch to the back of her hand as he scooped up the cards, a shoulder brush when he leaned in, even a bump of heads when they fought out a game of Snerts, resulting in shared laughter.

He was thirteen and she was seventeen, and Bill didn't think that this was the beginning of a lifelong romance. But it did Tim no harm for his first time to be with a young woman who, he well knew, had been brutalized in her previous sexual encounters, and who therefore would require patience and kindness. It helped that he was young and inexperienced enough to be entirely intimidated, and would therefore be very slow. And it did Amelia a world of good to discover the difference between a lout and a gentleman in bed. Bill had a shrewd idea as to what had started them down this road, and she had an even shrewder idea as to who first reached for whom.

Well, she was a poor guardian of teenage morality, no doubt, but Amelia was looking less like a forty-year-old barfly and more like a seventeen-year-old girl, and Bill couldn't regret that. It wasn't just the newfound discovery of good sex, of course; nothing was ever completely about sex, no matter what the Freudians said. The tai chi was giving her control over her body, a physical confidence. Moses had left the filleting of the day's salmon entirely up to her, and had viewed the results with nothing more than a disparaging grunt. From anyone else, that was like being awarded the Olympic gold medal, and judging from Amelia's flushed, proud face, she knew it. She hadn't been hit in four days. And a young man was looking at her with something close to adoration in his eyes.

Tim looked proud and confident, with no hint of the swagger so common among adolescent boys after their first score. Held together for the first terrible years of his life by some inner, unplumbed strength all his own, rescued by Wy in what sounded like the nick of time and given a home, regular meals, rules by which to abide and, above all, unconditional love, Tim had the makings of a truly good man.

"Amelia," Moses said.

Amelia looked up, her olive skin flushed with laughter. "Yes, uncle?"

"It's Sunday," he said. "We go home tomorrow."

Her smile faded. "Yes, uncle. I know."

On the floor Tim straightened.

"Do you go back to your husband tomorrow?"

Amelia sat up and pushed her hair behind an ear. A log split in the stove and hissed and spit when the flames hit sap. The damper flapped when a gust of wind tangled itself in the chimney. Boughs creaked outside.

"No, uncle," she said. "I won't go back to Darren."

Bill felt Moses stiffen, she thought with momentary surprise, and smiled to herself. "You sound pretty sure of yourself."

"I am." She said the words as if she was taking a vow.

It was amazing what four days of tai chi, sweats and fishing would do for the self-confidence, Moses thought complacently. The voices whispered a warning. He ignored them. This time they would be wrong. It had happened before, not often, but often enough to allow him to retain some hope in the face of unrelenting forebodings of death and disaster.

Bug off, he thought, and somewhat to his surprise, they did. And he wasn't even drunk.

Across the room Moses murmured something in Bill's ear, and she laughed. "Do you think they know we saw?" Tim whispered.

Amelia looked at the older couple. "I hope not." But she wondered. She'd seen Bill looking at her with a speculative glint in her eyes, and when she came back from the outhouse this evening her knapsack had been moved and the pills inside had shifted location. She didn't mind; she didn't want to be pregnant, either. She didn't know what she wanted, exactly, but then it had been so long since she had felt the courage to want anything.

Five months ago she had married Darren Gearhart with no desire other than to be a good wife and the mother of his children. She had wanted to sleep with him, too, and she now knew enough to know he had wanted to sleep with her. If he hadn't, he would never have married her. The realization didn't hurt as much as it once had.

A good wife, she had thought, meant keeping a clean, neat house, serving good meals on time, keeping the checkbook balanced. The second shock, after her wedding night, came when he told her to close her bank account, one she had been building since she first began to earn money as a baby-sitter at the age of twelve, and deposit its holdings into his own. She asked, timidly, if he would put her name on it, too. That was the first time he had hit her. It didn't hurt much, not like later, but it was the third shock, and then the shocks piled up so thick and fast that she lost the ability to differentiate between them.

She no longer had money of her own, there was only his money, doled out a few grudging dollars at a time. If she couldn't stretch them to cover the purchase of food and the maintenance of the trailer they lived in, she had to ask for more, and she learned quickly that she didn't ever want to ask for more. She learned not to visit her mother, too; he would either accompany her and be so rude that she would leave before she was too embarrassed, or on those few occasions when she managed to slip her leash and go off on her own, he would track her down and take her home.

Her mother knew, though. Amelia remembered her father. Oh yes, her mother knew, all right.

If Darren wasn't yelling at her, he was hitting her. If he wasn't hitting her, he was fucking her. It never stopped. She had thought he would be gone fishing most of the summer, but he'd been fired off the *Waltzing Matilda* practically before the season began. The skipper of the *Matilda* was Amelia's uncle's oldest son, and he had sought her out afterward, to apologize, she thought, but Darren had picked a fight with him and run him off before he could say so.

The five months had seemed like five years, and there had seemed no end to them. She could no longer sleep through the night, starting at noises when he wasn't next to her, and under constant assault of one kind or another when he was.

She'd been sleeping at fish camp, four dreamless nights of uninterrupted unconsciousness, in a bunk with clean sheets and a soft pillow all her own. She looked at Moses and felt something as close to love as she'd ever felt for a man. She thought how wrong people were who said he was an evil spirit. Even her mother, an elder who should have known better, had warned her children against him.

Tim's hands stopped shuffling the cards, and she looked up to see him watching her with grave eyes. "Are you okay?" he whispered.

She smiled. "Oh yeah," she whispered. "I'm perfect."

You sure are, he thought fervently.

To him, she was beautiful. The bruise on the side of her face had faded to a faint yellow and the dark shadows beneath her eyes were gone. Her hair, which she hadn't combed until her second day at fish camp, hung in a sleek, shining, black fall. Her olive cheeks were darker after three days spent outside and she moved with a new assurance. She looked him straight in the eye and smiled, and he had a hard time not ducking his head. He couldn't stop the flush that rose to his own cheeks.

"It was so good," he whispered.

"Yes," she said. She stretched a little in memory, her breasts pushing at the front of her shirt. "Yes, it was. The second time especially."

He swallowed. "Yeah." He shuffled the cards and they went all over the place. He bent over, picking them up, glad of the opportunity to hide his expression. "Amelia?"

"What?"

He gathered together all his courage and whispered her own question back at her. "Can we do it again?"

He heard her inhale, her involuntary, delighted and slightly surprised chuckle, and then Moses got to his feet, giving Bill a surreptitious tickle on the way up. "Come on, boy, time to bring in some more wood."

The last thing Tim wanted to do was leave before his question was answered, but he rose obediently and followed Moses into the storm. A gust of wind ripped the door from his hand and slammed it shut. "Moses!"

"What? And come on, let's get that goddamn wood before we both freeze our nuts off." He nudged Tim, his grin a white blur in a dark smudge. "Especially now that you know what they're for."

Tim was glad the darkness hid his flush. He should have known the old man would see, would know. He turned his head into the wind, feeling drops of moisture cool his cheeks. "Is that snow, Moses?"

"Feels like," the old man said, allowing the change of subject, much to Tim's relief. He rooted through the woodpile, going down a layer in search of the dry stuff, and stacked Tim's arms full.

"It's too early for snow," Tim said.

Moses added another piece of wood, and Tim could no longer see the blur. "It's never too early for snow out here."

A bird called, barley audible over the wind, a low note, followed by clicking sounds, the sound of bare branches rubbing together.

Moses, his arms full of wood, stood still, looking to the west.

"What?" Tim said.

"I thought I heard—"

"What?" The snow stung Tim's cheeks and he shivered.

Moses looked at him. "Go on, get back in the house."

Tim went inside ahead of him. Moses stood on the front porch for a minute longer, listening, but the raven didn't speak again.

They built up the fire and Amelia made more cocoa, lumpy, just the way Tim liked it. He looked at her with his heart in his eyes.

She looked up and saw him. The color in her cheeks deepened, and her smile was part shyness, part mischief and part warm wealth of shared knowledge.

Moses shoved the table into a corner and tossed blankets and pillows down on the floor. He turned down all the lanterns and opened the fire door. They gathered in a half circle around the flames, light flickering across their faces. "Story time," Moses said with that evil grin.

Bill settled down next to him. "Which one?"

Moses sampled his cocoa. "No contest. On a night like this, Uuiliriq."

"The Hairy Man? Oh brother."

Tim jumped. Amelia gave him a questioning look.

"Quiet, woman." Moses fixed a piercing eye on the two younger members of the group, and began to speak.

It was hard to say, afterward, just what it was about his voice that so compelled the attention. It dropped to a low tone you had to strain to hear, it fell into a cadenced rhythm that had your head nodding in almost hypnotic attention. He donned finger fans, made of woven straw and trimmed with caribou ruff, and used them to help tell the story, palms out, forefingers crooked around the tiny handles, hands moving in minute, precise jerks back and forth, up and down, side to side, expressing joy, fear, laughter, pain. Once Tim thought he heard drums sounding faintly in the background. Once Amelia looked around for the other singers. Even Bill was seduced, hearing the stamp of mukluks, the rustle of kuspuks, the cheers of the crowd.

It was an old story, never written down, known only to those who told it and those who listened, deep in the tiny settlements and villages of the Yupik. It was a story your grandfather told your father, and that your father told you, and that you would tell your children, in hopes that it would keep them safe inside after dark. It was a story that gave meaning to otherwise mysterious disappearances when it did not.

And it was a way to maintain a sense of cultural identity in a world increasingly white and Western.

"Uuiliriq lived in the mountains," Moses began.

"High in the mountains he lived.

"High in the mountains, in a dark cave.

"High in the mountains, in a dark cave.

"That cave so high, nobody climb there.

"That cave so high, nobody see it.

"That cave so high, nobody find it.

"Only Uuiliriq.

"All alone he live in this cave.

"He have no mothers.

"He have no fathers.

"He have no brothers.

"He have no sisters.

"All alone he.

"All alone he sleep.

"All alone long he sleep.

"Sometime he wake up."

Moses' voice deepened. "Sometime Uuiliriq he wake up.

"Sometime he wake up hungry."

Something not quite a shiver passed up Tim's spine. "Are you okay?" Amelia whispered.

He managed a smile and nodded.

"Sometime he wake up so hungry, he go get food."

The beat quickened.

"Sometime he leave that cave so high up in the mountains.

"Sometime he come down from those mountains.

"From those mountains sometime he come to village.

"One time he come to our village.

"Our little village by the river.

"The river she is wide.

"The river she is deep.

"The elders tell children to stay inside after dark.

"Children stay inside or the river will get them.

"But this one young boy he don't listen.

"This boy he wait till everybody sleeping.

"Everybody sleeping he go outside.

"Go outside he go down to the river.

"Can't catch me! he yell to her.

"Can't catch me! he yell to the lights in the sky.

"Can't catch me! he yell to the mountains.

"He yelling so loud.
"So loud Uuiliriq creep up behind.
"Creep up behind and grab him.
"Grab him and take him up the mountain.
"Up the mountain to that cave he got there.
"That cave so high, nobody climb there.
"That cave so high, nobody see it.
"That cave so high, nobody find it.
"The village it wakes.
"It wakes and that boy gone.
"The men they light torches.
"Light torches and climb those mountains.
"Climb those mountains and search all night long.
"All night long they see the torches from the village.
"From the village they see the torches go far away.
"Go far away and come back.
"Come back without that boy.
"Without that boy and his mother cry.
"His mother cry and his father cry.
"His father cry and his sisters cry.
"His sisters cry and his brothers cry.
"His brothers cry and his aunties cry.
"His aunties cry and his uncles cry.
"That boy gone.
"That boy long gone.
"That boy gone forever."

The fans slowed again, beating a dirge against the air. Moses'
voice dropped to the merest breath of sound.

"Some nights.
"Some night when dark outside.
"Some night when dark outside that village wake up.
"That village wake up and hear something.
"Hear something crying
"Crying far off in that night.
"Maybe that boy.

"Maybe that boy he crying for home.

"Crying for home.

"Those people they lay in their beds.

"They lay in their beds and they listen to that crying.

"They listen to that crying.

"But they don't go out."

The fans beat the air, the white strands of caribou fanning the air in precise, graceful arcs.

"Stay inside after dark.

"After dark stay inside.

"Stay inside after dark or Uuiliriq come.

"Uuiliriq come."

The fans stopped in midair. The room was still, the wind only a faint howl outside, the lamps the merest hiss of sound. Did a dark shape shift in the shadow near the door?

"AND GET YOU!"

Amelia screamed and grabbed Tim. Tim, to his everlasting shame, yelled and jumped. Bill spilled the rest of her cocoa and cursed roundly.

Moses fell backward laughing, a deep bellow of a laugh that rolled out of his chest and reverberated off the patchwork ceiling.

"Uncle!" Tim said. "You're scaring the women."

"Yeah, like you weren't peeing your pants afraid," Amelia said, and patted her chest as if reassuring her heart that everything was all right. "Uncle, you sure know how to tell a story."

Moses sat up again, still laughing, and stripped the fans from his fingers. "Gotcha," he said.

"Okay, that's it," Bill said, rising to her feet. "Story time's over. Everybody hit the rack. And as for you, old man." She leveled a glance at him. He grinned back at her irrepressibly.

"You've got to sleep sometime," she warned him.

She stoked the stove while Moses turned out the lanterns. A lecherous murmur and a reproving slap came from their bunk, followed by the sound of a long kiss and a rustle of covers as the two elders nestled together like spoons and settled in for the night.

Tim stretched out in his sleeping bag, arranging things so his head was near the head of Amelia's bunk. He wished he could crawl in with her, but he hadn't been invited. Besides, he didn't know how Bill and Moses would feel about it.

The howl of the wind, held in temporary abeyance by Moses' voice, was back with a vengeance, snarling and snapping, making the trees outside creak and the cabin shudder.

"I'm sure glad I'm not outside in this," he said unthinkingly.

"Me, too," Amelia whispered.

"You awake?"

"Yeah. You?"

"Yeah."

She was silent for a moment. "How come you jumped?"

"What? Oh. You jumped, too. So did Bill."

"Not then. Before. When he said the story was about the Little Hairy Man."

"Oh." Caught in the spell of the old man's story, he'd forgotten his initial reaction.

He was silent for a long time, so long that she thought he had fallen asleep. "In my village, there was this girl," he said finally. His head twisted on his pillow and he looked up at the face pressed against the side of the bunk. "She was teaching me Yupik."

"You didn't grow up speaking it?"

"My birth mother wouldn't. She said it was a dead language of a dead people, and if I wanted to get anywhere in life I had to speak English. She spoke only English at home."

His voice was matter-of-fact, but the undertone of bitterness betrayed him.

"But in school, you had to be fluent in both. So the teacher got a girl from the high school to teach me. She was really nice, so nice. She showed me how to learn. I never knew I could learn anything before her, but I could. She gave me that."

He stopped.

"Did you learn Yupik?" she said.

"Some. Before she went away."

"Went away? Where did she go?"

"I don't know. Nobody knew. One day she just wasn't there anymore."

"Did she—how did she leave?"

"Nobody knew," he repeated.

"Nobody found her?"

"They looked. But nobody found her." He looked up at her. "Some said it was the Hairy Man. That he came down from the mountains because he was hungry. And he took her."

They were both silent. "I'm sorry," she said finally.

"Yeah. Me, too."

"Her name was Christine," she heard him say just before she slid into sleep. "She was pretty."

And then, words so indistinct she might have dreamed them, "She looked like you."

Newenham, September 6

"I'm willing to try it if you are," Prince said hopefully.

Liam took one look at the clouds, so low that if he went outside and reached up he thought he might touch them, and said firmly, "I'm not."

"I'm grounded," Wy said. "At least until this afternoon."

Prince pounced. "Why, did you hear something on the forecast? Is it going to clear?"

Wy shook her head, almost amused. "Not likely. There's a gale warning out for Area 5A. It'll be moving north."

Prince stared out at the dark skies with a gloomy expression. The third interrogation of Teddy Engebretsen and John Kvichak the night before had produced no changes in their story, the result of which was that Prince now wanted very much to talk to Rebecca Hanover. She had shown up at Wy's house at first light on the off chance that the weather might look better out of Wy's window than it did from the trooper post. Liam had invited her to stay for breakfast.

"At least it isn't snowing anymore," Jo said, refilling coffee mugs all around.

A timer dinged and Bridget opened the oven door. The heavenly aroma of Bisquick coffee cake wafted through the room. Jim and Luke were sitting on the couch with their feet propped on the coffee table, Liam in the armchair. Jo replaced the coffeepot and perched on a stool at the counter next to Wy. Bridget cut the cake into squares and handed the squares around on saucers. For a while the only sounds were the dulcet growlings of Bob Edwards on the radio, the creaking of the house beneath the undiminished onslaught of wind, and grunts of pleasure as the coffee cake went down. Bridget was complimented lavishly all around, and she put her finger in her chin and curtsied in response.

Prince paced restlessly in front of the windows, until Liam said, "Why don't you go on down to the post?"

"What for?"

He shrugged. "Somebody might call in a triple homicide."

"Like we could respond in this," she said, but she picked up her hat.

When the door shut behind her Jim said, "What a hot dog."

Liam gave a tolerant shrug. "She's smart and quick and ambitious. All she needs is a little seasoning."

"She had two different homicides, one a multiple, the first day she got here," Jo said. "She got her name in the paper and everything."

"Thanks to you," Liam said.

Jo refused to curtsy, but she did bow her head in arrogant acceptance of what wasn't exactly an accolade. "In fact, you both did."

"Yeah, I was thrilled."

Jo snorted. "If you didn't want your name in the paper, you shouldn't have become a trooper."

"More coffee, anyone?" Bridget said brightly.

Jo gave Wy a long look. Wy wasn't talking much, and she noticed that her friend was keeping to the opposite side of whatever part of the room Liam was in. She wondered what had happened out at Nenevok Creek. She noticed Jim looking at Liam and wondering the same thing.

Bridget was still standing in front of her with the coffeepot and a smile. "Sorry," Jo said, and held out her mug. "Sure, and thanks."

Wy and Liam had come in separately the night before, and had exchanged perhaps ten words total before Liam went out to his camper for the night. There was no sneaking back in, either, not that there would have to be with Tim out of town. It wasn't like there hadn't been plenty of noise already to contend with from the back bedroom, she thought acidly. Not that she hadn't done her best to put Luke through his paces on the living room couch.

She looked at Luke. She should have known better. Beautiful men, like beautiful women, knew that their faces were their fortune. They didn't have to do anything but be beautiful. Luke, it must be admitted, was extremely beautiful, but beauty went only so far in bed, and even less far out of bed.

Bridget was beautiful, too, but she was also smart and funny. Jo hated to admit it, but Jim's taste in the opposite sex might be better than her own. "So you think Rebecca Hanover killed her husband and ran off because she didn't like being stuck out in the Bush for three months?" she said out loud.

"That's not for publication, Jo," Liam said sternly.

Jo's fair skin, the bane of her existence, flushed right up to the roots of her hair. "I heard you the first time," she said between clenched teeth.

He examined her expression for a moment, and then, amazingly, backed down. "I know. I'm sorry, Jo."

She managed a brief nod, and to salvage her pride added, "I didn't say I wouldn't write about it. But I won't use anything you tell us here today without your say-so." She looked at Wy, who was glaring at Liam.

"I know," Liam said again.

"I thought Woodward and Bernstein used two sources for every story," Jim said.

Jo appreciated the effort he was making to lighten the air. "They did."

"You don't?"

She matched his effort. "Not if the first source is a state trooper with twelve years on the job and a reputation for upholding truth, justice and the American way."

There was a round of nervous laughter. Everybody looked at Liam, who sighed. "Yeah, okay." He looked at Wy, who was studiously examining her coffee mug. His lips tightened.

"From the beginning," Jo prompted him. She didn't know what was going on there, but she was willing to act like the lightning rod for the time being.

Liam didn't strike. Instead, he told the story simply, beginning with the Mayday intercepted by the Alaska Airlines flight deck crew and his and Prince's arrival at the scene. He put together the case against Engebretsen and Kvichak in clipped, disinterested terms, including their passionate denials.

"I never met anyone who was arrested who ever was guilty of anything," Jo observed.

"Yeah. I know."

Liam's smile was thin and strained, and Wy tried not to feel guilty. What else could I do? she thought. He had to know. Maybe he's right, I should have told him sooner, but it's only five months since I saw him again, only a month that we've been together.

She thought back to the afternoon at the mining camp. I love you, Wy, Liam had said, and so she had told him, then and there, and he, at first disbelieving and then enraged, had stalked up to the cabin in a huff, ostensibly to search for evidence to help solve the mystery of Mark Hanover's murder but really, she knew full well, to put her far enough out of reach that he wouldn't be tempted to deck her.

She didn't blame him, but she wouldn't fall into the trap of blaming herself, either, not a second time. Shit happens. You can't let it define you, you can't let it define the rest of your life. She hadn't, and she wouldn't let him do so, either.

Jo's voice recalled her to the present. "But you still don't like them for it."

The trooper shrugged his shoulders. "I don't know. It doesn't feel right. Why'd they call in the Mayday? According to Wy the Hanovers weren't due to be picked up until Labor Day. If they did it, they could have left the body lying where it was, ready for the nearest grizzly to wander out of the woods and eat the evidence."

"In that case, where's Rebecca?" Jo said.

Labor Day, Wy thought, and remembered the last time she'd delivered supplies to Nenevok Creek. Three fishermen getting restive as she fought the cargo netting and the bungee cords. Rebecca watching with a wistful expression on her face, arms cradling the stack of magazines Wy had brought in for her. Mark Hanover coming up the path and—oh. "Oh hell," Wy said.

Everyone looked at her.

"I'm sorry," she said sheepishly. "I totally forgot."

"What?" Liam said.

"The fishermen were in a hurry to get to the lodge and I was humping it to get the plane unloaded and we'd hit an air pocket on the way in and the cargo had shifted a little in flight, you know, just enough to wedge itself into—"

"Wy," Liam said. "What did you forget?"

Wy took a deep breath. "The last time I made a supply run into Nenevok Creek, Mark Hanover pulled me to one side and said they might need another order of supplies, a big one this time. Like I said, my passengers were in a hurry and I wasn't paying much attention. I told him to get me a list and he said he would and we took off."

There was a brief, electric silence.

"You only just remembered this now?" Liam said.

"I'm sorry," Wy said helplessly. I've had other things on my mind, she thought, and knew by the shift of expression on his face that he had seen that thought reflected in her eyes.

"A big order of supplies," Jo said, her eyes bright, her nose all but twitching. "At the end of the summer? Nobody orders supplies at the end of the summer. You're just inviting the bears in, leaving a bunch of food sitting around your cabin."

"Unless," Liam said.

"Unless," Jim said, "you're ordering up enough to see you through the winter in that cabin."

"From what her friend Nina said," Liam said slowly, "Rebecca Hanover wasn't more than lukewarm about spending the summer out there."

"If he told her about this wonderful new idea just before they were scheduled to leave—" Jo said.

Liam looked at Wy. "Tell me everything you remember about Rebecca Hanover."

"I already did."

"Tell me again."

He was all trooper now, firm, implacable, totally focused on the job. He bore no resemblance whatever to the furious man who had raked her over the coals at Nenevok Creek. In one way, she welcomed it. In another, she did not. She got up and went to the corner desk from where she ran her business, and pulled out a tall red book filled with dated, lined pages. She opened it and flipped through May, until she found the day she wanted. "Here it is, May twenty-ninth, the Saturday before Memorial Day. Passengers Mark and Rebecca Hanover, along with two hundred pounds of freight, to Nenevok Creek."

Wy looked up. "She was frightened. First time she'd been in a small plane, I think. But he jollied her on board. They sat in the back—we had to take the Cessna because of all the freight—and I strapped some of their canned goods into the front seat to balance out the load. It was a clear day, maybe an eight-knot wind, easy flight, eighty-five minutes there and back again, no problem."

"How did she strike you?"

Her eyes narrowed in memory. "As a dyed-in-the-wool city girl," she said after a moment. "She's beautiful, blond hair, blue eyes, great figure. Immaculate manicure. Soft voice, called him honey a lot. She's not your typical Bush rat. Her husband had the gold bug, and she was along for the ride."

"Willingly?"

She considered. "If you mean by that, did he have a pair of handcuffs on her, no."

"But?"

"But." She met Liam's eyes straight on for the first time in forty-eight hours. "But she wasn't happy about his decision."

"She think it was pie in the sky? Gold mining is, mostly."

Wy shook her head. "Wasn't the money. She just didn't want to be out there. It was like pulling up a hothouse orchid and try-ing to transplant it on the moon. She knew it. He didn't." She looked down at the Day Timer, leafed through some more pages. "I dropped off supplies half a dozen times. Every time, she was waiting at the strip. I took her some newspapers and magazines and she was, well, almost pathetically grateful."

She closed the book and raised her head. "I don't think she killed him, Liam. She isn't the type."

"Everybody's the type, Wy, given the right provocation."

"I know you always say that," she said stubbornly, "but she loved him. They had this kind of, I don't know, sexual thing going on that practically gave off sparks. He was gorgeous, too, one good-looking hunk of man. What's more, I'd say he loved her as much as she did him."

"Never underestimate what three months in the Bush will do to a relationship," Jim observed. "You see the results in the front pages of her rag every day." He hooked a thumb at Jo.

"Hey," she said, faintly protesting. "I resemble that remark."

Wy put the book back on the desk. "Are you still absolutely sure Hanover's death has nothing to do with Opal's?"

His eyes went from her to the map on the wall behind her. "Different weapon. A long way to go on foot in a very short time. I could be wrong, but I don't think so."

The phone rang and Bridget answered it. Liam could hear Prince's voice. "One moment," Bridget said. "It's for you," she added unnecessarily, and handed it over.

Prince wasted no time in pleasantries. "I just got a call via the marine operator. She relayed a call from an old guy up at"—he heard the rustle of paper in the background—"at Weary River. Is that right, Weary River?"

He carried the walk-around phone to the map on the wall. "Yeah," he said, locating Weary River. About halfway between Rainbow and Russell. "I've got it."

"Well, this old guy, he's Italian or used to be before he homesteaded out at Weary River and turned American, and she couldn't hardly understand him but she thinks he called to say that he'd found a body." Prince's excitement crackled down the line.

"Where?"

"A place called Rainbow."

He moved his finger up. "Got it. Rainbow." He was very conscious of Wy looking over his shoulder and the rest of them crowding around behind her. "Who's dead?"

"A guy name of Peter Cole."

"Peter Cole?" He felt Wy's indrawn breath and looked at her. "Hold on." To Wy he said, "You know him?"

She nodded, dazed. "He's on my mail route." She swallowed and met his eyes in sick apprehension. "The same day I went to Kagati Lake and found Opal Nunapitchuk."

"You saw him that day?"

She shook her head. "I almost never do. He's a hermit, doesn't like being around people much. He left the bag to be picked up on the strip. I took it and left the incoming mailbag in its place."

"Is that any way to treat the U.S. mail?" Jim said.

Wy shrugged. "It's his way. He doesn't hurt anybody." She winced. "Or he didn't."

"Prince," Liam said into the phone. "How did Peter Cole die?"

Her voice was triumphant. "The old Italian guy said he was shot." She couldn't have been happier if Ted Bundy were loose in the Bay.

"With what?"

A little deflated, Prince said, "He didn't say, just that Cole was shot. He's got a pretty thick accent," she added. "It's not easy to understand him over the radio."

He was looking at the map, following the thick black line that marked Wy's mail route, some of the destinations printed on the map, some penciled in later by Wy. Kagati Lake. Russell. Weary River, where the old Italian guy homesteaded. He tapped the map. "What's his name, do you know?" he asked Wy.

"Julie Baldessario."

"Julie?"

"Giuliano. But everyone calls him Julie."

"He's a reliable kind of guy?"

She nodded. "He's about a million years old, came into the country after World War II. Lost his family in the Holocaust. Just looking for a little peace and quiet, I think."

"Good story," Jo said, interested.

Jim smacked her lightly on the arm, and she subsided.

"But he's very much all there," Wy said. "If he says he found Peter Cole shot, he found Peter Cole shot. The question is, what was Julie doing out in this?" She waved a hand at the storm outside.

Liam ignored her, continuing to trace the map with his forefinger. "Rainbow, Kemuk." His finger had to make a little jog to one side. "Nenevok Creek."

He stood up. "We've got dead people at Kagati Lake, Russell and Nenevok Creek. All were murdered. All were killed within five days of each other. Some nut is shooting his way from settlement to settlement."

Wy was still staring at the map. Her face was white.

"Wy?" he said, touching her arm. "Wy, what is it?"

Mute, she pointed.

Her mail route took a dogleg between Rainbow and Kemuk and another between Warehouse Mountain, Kokwok and Akamanuk, but south of Akamanuk . . .

South of Akamanuk was Old Man Creek.

EIGHTEEN

Wood River Mountains, September 6

She was so cold.

She couldn't feel her hands anymore. Her feet had been numb since the night before.

She knew a storm was coming the previous afternoon when the low, dark clouds took over the sky and the wind began to bite into her flesh, but she'd never been outside in a storm before and she had had no idea how cold it would be.

She'd found rudimentary shelter in a hollow against the side of the uprooted cottonwood. What little wit she had left had murmured that something else might regard that hollow as its own, but she was too tired and too hungry and too cold to care. She found a long branch and propped it against the trunk over the hollow. She found other branches and leaned them against the first. She scraped together a covering of pine needles and fallen leaves and more branches, and then she crawled beneath it and curled into a sodden ball, shoving her hands between her thighs. If he found her, he found her. She had to rest. And she could go no further in the dark. She had fallen the night before and hurt her leg. She could still walk, but for a few paralyzing moments she had thought that it was broken, that she would be unable to move, to run, to flee, to fight if need be.

If he had come on her then, he would have had her.

Somehow, she had managed to pull herself to her feet and stagger on. She knew he wasn't far behind her. She could feel him coming, feel his rage, feel his hands on her, his penis thrusting into her, and she simply could not bear to endure that again. Better to die out here in the wilderness. Mark was dead—no, no, don't think of Mark, bleeding his life away while she went like a lamb to his slaughterer—she might as well be, too. All she wanted now was to die in peace, and not to be buried next to all the other Elaines in that sun-dappled dell of death.

In some part of her mind, the part that was still able to wonder, to think, she was amazed that she had made it this far. She couldn't believe that she had escaped in the first place. Squirting the Windex into his eyes had been pure instinct; she hadn't even known she had still been carrying it.

She wondered what was in it, in Windex. Alcohol, maybe, that was why it evaporated so fast. And why it stung the eyes so much. Who made it? Johnson and Johnson? Procter and Gamble? She would write their president a letter of appreciation, whoever they were and whomever he was. She would give a testimonial. She would clean her windows with Windex for the rest of her life She'd order it by the case, by the pallet, by the truckload—

Her stomach growled. Shut up. Shut up shut up shut up. I know you're hungry. So am I. We don't have any food, so just shut up.

She'd found some highbush cranberries that morning and gobbled them down, equally oblivious to the piles of bear scat with cranberry seeds in them and the seeds themselves, which took up most of the fruit. They were so tart as to be nearly sour, but they gave her a spurt of energy that finally got her out of the valley.

She was on the downside of a set of rolling foothills now. Before her spread an immense flat marsh with a wide river snaking across it. She knew the sun came up in the east, and she also knew that this was Alaska, that it was September and the sunrise was moving steadily south. Bristol Bay lay to the southeast. Newenham was in the southeast. They had changed planes in Newenham. There were houses in Newenham, warm houses, and stores, stores with food on the shelves, and running water, hot water, and telephones and television and maybe even a bead store.

From something Mark had said once—no, no, don't think of Mark, facedown in the icy water—she knew enough to follow the rill downstream to a creek, the creek downstream to a river, the river downstream to the sea and civilization. And she knew that he knew it, too, and would be hard on her heels.

Her stomach growled again. Shut up shut up shut up. She found a stand of fireweed, and she remembered from the herb book that Natives ate the pith. She'd paused precious moments in her flight to strip the leaves and crack the stems, only to find the marrow woody. She ate it anyway, and dug up the roots because the book had said those were edible, too. The taste of the dirt was cool and metallic. Later she stumbled into a patch of wild celery, something her friend at work had called pushki, and she picked some and peeled it and ate it. It, too, was wooden and tasteless. Blisters were already forming where one of the leaves had brushed her arm. Because she was trying not to follow the creeks downhill too closely, she had no water to wash until it was too late.

And then there was the blood.

It wasn't all hers.

The bear had come out of nowhere, rising up out of the dense thicket of alders like a colossus, spreading his arms wide, claws extended, roaring out his rage and fear at her trespass. He'd been eating a snowshoe hare. He swiped at her with one taloned paw and sent her tumbling head over heels, until she crashed into the trunk of a birch tree. She was dizzy and disoriented, too stunned to move. She could feel the wound on her shoulder and back, but it was more of a dull ache than a biting pain.

The bear growled and snarled and tore up a couple of alders. She heard him, but could not be stirred to move.

After a while his grumblings faded into the distance.

She'd been lying there waiting for him to come over and finish her off. She was even glad her flight was over. No one would ever know now what had happened to her, but she was too tired and too cold and too hungry to care.

When the bear left, it took her a while to believe it. Why hadn't he finished off his kill? Had the smell of human startled and surprised him so violently that he was actually afraid of her; weak, starving, freezing, defenseless Rebecca Hanover? So afraid that he'd run off and left his meal behind?

She raised her head. The rabbit was still there, its body torn almost in two, red flesh gleaming between stained brown fur only beginning to turn winter white. She could smell its blood.

Her stomach growled.

Raw meat was harder to chew than cooked.

If you're going to be lost in the Bush, Rebecca, she thought now, be lost in the early summer. Chances of finding food are better then, if you're too squeamish to shoot anything. Mark had said that with a smile when they'd first—no, no, don't think about Mark, or Mark's smile, or the way he—

The wind roared overhead and there was a loud crash. She went totally still, not blinking, not breathing, straining to hear over the wind and the moan of the trees. It could have been a branch falling. That was it, a branch, breaking off and falling to the ground. She willed herself to relax, and discovered that her hands had thawed enough to feel the pushki blisters on her right arm. The thorns stung, too, the thorns she'd picked up when she stumbled into a patch of devil's club. Tiny thorns, on the stems and the undersides of the leaves, so little she hadn't noticed them, so little she could barely see them after they were embedded in her skin, so little they ought not to hurt as much as they did.

She burrowed down again, in search of some particle of warmth left over from the morning sun.

She should have taken her gun down to the creek that morning. What morning was that, exactly? There had been no clocks at the little cabin in the canyon, and no calendar. Days had passed, but maybe weeks. She didn't know anymore.

One thing she did know. The man who had killed her husband and kidnapped and raped her repeatedly was still after her. Her escape had been an affront to his pride, and if she had any doubt of his determination to keep her forever, it had been banished by the sight of those wooden markers.

All Elaines. He had called her Elaine. All those Elaines. Twelve. My god, twelve of them. Twelve women before her. Had he kidnapped them all? Raped them all? Buried them all? Fashioned markers for them all? Why had no one noticed? Why had no one cared? There were mothers there, she was sure of it, daughters, nieces, aunts. Why had no one come looking for them? Where were their fathers, their mothers, their sisters and brothers? Where were their friends? Where were the police, and the state troopers, and the FBI? Where was *America's Most Wanted*? Where was *Cops*? Where was *60* goddamn *Minutes*?

She knew one more thing. Wounded, cold, hungry, huddled beneath a few branches and leaves, hundreds of miles from help, her own death one degree in temperature away, she knew she was luckier than anyone buried beneath those perfect wooden markers at the head of that perfect little canyon, a quick walk from the front door of that perfect little house.

Something rumbled in the pit of her belly. At first she thought it was a reaction to the rabbit. It took a moment to recognize it as anger, an emotion she had last felt aimed at Mark. She shied away from the memory at first, but it was such a tiny presence, barely a spark. She wrapped her arms around her middle and curled around it, creating a protective shield. The spark caught and grew, warming her.

If he doesn't catch me.

If I don't starve to death.

If I don't die of exposure.

If I make it out of here.

If all those things, it will be because of you, Elaine.

The words ran through her mind again and again and at some point the "if" changed, faded, disappeared.

I won't let him catch me.

I won't starve to death.

I won't die of exposure.

I will make it out of here.

I will beat him, Elaine.

I will beat him for you.

Here it was in the middle of the first fall storm, and his Elaine was right out in the middle of it. She wasn't strong enough to brave the wind and the rain, and if his weather sense was not mistaken—and it hardly ever was—it would snow before morning. He bent his head against the storm and plodded patiently on.

She had to have water, and it had to be running water, so she had to stay close to the drainage system. Really, it was simply a matter of following her downhill, and she left enough tumbled rocks, broken branches and trampled grass to make that easy enough. He was worried, though; she had no jacket, no gloves, no sleeping bag. The high-bush cranberry patch hadn't been that big, and cranberries would not sustain her for long. She was probably hungry. His heart ached for her. Poor little girl.

Yes, of course, she had been naughty, and she had to be punished. She had broken a rule and she would have to pay for it. She always did.

Still, he couldn't help feeling sorry for her. He'd seen three bears and at least a dozen moose. She had been lucky enough so far, but it was only a matter of time before she ran into something she couldn't handle. He would be there for her.

Kind but firm, that was the best way. She would be nervous, perhaps even a little rebellious at first, but that was only natural. Deep down, she knew how things were.

And if she had forgotten, he would have to teach her.

Again.

He smiled into the upturned collar of his jacket, and plodded on.

NINETEEN

"You're not going," Liam said.

Wy looked at him, her face empty of all expression. "That's my son up there. You can't stop me." She walked over to the map of southwest Alaska. They'd driven to the post with Prince, who was standing with her arms folded, shaking her head.

Wy pointed. "The airstrip for the Old Man Creek fish camp is Portage Creek. The fish camp is about four miles downriver from the strip. Moses keeps his skiff at Portage, but it'll be at the fish camp now."

"So even if you are crazy enough to get in the air in the first place," Prince said, "and even if you're lucky enough to get down in one piece, you've got to get from the airstrip to the fish camp. How?"

"There will be a boat. There's always a skiff, somebody's dory, something that floats that somebody leaves behind."

"You don't know that for sure. What if you get out there and this is the first time there isn't? And what makes you so sure anyone is heading in that direction anyway? That's a hell of a long way to hike through a storm. Especially when there are other settlements along the way."

"Look," Wy said, her tone so patient that Prince gritted her

227

teeth. "Dead woman at Kagati Lake. Dead man at Rainbow. Dead man at Nenevok Creek. Connect the dots." She snapped her fingers impatiently and Liam tossed her a pen. She drew a line between the three settlements. "Old Man Creek is the only dry ground on the Scandinavian Slough besides Portage Creek, and the creek is on the wrong side of the slough. The rest of the area is just one big swamp. Everyone in the Bay and on the river knows this, and by now she has to know that everyone in the Bay and on the river knows that some nutcase is killing people. The river is the best road out of here, she hits it, steals a boat, floats downstream and is home free. It's logical for her to head in that direction."

"You keep saying 'her' and 'she,' like one person killed all three people and that person is Rebecca Hanover," Prince said. "She wasn't anywhere near Kagati Lake. She couldn't have killed Opal Nunapitchuk. And she didn't have any reason to, no motive, nothing. Not to mention which, you just got done painting the most heartrending picture of Little Miss City Girl, who doesn't know squat about surviving a trek through the Bush. How is she supposed to know where she's going? What does she think she's going to find when she gets there?"

Wy's temper flared. "Look. There is a trail of bodies on a line heading southeast. The last body reported found—and please note we have no idea if it's the last body to be found—is lying twelve miles from Old Man Creek. You're right, I don't know that Rebecca Hanover killed her husband, let alone Opal or Peter. Hell, for all we know, maybe she's got a lover, maybe they're in it together, maybe he killed Opal and Pete to make it look like there is a crazed killer on the loose. I don't know and I don't care. I am not taking any chances with Tim's safety." She tossed Liam's pen back. He snatched it out of the air before it skewered his eye. "I don't care what the two of you do or don't do. I'm getting in the air and I'm going to Portage Creek. I'll find a way to Old Man Creek when I get there."

"You can't do that."

"The hell I can't," she said curtly, opening the door. The wind snatched it from her hand and slammed it against the wall. "I'm a private pilot flying alone. There's no law against that. Yet."

The wind snatched the door from her hand a second time and slammed it shut behind her. When Liam wrenched it open again to follow, a raven, riding out the wind on the bough of a spruce tree, croaked overhead. For once, Liam didn't even look up.

Little Muklung River, September 6

She didn't, couldn't know how far she had come.

All sense of direction had been lost in the fog and the snow.

She knew she was leaving footprints to follow. The weather had betrayed her, a storm with snow in September, how could that be? Until then, she'd had a chance.

Now all she wanted was warmth and food. Coffee. Hot coffee, creamy with half-and-half and sweet with a heaping spoonful of sugar, two spoonfuls, three. She could almost smell it, and her mouth watered.

There was a river. She was following it downstream, although she knew he would be following it, too, knew that her footprints in the new-fallen snow left a track a child could follow.

The biggest battle now was to put one foot in front of the other. The left foot had lost all feeling, but that wasn't surprising, as she'd lost her left shoe in a half-frozen bog a mile back. Or maybe it was yesterday.

She stepped slowly, with all the deliberation of a drunk.

There was the sound of water running swiftly between banks, as if the creek had widened suddenly. She looked, but it wasn't so. She had long ago stopped believing her eyes. Now she could not believe her ears.

But what about her nose? She was sure she could smell the coffee now. She closed her eyes and inhaled. Coffee and wood-smoke. And fish.

There was a sense of brightness before her, or rather a thinning of the gloom. She squinted.

She was in a clearing.

There was a cabin in the clearing.

There was a light in the cabin window, and movement behind that light.

She stopped dead and stared, disbelieving. Was it another hallucination? She'd had so many, of Mark holding out his hand and smiling, of Nina laughing, of Linda's table strewn with beads, of her mother's fried chicken, of Maalaea Bay on Maui, where she had spent so many vacations, and where it was so very, very warm.

She took a hesitant step.

The cabin did not vanish into the snow and the fog. There might even be voices.

There was a door.

She stumbled into a run.

Old Man Creek, September 6

"Hey!"

"What? You unnatural brat," Moses added, somewhat unfairly, since he'd been awake for an hour.

"It snowed!" Tim opened the door wider. "Look!"

The snow lay two inches on the ground, and the pure, pristine white lightened the low, leaden look of the sky.

Moses came to stand behind him. "And more coming, I bet." The snow swirled up in a sudden gust of wind and he shivered. "Come on, get out or get in."

"I gotta pee," Tim said, and dashed around the corner.

Amelia yawned and stretched. Moses looked at her approvingly, or as close to approvingly as he ever looked at anyone. The bruises had nearly faded from her face, there was color in her cheeks, and even rumpled with sleep her hair had regained a healthy shine. She looked good. "You look good," he said.

She was startled, and a little wary. "Thank you, uncle."

"Get your pants on, let's stand a little post while my woman makes us some coffee."

Bill sent him a haughty look, and he grinned.

They assumed the position, and Tim walked in. "Oh man. It's too small in here to do tai chi."

"I've done form in airplane bathrooms," Moses said. "Where there ain't even enough room to crap, I might add. There's all the room in the world. Get your butt over here."

Grumbling, Tim complied, and Bill noticed that both kids were moving more easily. The price of a good teacher is above rubies, she thought. She made coffee then, but only because she wanted some herself. *My woman*, indeed.

She looked out the small window over the counter. Gray skies, swirling snow, and only yesterday it had been Indian summer. The thermometer mounted to the outside wall of the cabin read thirty-nine degrees. The snow would be gone by noon. She peered skyward. The storm looked as if it were taking five before turning around into a real nor'wester.

She lit the Coleman stove and put the pot on to boil before checking the woodstove. The wood box was nearly empty after she stoked the fire. "Hey guys, sorry to interrupt, but we're about out of wood."

"Then go get some," Moses growled.

She turned and gave him a smile. "Your woman gets the coffee made. Her man gets the wood in."

That surprised him into a laugh and he stood up. "I can't be freezing my ass off out there alone. Come on, boy."

He and Tim donned jackets and went outside. Amelia continued to stand post, forearms perpendicular to her torso, forming a gentle curve, legs bent with her knees directly over her toes. Bill admired her for a moment before going back to the counter and getting out the ingredients for her famous oatmeal. The secret was lots of butter and brown sugar, but steel-cut rolled oats were also very important, as was the evaporated milk. Heart attack in a bowl, she thought fondly, and dumped raisins into the pot.

"Bill?"

"What, honey?"

"How did you come to Newenham?"

Bill turned with the bag of oats in her hands to meet Amelia's inquiring gaze. "What brought that up?"

"I don't know," Amelia said. "No reason, I guess."

Bill looked at her thoughtfully. She was asking for something, Bill wasn't sure what, exactly, but she was asking, and Bill had the feeling that Amelia hadn't asked for much in her life. She turned back to the counter. "I was married once. To an Army officer. It didn't work out. I left him, and came to Newenham. I've been here ever since."

"Why did you leave him?"

"He hit me," Bill said matter-of-factly. She measured the oatmeal, added more because she hated soupy oatmeal, shook some salt into it, stirred both into the raisins.

Amelia's breath sucked in. "He hit you?"

"That's what I said."

"Somebody actually hit you?"

The mixed note of disbelief and awe in Amelia's voice made Bill grin out the window. "Yeah."

"What did you do?"

"I told you. I left him."

"After the first time?"

"Yeah. You only get one shot at me."

A brief silence. "I let my husband hit me again and again and again."

Bill sighed. She covered the pot and set it on the stove. She turned and leaned back against the counter and folded her arms. "What are you going to do about it?"

"What do you mean?"

"You told Moses you weren't going back to your husband. Did you mean it?"

"I meant it."

"You sure?"

"I'm sure."

"Okay, then. You've taken action. You've made a decision. Stick to it."

Amelia looked at her. "You don't think I will."

Bill shook her head, let out a breath. "Amelia, I don't know you well enough to say what you will or you won't do. I will say that I've seen a lot of women in your position, and that I've seen a lot of women take it and take it and take it. I've even seen a few men in that kind of situation. It's never pretty. But it wouldn't happen if the person letting it happen didn't get something out of it."

"I didn't get anything out of it except hurt."

Bill raised her eyebrows.

"I didn't want to get hurt! I didn't like it!"

Bill shrugged. "Then don't go back." She unfolded her arms and stood straight. "Understand one thing, Amelia. Whatever happened to you in your marriage, whatever happened to you before that"—Amelia went white beneath her newly acquired tan—"none of that matters a good goddamn. It's what you do now that counts. It's what you do tomorrow. It's your life. Moses has given you a breather. What happens when we leave here is up to you."

"I know that."

"Good." Bill peered through the window. The woodshed was around back and she couldn't see the menfolk, but she heard Moses curse and Tim's laughing oath and was satisfied.

"Why do you want to go to New Orleans?"

"What?"

Bill turned to see Amelia pointing at the Frommer's guide to New Orleans lying open on the bunk. "Oh. Why? Why not? Best music, best food in this hemisphere. Who wouldn't want to go?"

"What's it like there?"

"I don't know. I've never been."

"When are you going?"

"I don't know. Sometime. Have to get free of the bar."

"Dottie's taking care of the bar right now," Amelia pointed out.

Bill turned, half laughing, half exasperated. "What's going on? You want to come?"

Amelia's eyes lit up. "Sure!"

Bill shrugged. "Okay. Start saving your money for a ticket."

"Oh." The light in the girl's eyes faded. "I don't have a job."

"Get one."

A silence. "Yeah," Amelia said slowly. "I could do that."

A rustle of clothing told Bill that the girl was getting dressed. "One more thing."

"What?"

Bill turned to meet her eyes. "Don't hurt that boy out there. Not any more than you have to, anyway."

The girl flushed. "I won't."

"Good."

"Bill—"?

"What?"

"We saw you," the girl said in a low voice. "You and uncle. On the porch. When we were coming back from the pond." She sneaked a look through her hair and saw that Bill looked more amused than appalled.

"You did, did you? That must have been an eyeful."

"I—we—"

"Never mind," Bill said. "I can guess." She turned. "It was okay?"

Amelia blushed a deep vivid red this time. "Yes." She hesitated.

"Go ahead. Tell. Ask. Whatever you need to know."

"We—well, we did it twice."

"Ah, to be a teenager again," Bill murmured.

"What?"

"Never mind."

"It was okay," Amelia said, the wondering tone back in her voice. "It didn't even hurt. And the second time . . . it even felt *good*."

"It's supposed to."

"It is?"

"Yes," Bill said firmly.

"Oh."

"Amelia."

The girl raised her head from contemplation of her clasped hands.

"You're seventeen, you've been to school, you know all the dangers. Hell, you have to know about the STD problems in the Bush, especially AIDS."

The girl nodded.

"Be careful, okay? Just be careful."

Amelia stood up, very solemn. "I promise, Bill," she said, as if she were taking an oath. "I promise I will be careful."

"I checked your day pack," Bill said.

Amelia ducked her head, her face flushing. "I thought maybe you did."

"I notice your prescription runs out this month."

"I have more at home." Amelia paused. "My husband doesn't want kids."

Bill nodded. "Do you?"

"Yes. Someday. Not now." The response was automatic, and Bill watched the girl listen to herself say the words. "Maybe," she said slowly. "I don't really know that I do want to have kids."

Bill nodded, as if Amelia had confirmed some inner conclusion. "We have choices about that nowadays. Get the prescription refilled."

"I will," Amelia said, still with that look of surprise. "I will," she said again, more firmly.

There was a noise at the door and Amelia looked alarmed. "Don't worry," Bill said, grinning. "This was strictly girl talk."

Amelia looked relieved.

The door opened and a third woman fell into the room.

At first they couldn't tell she was a woman, she was so covered in snow and frost and mud. Leaves and twigs were caught in hair so lank and matted they couldn't tell what color it was. Her blue jeans were soaked through. She was wearing tennis shoes, one of which was missing, and the white anklet on that foot was torn and the flesh beneath bleeding. Her shirt was ripped at the left shoulder, the same with the T-shirt under it, revealing a long tear of flesh, reaching from the top of the shoulder to halfway down the back. A flap of skin hung loose, to show the shoulder bone gleaming whitely.

They were caught motionless in shock. The woman looked up at them and opened her mouth. Her voice was the merest croak of sound. "Help."

She tried to say more, but couldn't. "Help," she said again, and lay her head down on the floor and closed her eyes.

TWENTY

Portage Creek, September 6

The strain of holding the plane more or less level was beginning to tell in her arms and legs. The pedals pushed hard against the soles of her feet, the yoke pulled steadily against the grip of her hands, and she was constantly on the alert, constantly adjusting her limbs to meet the demands the weather was putting on the exterior surfaces of the aircraft.

She risked a look at Liam. He was staring straight ahead with a grim expression. His blue eyes were narrowed, as if in concentration, as if by concentrating on the control panel he could by sheer effort of will make the plane fly straight and true. His knuckles were white where his hands were knotted on the edge of his seat.

She'd taken the Cessna. Heavier plane, more power. Faster, too, although that didn't seem to matter much. The wind was gusting thirty to thirty-five knots out of the southeast, and the Cessna was being continually buffeted from the right, which meant she continually had to correct for drift.

She glanced down at the GPS, and thanked whatever the gods might be for it. The digital readout recorded their progress. She'd logged in the latitude and longitude of their destination, and it would tell her exactly and precisely when they had arrived, a good thing since they sure as hell weren't going to see it very far ahead.

So it wasn't like they were forced into dead reckoning, although the weather on the outside of the cabin made it feel like it. Torn wisps of fog kept the ceiling at a hundred feet. She was maintaining an altitude of fifty feet and even then she wasn't always sure which way was up. The snow on the ground merged with the clouds and the fog to form a sphere of white all around them. She didn't look up from the instrument panel. She was afraid to, afraid she would lose all sense of where the earth was, and fly straight into it.

She couldn't do that. Tim was at fish camp. So was Moses. So were Bill and Amelia, for that matter.

She was following the river in hopes that she would spot the fish camp dock. If she could just locate the cabin, she could buzz it, open the window, yell a warning. Tim, be careful, she thought. Watch your back. Look out for yourself.

They'd only found each other two years ago. Two years filled with joy and laughter, rage and tears. Two years of getting used to sharing her home with an adolescent boy, the equivalent of one gigantic nerve ending rubbing up against the world. She was doing a good job, she was sure she was, but she'd only had him two years. He had just turned thirteen, and she wanted him for another five, she wanted to care for him until it was time for him to go out into the world. She wanted to give him a chance, the same chance her adoptive parents had given her when they rescued her from her birth parents. What was the point of returning to Newenham to live if she couldn't help out her own?

And she loved him. Tim, oh Tim, please, please be all right. Please let whoever this crazy killer is miss the fish camp. Please let him be lost and stumbling around a hundred miles from here, or on his way to Acapulco. Please let this goddamn fog lift.

The marine forecast for Area 6 had been less than encouraging. A storm warning, south winds at fifty knots, seas at twenty-two feet, rain. The low was a hundred miles north of Dutch Harbor and moving up the Alaska Peninsula. Oh joy.

Oh fog. Oh fucking fog. She was flying blind but for the digital readout mounted to the control panel. She watched it more than she looked through the windshield because the view through the windshield never changed, fog and more goddamn fucking fog. The little green numbers ticked off steadily, one at a time, reassuring her that she was on course and nearing the location she had punched in, that she was maintaining her altitude, that her ground speed was a hundred and five. She believed the readout. She believed it implicitly. Her faith was committed, fervent, and necessary. She might even buy stock in Geo Star. If they got out of this alive. Which of course they would, because she believed.

The minutes inched by a second at a time, with more minutes stretching ahead.

"I'm sorry," she said suddenly.

It took him a minute to respond, she suspected because he was too terrified to open his mouth, afraid that the physical act of speech might somehow affect the motion of the aircraft and send them plummeting down. "What for?"

"For not telling you sooner."

He did look at her then. "Jesus, Wy. That's not why I'm pissed."

A strong gust blew the tail around to the left. Wy corrected the attitude of the plane automatically. "Then why are you?"

"Because you didn't trust me enough to understand."

"It wasn't that." She risked looking away from the GPA for a moment to meet his eyes. "Liam, think about it. We haven't known each other that long, we've been together even less than that. I—"

"I know all I need to know," he said.

"Evidently not."

A gust of wind shook the craft. Liam set his teeth and stared out into the whirling white maelstrom. "So you've been married before. So what?"

"If that's how you feel, why the attitude?" she demanded.

"It was Gary, wasn't it? Jo's brother? The guy I met on the river last month?"

"Yes."

He thought of the good-looking man, of his proprietary air around Wy that had so irritated Liam. "The divorce wasn't his idea, was it?"

"No."

"He'd still be married to you if he could be."

Her capable hands adjusted the throttle, fine-tuned the prop pitch. The Cessna seemed to respond, their passage through the vortex smooth out an infinitesimal amount. "I don't know. Probably." She risked another glance. "But. You will notice that he is not. Things end. We move on."

"You're starting to sound like Moses," he muttered.

"I was pregnant," she told him suddenly.

"What?" He stared at her. "What did you say?"

He is thinking about something other than a fiery plane crash now, she thought with a flash of grim amusement. "I was pregnant, that's the only reason Gary and I got married. I liked him, I loved Jo's whole family, but I had plans for what I wanted to do with my life, and they sure as hell didn't include marriage and children, not then. But I got pregnant, and I made the mistake of telling my parents, and they insisted on marriage. So did his. Pretty traditional people, both sets of parents."

"What happened?"

The plane hit an updraft and they were borne irresistibly upward, a hundred feet in a snap of the fingers, magic. She coaxed the plane back to fifty feet, then wiped her palms on her jeans, one at a time, and tried to put her hands back on the yoke with something less than the grip of a dead man. Liam, she noticed, was looking at her instead of monitoring the altimeter. She wasn't sure he'd even noticed the updraft.

"I lost the baby," she said. "In the beginning of the sixth month." She took a deep breath, held it, and then let it out, one slow molecule at a time. "They let it rot inside me. Just rot away, into nothingness, nonbeing. My belly got smaller and smaller. And then it was gone."

His eyes were stricken. He tried to say something, failed, had to start over. "God, I'm sorry, Wy."

"The marriage, such as it was, didn't last much longer. Gary didn't fight me on it."

"But he's always there, waiting," Liam guessed, and smiled humorlessly when he saw the acknowledgment in her eyes. "Smart, good-looking guy like that. Why didn't you stay with him?"

"Because I was more in love with his family than I was with him, and after the baby died I realized that. It was a girl."

"What?"

"The baby. It was a girl. They told me after one of the tests."

He was instantly overwhelmed by the vision of a tiny Wy, all dark blond hair and big gray eyes and dimples. "Goddamn it," he said. "Goddamn it, Wy."

Her voice was strained. "Afterward the doctor talked to me. He said something went wrong."

"What?"

She shook her head. "He used a lot of medical terminology, but what he said was, I couldn't have any more children." She turned to meet his eyes. "Not ever, Liam. No babies out of this belly. Not ever."

They stared at each other.

The GPS beeped, loud enough to be heard over the wind buffeting the plane, and they both jumped. Wy looked down and saw the coordinates of the Portage Creek airstrip flashing on the digital readout. She peered through the windshield. Nothing but fog. She checked the altimeter. Fifty feet, sixty feet, fifty-five feet, she couldn't maintain a steady fifty in this wind.

The GPS stopped beeping. They'd overshot the strip. Climb and bank or just bank? Fifty feet in the air in winds gusting to forty was not the place to indulge in turns, however gentle, and however flat the terrain. She increased power and pulled back on the yoke. The wind slammed into the side of the plane and the tail crabbed around, but they climbed to a hundred feet. "Hold on," she said, unnecessarily because Liam would have been holding on with his teeth if he could have, and put the plane into a full-power left turn.

The rudder fought her for every degree of turn. The wind howled its delight, slapped the underside of the right wing with all its force, the right wing came up and for a moment Wy thought the Cessna was going into a snap roll. She increased power, kept her stranglehold on the yoke and her feet firm on the rudder pedals, and prayed that the rudder wouldn't rip off. The wind had them by the scruff of the neck and they were being shaken and tossed and jostled and jarred and jolted all over the place, their seat belts and a minimal amount of centrifugal force the only things keeping them in their seats.

They hit another updraft, a small one but strong enough to jerk the plane up five feet. Liam's head banged against the window with the sudden movement. "Jesus Christ, Wy! This is gonna tear her apart!"

"Don't worry! She'll hold together!" You heard me, baby, she thought. Hold together.

The Cessna came around, slowly, screaming in every seam and rivet, but she came around. This time Wy didn't screw around, she took it down to the deck, twenty feet off the ground, flying every foot of the way, hopping the tops of trees, fighting her way around torn wisps of fog, straining her eyes in search of eighteen hundred feet of gravel strip, thirty feet wide with spruce and birch and alder and cottonwoods crowding the sides and one end ending in the Nushagak River.

It appeared suddenly out of the mist, so like an apparition and so much what she wanted to see that for a moment she doubted it.

"There!" Liam yelled.

"I see it," she said, and went in for a full-power approach.

The first time the wind blew so hard and so steadily down the airstrip that the Cessna had too much lift to land.

"I can't get her down at full power," she shouted to Liam. "We have to go around."

"Do what you have to," he said. "Never mind me, just get us down."

She risked a look at him and saw that his face was white but determined. He looked like he thought he might die, but that there was nothing he could do about it.

"We're fine," she said.

"I know." Nothing he could do but trust her.

They were coming off the end of the runway now, gaining altitude but not enough to lose the airstrip. They went into another left turn and the wind slammed into them again. This time they were more ready for it, braced. Wy felt like she was riding a bucking bronco, only higher.

"You ever go sailing?" Liam shouted.

"What?"

"Sailing, like on a sailboat."

"No," she said, working the yoke and the rudder in subtle movements, trying for the best altitude to produce the most forward motion and the least turbulence. The horizon, a mass of dark green intersecting with a mass of dirty white, tilted up.

Liam kept shouting. "When the wind's blowing, the sailboat heels over, to the right or to the left, depending on the tack the boat is taking into the wind. Why doesn't the boat go all the way over and swamp, you ask?"

She was bringing the Cessna around to a southwesterly heading before the storm blew them to Anchorage, but she shouted back, "Why?"

"There's a part of the hull that sticks down like a sword out of the center of the keel. It's filled with lead. Ballast."

"Oh. Right. Good." Their airspeed kept fluctuating, and she had no idea what their true ground speed was. Her biceps were beginning to tremble from the strain of hauling so long and so steadily on the yoke.

"I never think there's enough ballast," he shouted.

"What?"

"I never think there's enough ballast on a sailboat. I always think it's going to go all the way over. It never does."

They were lined up with the runway again, although they kept sliding north and Wy kept having to correct. She came in full power again because she didn't dare do anything else. This time the gear touched down, not just once but three times, hard enough every time so that it felt like the struts were going to come up through the wings.

Trees flashed past, the gravel strip screamed beneath them, the Cessna keeping on the straight and narrow only when it was crossing it.

"Wy?" Liam said.

The end of the runway was fast approaching.

"Wy?" Liam said.

So was the Nushagak River.

"Wy!"

She waited until the last possible moment to cut power. When she did, they had maybe a hundred feet of runway left. She pushed in the throttle and kicked right rudder simultaneously. The Cessna pulled hard right. A gust of wind came screaming down the runway and hit the tail. It raised up, enough to pull the plane up off its right wheel. The left wingtip dipped toward the ground. They were still rolling.

"Wy?"

The gust seemed never-ending, pushing, pushing, pushing. The left wing of the plane dipped lower and lower, and they were still rolling, right toward a stand of three large cottonwoods. She cut power completely. The prop stopped straight up and down.

"Wy?"

Momentum kept them moving. Ground loop, she thought, goddamnit a goddamn groundloop, we'll be okay but what about my goddamn plane goddamnit. "We'll be okay Liam we'll be okay we'llbeokaywe'llbeokay oh shit!"

The Cessna paused, poised on nose and left gear, the left wing barely a foot from the ground. It seemed that everything was holding its breath. Wy, Liam, the Cessna, even the wind.

The wind died. Just like that. Stopped in mid-roar, for that precious second the Cessna needed to recover. The tail settled down, the right gear fell back on the runway with a thump, and the left wing came up.

They were still rolling. Wy hit left rudder hard, swerving to avoid the cottonwoods, only to run into a stand of alders. Smaller trees, but still trees. The Cessna hit them hard enough to bury its nose up to the leading edge of the wings. They bounced back once from the impact, and stopped.

They sat there for a moment in silence. The wind as suddenly started up again, a long, angry howl.

"You're a good pilot, Wy," Liam said finally, in a conversational tone.

"The best," she said in a very faint voice.

"I wonder if my heart is ever going to get back to normal sinus rhythm," he said, still in that same conversational tone.

"I wonder if mine's going to start beating again anytime soon."

They sat for another moment, trying to grasp the fact that they were still alive, and trying to remember what it was they were supposed to do next.

Tim. That's why they were here. Tim. There was a crazed killer on the loose who might hurt Tim. Moses. Bill. Amelia.

Wy stirred. "We'd better get going, see if we can find a boat." She unstrapped her seat belt with hands that did not seem to belong to her. The door was hard to open against the alder branches crowded up against it, but once the wind caught an edge she had to hang on so it wouldn't be yanked out of her grasp. On the other side of the plane Liam was having the same problem. A branch caught at his uniform, ripping a hole in his sleeve, and he cursed.

Wy tugged a backpack from the cargo compartment and pulled it on. Liam did the same with his. They were both wearing heavy boots and jackets. She forced the smaller door shut and turned to leave.

"What about the plane?" Liam said.

"Leave it," she shouted back. "Those alders are probably better than a tie-down in this wind. Come on."

He paused, looking up.

"What?" she shouted.

"Did you hear it?"

"Hear what?"

He stared over her shoulder. "Nothing." Any sensible bird out in this wouldn't waste time croaking out hellos, he'd be keeping his beak shut and his head down.

They staggered down the strip, bent double into the wind. It wasn't very cold, Wy thought dimly, and noticed that the four inches of snow that had fallen overnight had almost completely melted away. "Chinook?" she yelled.

"It feels like it," he yelled back. "Did the forecast call for it?"

"No."

"Figures."

The runway ended in a small berm overgrown with more alders and salmonberry and raspberry bushes. The red and yellow fruits seemed almost incongruous on such a day, hanging in fat succulent clumps from stalks bowed beneath their weight. Bears, Wy thought suddenly. "Bears," she said out loud.

"Shit! Where?"

"Berries," she said, pointing. It was hard to get words out, the wind snatched her breath away.

"Oh. Yeah. Right. Where's the dock?"

"Over the berm."

They found the path and struggled down it. It terminated in a dock, a rectangular pier surfaced with one-by-twelve wooden planks. There was no boat.

"Shit!"

"Well, great," Liam said, more tired than annoyed. "What do we do now?"

"There has to be a boat, there has to be. It's September, there's nobody left on this part of the river except Moses." She turned and let the wind blow her ashore.

"Where are you going? Wy, wait, wait for me!" He lumbered after her, to find her wading through the brush along the river. "What are you doing?"

"I'm looking for a boat," she said. There was a crash of brush ten feet to her right, a hasty scramble of feet and big body, a panicked breaking of branches; Wy didn't even look around. Liam never did see what creature's hiding place they disturbed. "There has to be one, Liam, a lot of people with fish camps leave their boats here over the winter. They pull them up on the bank and—" She stopped, so suddenly that he ran into her.

He looked over her shoulder, and there was an old wooden skiff, about twelve feet long, he estimated, lying hull up on a trampled patch of ground.

Wy was already bending down and hooking her hands beneath the gunnel. He moved forward to stand next to her. "Ready? One, two, heave!"

The boat was heavy and went over reluctantly, but Wy was determined and over it went, landing with a thump and rocking a little on its rounded hull before coming to a rest. She went to the bow and found the bowline threaded through a crossbar nailed inside the prow. "Come on," she said, and started hauling.

He picked up the pair of oars that had been lying on the ground beneath the boat and tossed them in. He pushed from the stern, going knee deep into mud. Great, there went his uniform pants. It wasn't twenty feet to the edge of the river and the boat slid easily into the water.

The surface of the river was choppy, and the current was strong. They began drifting downstream immediately. Oarlocks dangled from twine and Liam slipped them into their respective holes. The oars went in. "Do you know how to row?"

"No," Wy said, the wind ripping the words out of her mouth almost before they were said. "It can't be that hard, though." She sat down on the thwart and grabbed both oars, pushing forward. The blades dipped in the water, skimmed the surface, splashed a lot of water around and didn't provide any thrust. She looked up, surprised.

For the first time in days Liam felt like smiling. "Here," he said. "Let me try."

"No," she said. "I'll get it, I just need to—"

"Wy. Get up."

Something in his voice made her comply. He remained standing, face forward, and the oars dipped, rose, dipped, rose. The chop hit the bow with regular taps as they moved smoothly forward.

"You've done this before," she said.

"I like boats," he said.

"Better than planes."

"A whole hell of a lot better than planes."

"I'm going to teach Tim how to fly," she said.

"Are you? Good."

Wavelets slapped at the hull. Liam felt a coldness around his feet and looked down to see that they were taking on water. Not a lot, and not very fast, but there was some in the bottom of the boat that hadn't been there when they shoved off from the airstrip. "Wy?"

"Oh great." She found a bailing can cut from a Clorox bottle wedged beneath the bow thwart and started scooping up water and emptying it over the side. A log thudded into the skiff and they both held their breath, waiting for a hole to open up and the leak to become a gush. It didn't happen. Cold sweat trickled into Liam's eyes and he wiped his forehead against his arm. The wind took the opportunity to gust hard against the port side and push the stern halfway around, so that the bow was headed toward the south shore of the river. Liam battled it back, shoulder and arm muscles straining as he pushed hard on the port oar, the starboard oar horizontal and motionless above the surface, water dripping from the blade. "How far is the fish camp from the airstrip, again?" he said when they were straightened out and headed downstream once more. He was proud that his voice remained level.

"About four miles," she said. "Why don't I teach you, too? Make it a family affair? If you understand it, if you can control it, it won't frighten you as much."

"Do you have any idea how fast this river runs?"

She sighed. "No. Why?"

He rested the oars to check his watch. "We went into the water twenty minutes ago. I'm trying to figure when we'll make the fish camp."

"It's the first dock on the north shore of the river after Portage Creek."

The wind roared overhead and snatched the words from her mouth so that he could barely hear them. "So we hug the right bank and hope we bump into it."

"Yeah."

Hopeless, he thought, and as if to underline the thought, there was a gust of wind so hard it spun the skiff around like a top. Wy was thrown against the side and lost her grip on the bailer, which went over the side. "Are you okay?" Liam said when they stopped spinning.

"Yeah," she said, straightening. "I lost the bailer."

"I saw." He looked around, eyes tearing from the wind. They seemed to be in the center of the river, no bank, no trees to guide them. "Which way is downstream?"

She looked left, right. "I don't know."

It was so dark and the surface was so choppy that it was impossible to tell which way the current was going, and the wind was blowing so hard that it negated the current anyway.

Then there was a brief, tantalizing lull in the wind and he heard a sound, a creaking branch, or maybe the k-kk-kkrak of a raven.

What the hell. He rowed toward it. Trees, shaken roughly in a giant's hand, loomed up out of the darkness. He put the starboard side parallel to them and began to row again.

Liam bent his head and rowed into the wind and the darkness. Push, lift, swing forward, dip, push. Push, push hard, push the water under them, behind them, away, away, along the wide Nushagak. Didn't quite have the ring of the Missouri, he thought dimly. Push, lift, swing, dip, push. His shoulders were aching, his arms numb. If only he could row with his legs, his tai chi-conditioned legs. His thighs were like iron, his calves like steel. From the waist down he'd never been in such good shape.

A high chair bolted to the thwart. Like a dentist's chair, only not as heavy. Stirrups on the oar handles. Sit in the chair, put your feet in the stirrups and push, lift, swing, dip, push. If he got out of this alive, he'd patent the son of a bitch.

"Liam?" Wy's voice came to him from far away. "Liam?"

He realized she was standing stock-still, her head cocked as if she was listening. The oars came up and he paused, trying to hear what she did. "What? What is it?"

"Nothing," she said, and he could hear the tired smile in her voice. "Nothing at all."

It took him a minute to comprehend what she meant. Some-time, somehow the wind had died down completely. Stopped, as if someone had thrown a switch. The surface of the river had smoothed out, hardly any chop left.

"What happened?" he said, dazed.

"It stopped," she said, sounding as punchy as he felt. "It stopped."

One minute later, as if in compensation, they floated into a gloomy soup of fog. It parted grudgingly before them and closed in again greedily behind them as they passed through it, and Liam had the sensation of being swallowed alive. He knew a sud-den sympathy for Jonah. Water sloshed at his feet.

Moisture condensed on their faces and hands in tiny droplets. They couldn't see ten feet in any direction. Liam kept them as close to the bank as he dared. The riverbank undulated in curv-ing S's, flirting with sandbanks, opening suddenly into the mouths of creeks—the wrong creek, time after time. They heard the sound of an occasional fish jump, the lost cry of a goose, the rustle of brush as something moved through a thicket. No croaking of ravens, though.

"I feel like Charon," Liam said, his voice hushed.

Her laugh was forced. "Where is Cerberus?"

"That was him before. The wind. Sounded like a three-headed dog howling to me."

This time her laugh wasn't quite as forced. "Now that you mention it . . ."

He could barely see her through the mists that curled between them, a ghostly outline in the bow. To keep her talking, he said, maybe at random, maybe not, "Do you remember your mother?"

"Not much."

"Was your father around?"

"No." There was a brief silence. "I don't remember him at all."

"Lucky," he said, thinking of his own father.

Her voice came gently out of the night and the fog. "He's not that bad, Liam."

"Yeah, well, whatever." She didn't know what he knew about his father and what Colonel Charles Campbell would do, had done, for promotion. She didn't know why he had made her fly him out to that archaeological dig south of Newenham and west of Chinook Air Force Base when his father had left this summer. Wy had met Charles twice. She didn't know him the way he did.

"You named your son for him," her disembodied voice reminded him.

"That was Jenny's idea."

"You could have changed her mind."

"Yeah." He rowed. "Yeah, I suppose I could have. And the fact that I didn't says something."

"He's your father."

"Yeah. He is that. Did you ever know who yours was?"

A raven croaked suddenly from overhead and Liam started violently, jerking the oars free of the water. Water splashed, catching both him and Wy. The stern of the skiff started to drift. The dock loomed up suddenly out of the fog, materializing into a dark rectangular shape off the starboard bow.

They both saw it at the same time. "There!"

He pulled for shore with short, powerful strokes, and a moment later they were alongside. Liam shipped the oars while Wy fastened the bowline off to a cleat on the dock. She trotted up the dock, Liam right behind her, and they threaded their way up the path that followed the creek. Moments later they emerged into the clearing and there was the cabin. She paused just long enough to grin at him. "I told you we could make it."

He kissed her. He hadn't meant to, but he did it anyway. "I'll never doubt you again." He added, following her to the door, "I'll never fly into a storm with you again, either."

"I swear I hear voices," they heard someone say, and the door of the cabin opened as they walked up the steps.

Bill stood there, astonished. "What the hell are you two doing here? And how the hell did you get here?"

TWENTY-ONE

Newenham, September 6

"Do you think the wind's slowing down a little?"

"In the last five minutes since you asked, no."

"Wy's going to be seriously pissed if you break her computer."

Jim spared a glance over his shoulder. "Oh, please."

Jo, pacing restlessly back and forth across the living room of Wy's house, glared at the back of his head as he sat hunched over the monitor. "What are you doing, anyway?"

"Destroying your credit rating."

She halted. "What?"

He grinned at the screen. "Relax, Dunaway, it was joke."

Suspiciously, she came to peer over his shoulder. "It better be." She squinted. "For god's sake. Isn't that the state troopers' database?"

"Yes."

"How did you get in?"

"Talent, Dunaway, loads and loads of talent." He scrolled down.

"Liam gave you the password."

He snorted. "The perfect cop breaking faith with his own force? Give me a break."

"You hacked in?" Jo glanced around nervously, as if expecting

253

the FBI to break down the front door in the next moment. "You can get arrested for that."

"They'll have to catch me first." He turned and they practically bumped noses. For that single moment, time seemed to stop. She could feel his breath on her face. He could see every separate dark blond lash on her eyelids. For a frozen moment, neither of them moved. Bridget and Luke, playing a noisy game of cribbage at the kitchen counter, seemed to fade from the room.

She jerked back, eyes wide with dismay.

"Well, well," he said, just as startled but quicker to recover.

"Well, well, nothing," she said. She took what she hoped was an unobtrusive step backward. "I asked you what you were looking at."

You, he thought. And now that I am, I won't stop until I get you. But he was a patient man, and there was a time and a place for everything. Not here, not now. But somewhere and soon. "Disappearances," he said, turning back to the computer.

"Disappearances?" She took a cautious step forward, positioning herself so that she could just barely read the text on the screen over his shoulder, but far enough away to run if she had to. Not that she would, she wasn't a coward.

"Yeah."

"What disappearances?"

"Women. Young women. Gone missing. All from the Bristol Bay area." Unconsciously, she took another step forward, and he smiled to himself when he felt her warmth at his shoulder.

"You mean like Rebecca Hanover?"

"I mean exactly like Rebecca Hanover." He sat back. The fuzz of her sweater brushed the back of his head. She didn't notice. He did. "Last night at dinner you were talking about another woman who went missing."

"Stella Silverthorne."

"Yeah. Then Wy was talking about the daughter of the postmistress that got killed, what was her name . . ."

Jo's reportorial instincts were kicking in, the mental Rolodex whirring, click, stop. "Ruby Nunapitchuk."

"Yeah."

"I remember that story. The dad took the kids out hunting, right? Two sons and two daughters?"

"Yeah, and lost one of the daughters."

"They never found the body."

"Nope." He nodded at the screen. "Bill Billington ruled on a presumptive death hearing the following spring. Accidental death due to misadventure. The parents filed an appeal, which was denied."

"What was the basis of their appeal?"

"You ever talk to a magistrate about presumptive death hearings?"

She shook her head.

"Nobody wants to believe in accidental death. It's too—it's too—"

"Accidental?" she suggested.

"Smart-ass," he said, "but yeah. You lose somebody you love, you want there to be a reason. He can't have fallen into a glacier, or off a boat, or down a mountain. Death can't be that random, that irrational, not for a lot of people."

"Makes sense."

"Ha, ha. Sit down with Bill sometime, get her to tell you some of the arguments surviving family members have put forward to vacate a judgment of accidental death. They come in two kinds: weird, and weirder. He was pushed into that glacier, he was dumped off that boat, he was tripped down that mountain. He was about to take over the glacier tour company, and the current owner bumped him off. He seduced the boat captain's daughter, and the captain keelhauled him. The climb leader had designs on his body, and when he wouldn't put out, cut the rope between them."

"Sounds like a story." He shook his head in feigned exasperation at her single-mindedness. She grinned. Their eyes met. The grin faded. "Yes. Well. So you started looking up missing women."

Dana Stabenow

"Women missing in the Bristol Bay area," he said. He tilted the chair back, coming solidly up against her, and linked his hands behind his head. She was still for a moment before moving back, but not that much back. His dark hair stood up in a rooster tail from repeated impatient pullings, and he was frowning behind his glasses. "It didn't hit me until last night, when you were telling us the story about Finn Grant and his lost hunting party, and how one of the women was never found. Interesting, I thought, two women missing in the Bush, same general area, only four years apart. Then I remembered what Wy said about the postmistress's daughter, and how she was lost eight years ago."

Jo was skeptical but interested. "Okay, how many of these women missing in the Bristol Bay area have you found?"

He sat forward and rested his elbows on his knees, frowning down at his clasped hands. "Seven. Altogether."

"Seven?" Her tolerant smile and indulgent tone of voice vanished. One quick step had her back at his shoulder. "Show me."

He was more troubled by his discovery than he was triumphant at having piqued her interest. "I accessed the missing persons records for the judicial district for the last twenty-five years, which is as far back as they've got in the data base. Ruby Nunapitchuk eight years ago, Stella Silverthorne five years ago, Rebecca Hanover four days ago."

"All women."

"All young women," he said. "Rebecca Hanover is thirty-two. Ruby Nunapitchuk was seventeen. Stella Silverthorne was twenty-six."

"Opal was fifty-six."

"Yeah, she was the oldest by about twenty years."

"She might not have looked her age, though," Jo said slowly. "Wait a minute." She rolled the chair back with him on it and pulled open the drawer. A pad of yellow sticky notes and a pen later, she shoved both back in.

"Just move me out of your way if I'm in it," he said, ruffled.

She wasn't listening, staring instead at the map on Wy's wall.

"Okay," she said, scribbling. One sticky note with a name and a date went on the map at Nenevok Creek, another at Kagati Lake, a third at Weary River. "All right. Who else?"

"I worked backwards, most recent reported disappearances first. Cheryl Montgomery disappeared right off of Four Lake two years ago. She was an experienced backwoodsman, too, someone you wouldn't think of getting lost."

Jo inspected the face smiling up at her from the monitor. "She's lovely."

"Yeah. And lost."

"Okay." A fourth sticky note at Four Lake. "Who else?"

"In 1992, Brandi—with an *i*—Whitaker was mushing the Kuskokwim 500. She disappeared along with her whole team. Everybody figured they'd fallen into a lead. There wasn't much fuss; she didn't have much family and she wasn't that good a musher."

A fifth sticky note went up. "Next?"

"In 1991, Ruby Nunapitchuk. Then back four years, and Kristen Anderson goes missing. Fisherman's wife, out of Koggiling. She was alone at fish camp. When her husband came to pick her up, she was gone. Salmon on the drying racks, but the fire had been cold for at least a day. Again, there is no hint of foul play in the case file. They had a good reputation in Koggiling. Three kids, sober, well liked."

A sixth sticky note.

"And then as far back as I've been so far, 1986, Paulette Gustafson."

"Same year as Whitaker?"

"Yeah."

Then it hit her. "Gustafson?"

"Yeah?"

"As in former state senator Ted Gustafson?"

"Yeah."

"Wy mentioned him. He's on her mail route. The diabetic."

"Yeah."

257

"I can't believe she stayed missing for long."

"She still is, despite what looks like a full-scale search effort from everyone from the Alaska state troopers to the FBI."

"The FBI?"

He shrugged. "There are references made to them; I haven't tracked them down yet."

"What was she doing here?"

"Visiting high school friends. She was a bit of a rounder, it sounds like. She and a group of her old high school buddies drove up to the One Lake campground, had from what all accounts say was one hell of a party, and when everybody woke up three days later to pack up and go home, Paulette Gustafson was missing."

"They never found her."

"Nope."

A seventh sticky note. Jo stood back and stared at the map, festooned now with what she considered to be entirely too many little yellow flags. "Seven in, what, twelve years?"

"Thirteen. And this is only so far as we know, remember. Only what has made it into the trooper data bank."

Behind them, Bridget toted up some impossible score and pegged out, and suffered Luke's mock displeasure with a complacent air.

Jo took a deep, careful breath. "You mean—"

"I mean there might be more," he said bluntly. "How many little villages out there who never call the troopers if they can possibly help it? How many kids drown in the river without anybody ever knowing, with their people chalking it up to Maniilaq or whatever malevolent spirit happens to be flitting through at that time of year? A lot of these folks haven't made it into the twentieth century yet, Jo, never mind the twenty-first."

She stared at the map, her skin cold. "Seven women, all young, all disappeared within sixty miles of one another, all within the space of thirteen years." She looked at him. "How can no one have noticed?"

He shook his head. "None of them are related. Half of them are from Anchorage. Four, five of them were engaging in high-risk activities, hunting, canoeing, mushing. You're a reporter, Jo, you've written enough stories about this kind of thing, you know it happens."

She pointed, one at a time. "Paulette Gustafson, 1986. Same year, Kristen Anderson. A five-year gap between her and Ruby Nunapitchuk in 1991. A year after her, Brandi Whitaker. Two years after Brandi, Stella Silverthorne. Three years after Stella, Cheryl Montgomery."

"And now, two years later, Rebecca Hanover."

They stared at the map in silence for a moment. The shuffle of cards and the murmur of voices behind them seemed very far away.

She looked at him, her eyes glittering. "Seven times is a serial killer, Jim. We need to talk to Liam."

He looked past her out the window. "Right about now, he should be busting up the party at Old Man Creek. If Wy managed to get them down without wrecking the plane."

Jo didn't even bristle. "Then let's go see Prince."

Old Man Creek, September 6

"Where's Tim?" Wy shoved past Liam into the cabin. Tim was sitting at the table, across from Amelia, one hand full of cards, his mouth open as he stared up at Wy. She felt a sense of overwhelming relief sweep over her, a relaxation of a thrumming, all-consuming tension she didn't even know she had been experiencing. She didn't miss a step, she walked straight to him and pulled him up into her arms. "Oh, Tim," she said, rocking him a little. "Oh, Tim."

He squirmed in her embrace. "Mom, c'mon." He slanted a sideways look at the girl across the table.

Liam's eyes went to the woman lying in the bunk. "Who is that?" he said sharply.

She didn't stir, but Bill snapped, "Keep your voice down."

"Who is it?"

"We don't know. She staggered in here about four hours ago and passed out."

Liam nudged Wy. "Is that her?"

She tore her eyes from Tim and walked over to the bunk to look down into the woman's face. "Yes. This is Rebecca Hanover."

"Is that her name?" Bill said.

"Is she armed?" Liam said.

Moses surveyed him with an irritated expression. " 'Is she armed?' She's damn near dead, is what she is."

"Her husband is dead. Murdered. Blasted away with a shotgun."

They all looked at Rebecca Hanover. Her eyes moved restlessly beneath closed lids. Her skin was waxen, her hair tangled with twigs and pine needles. She whimpered a little, stirred, one hand half raised in a protective gesture. They could see the broken nails, the dried blood and dirt beneath them. One shoulder was bandaged. She subsided again into an uneasy sleep.

"Sanctuary," Tim said.

Everyone turned to look at him. He flushed. "That's what she said. It's the only thing she said after we got her into the bed. 'Sanctuary.' "

"What's that mean?" Amelia said.

"In olden times," Tim said, "people who were being chased could run into a church and the cops couldn't get them. Sanctuary. I read about it in a book once," he added.

"Oh." Amelia had never read anything that hadn't been assigned as homework. "Could bad guys run into the church, too?"

Tim looked at Bill. "Yes," she said. "Bad guys could run into the church, too."

Amelia looked at Rebecca Hanover, and with the devastating single-mindedness of the young said, "So just because they ask for sanctuary doesn't mean they didn't do it."

Liam started forward, hand out to wake Rebecca Hanover. Moses got in his way. "I've got to talk to her, Moses," Liam said.

"No you don't," Moses said. "She didn't kill anybody."

The voices tell you so? Liam wanted to say. "At the very least," he said, "she's a material witness to the death of her husband. I have to talk to her. Let me wake her up."

"She'll wake up in her own good time," Moses said flatly. "And no," he said pointedly, "they didn't. They haven't been real mouthy on this trip."

Liam cleared his throat and couldn't think of anything else to say.

Standoff.

"No one is going anywhere in this pea soup anyway," Bill said practically, defusing the tension. "You'll have plenty of time to wait for her to wake up. She's not going anywhere. Amelia, make some more coffee. Tim, get down two more mugs. Are you hungry? How about a tuna fish sandwich? I'll just—"

"What's that?" Wy turned her head, listening.

"What?" Bill moved forward a step, and cursed the apprehensive note in her voice. She was nervous. She couldn't remember the last time she'd been nervous. She couldn't have said why she was now.

Into it floated a voice, high, thin, thready. "Elaine. Elaine the fair. Elaine the lovable. Elaine, the lily maid. Come out, Elaine. Come out."

On the bed, Rebecca whimpered without waking, her legs pumping against the blankets.

"What the hell?" Moses said, and went to the door.

"No, wait—" Liam said.

But Moses was before him and pulled the door open. "There's no one named Elaine in here, but come on in and get out of the snow!"

The door pushed open against him and a man stood there.

"Gun!" Liam shouted, and Moses dropped into form one second too late. The weapon fired, the noise of the shot deafening everyone in the cabin, and Moses, foot half raised in something Liam recognized as the beginning of Kick Horizontally, crumpled to the floor without a sound.

Bill made a sound low in her throat and moved forward.

"Hold it," the man said.

She either ignored him or didn't hear him, dropping to her knees next to the old man, who suddenly looked infinitely older, whose blood welled red from beneath the fingers pressed to his side.

The man had a brown, seamed face surrounded by a halo of tangled, dirty gray hair, hair repeated in the collar of his shirt and on the backs of the hands gripping the rifle. A Browning, Liam noted. A semi-automatic, .270 maybe, or a .30-06. What did one of those hold, four rounds? Three, in magnum. He looked Moses, at his wound. Not magnum. Three left, then.

"Uuiliriq," Tim breathed. "It's the Hairy Man, Mom."

Amelia's eyes were enormous in her small face.

Mad eyes looked at Liam, saw the weapon strapped to his side and raised his rifle. "Lose the gun, son." The words sounded rusty with disuse.

Liam didn't move.

With uncanny instinct, the man took two steps forward and jammed the barrel of the rifle beneath Wy's chin. She rose swiftly to her feet, to stand on tiptoe. Her eyes were wide but she looked more angry than frightened. His Wy. His own Wy, nobody else's. Liam felt an answering anger kindle inside him.

The smell of the man filled the cabin, woodsmoke, dead fish, dried blood, sweat. Later, Liam would think it was that smell more than anything that made him pull out his weapon and lay it on the floor.

"Kick it to me," the man said.

Liam managed to put enough of a spin on the kick that it slid to the opposite corner of the cabin, coming to rest beneath the bunk where Rebecca Hanover lay, motionless now, even her eyes still beneath their lids.

The man followed the path of the pistol with steady steps, and paused next to the bed. "Elaine." His voice was low but audible to them all. "Oh, my Elaine. Why did you do this to yourself ?"

He reached out a hand as if to brush the hair from her face, and she exploded into action, launching herself at him too quickly for him to raise the weapon. They both went crashing to the floor.

Liam went for the rifle, but the ragged man threw off Rebecca, who thudded hard into the wall, slid down and lay still. The ragged man got to the rifle a split second before Liam, but didn't have time to aim before the rifle fired a second time. The shot boomed in the close confines of the room. Behind him Liam heard someone cry out, a soft thud as a body hit the floor. A second later, like Moses a second too late, he tackled the man and grabbed for the rifle, his hands closing around the barrel, warm from the two shots.

The ragged man was incredibly strong. They were close enough to touch, to kiss if they'd wanted to. The ragged man's mouth was open in a rictus of a grin. He shifted his weight suddenly. Liam lost his balance and fell heavily to one side, maintaining through sheer will his grip on the rifle barrel. The ragged man snarled and the barrel inched down and there was nothing Liam could do to stop it. The rifle fired again, almost jolting his grip loose. His hands stung but he held on. One shot left.

Wy had been going for Moses' .30-06, mounted on a rack next to the door. The third shot had caught the .30-06 squarely on the breech, shattering it.

Wy cursed and hefted the rifle by the barrel in a strong batter's grip. If it couldn't shoot, it could club.

The ragged man twisted like a fish, dropping the rifle in a sudden movement and closing his hands around Liam's throat. In an instinctive gesture, Liam dropped the barrel to grab for the ragged man's wrists. The rifle was held between them by the press of their bodies, so tightly that it couldn't fall. Liam was choking, his face a dull red, his hands clawing.

"Leave him go!" Wy shouted, and made good on her words

when she swung the rifle. The butt connected with the ragged man's skull with a satisfyingly solid smack.

His hands loosened from around Liam's throat. He rolled to one side to lie on his back on the floor and blink up at the ceiling in a puzzled way.

Wy reached him first, kicking his rifle out of reach. "You son of a bitch!" she said fiercely.

He ignored her, turning his head to look at Rebecca Hanover sprawled in an ungainly heap, only just beginning to blink her way back into consciousness. "Elaine the fair, Elaine the lovable," he said dreamily. "Elaine, the lily maid of Astolat. My own Elaine."

Behind them, Moses had crawled to Amelia and was cradling her in his arms. Tim knelt at his side, his face white and shocked. Blood had gathered and pooled on the floor beneath all three of them, but it had ceased now to flow.

"Goddamn it," Moses said, in a tired voice Bill had never heard before. "Goddamn it all to hell."

He put back his head and yelled, "You have to be right, don't you, you sons a bitches! You just have to be right!"

Bill put her hands on his shoulders. "Hush, old man," she said. "Hush now."

"Goddamn it," he said again.

He closed his eyes and rested his head on Bill's breast.

TWENTY-TWO

Newenham, September 16

Liam came in at ten that evening. "She found it," he said flatly, and disappeared into the bathroom.

"Would you like to sleep in the camper tonight?" she said suddenly.

His nose startled out of *The Lost Wagon*, Tim looked up from where he was curled on the couch and said, "What?"

"Sleep in the camper tonight," she said. "That's an order."

He looked toward the bathroom, and when he spoke she could have wept at the effort it took him to make the joke. "What's it worth to you?"

"A smack upside the head," she said, grabbing for him.

He hot-footed it out of reach, not quite smiling but nearly there. He loved sleeping in the trailer, having his own little self-contained house around him.

She eased the bathroom door open and slipped inside. Liam was outlined behind the curtain, hands propped on the wall on either side of the shower head, head bent beneath the stream of steaming water. She stripped and stepped into the tub behind him.

He jumped when he felt her hands on him, but he was instantly responsive. He tried to turn, tried to reach for her, and she

265

wouldn't let him. It was part seduction, part subjugation and part the staking of a claim. He recognized it for what it was and the sum of all its parts, and he let her have her way with him.

She made him a late supper of cold moose roast sandwiches and Corona, and then they made love again on the living room couch, a fire in the fireplace and the curtains open to the river and sky. "My turn," he murmured.

"Do your worst," she whispered, lying back.

"God," he said later, "the worst day fucking is better than the best day fishing."

She shoved him off the couch and he landed smack on his bare ass, yelping and laughing. She hung over the side, looking at him. "Can you talk about it now?"

"Yeah." The laughter faded. He climbed back up on the couch and snuggled next to her. Her hair was a wild tangle that tickled his nose, and her elbow was jabbing uncomfortably into his chest. He cupped a palm around her breast and trailed a finger down her spine. Her thigh was between his and pressed up against him, his was pressed against her. Marking their spots. He could live with the elbow and the tickly hair.

"We were about to pack it in for the day, but she insisted we stay out as long as there was light to see by. She spotted it up this canyon, nearly a ravine, totally overgrown. We couldn't have made it in a plane."

"No strip?"

"No strip. He liked his privacy, the sick little bastard. Search and Rescue had to set the chopper down nearly a mile out. We hiked in, and it wasn't easy. I don't know how she got away."

"She told us. Windex."

A faint laugh rumbled up out of his chest. "Right. Your all-purpose cleaner and killer deterrent."

She trailed a fingertip down the crack of his behind, and he twitched, distracted, as she had meant him to be.

"Guy's a master builder, I'll say that for him. Everything hand-hewn, fitted together like pieces of a puzzle. And literally invisible from the air. You couldn't even see the smoke rising from the chimney."

"Fine, he can bid on the addition to Spring Creek. That ought to be a lifetime guarantee of work."

"If he doesn't get off by reason of insanity."

"He couldn't. They wouldn't!"

He said nothing.

After a moment, she said, "Were there twelve graves, like she said?"

His chest rose and fell on a sigh. "Yes. There wasn't time to dig them up this afternoon. We logged the location on the GPS. We'll go back tomorrow with shovels and body bags."

He rolled over, pinning her to the back of the sofa, nudging her legs apart to slide smoothly home. Something between a gasp and a moan caught in the back of her throat, and he smiled at her. "Why is it we're screwing around on this couch when there is a perfectly good bed in your bedroom?"

"You tell me," she whispered back, and pushed back, rolling so that she was on top. She rode him, she rode him hard, so that his only thought, at least for those precious few minutes, was of her and only of her, and when he came she was watching, waiting for it, and she whispered, "I love you, Liam," and followed him over.

The next day Liam returned to the perfect little cabin in the perfect little canyon. They disinterred the bodies, one beneath each of the wooden markers. There were no years carved into the markers, only the name and the line of verse, repeated twelve times, barely legible on the earlier markers, crisp and clean around the edges on the more recent ones.

They found a small arsenal in a concealed locker in the crawl space beneath the cabin, one that appeared to have been acquired along with the victims. The BAR Hairy Man (the killer was resisting all attempts at identification) was carrying at Old Man had been registered three years before in Cheryl Montgomery's name. A twenty-two pistol was eventually proved to have been the weapon that killed Opal Nunapitchuk; later another of the victim's parents identified it as having belonged to the victim's grandmother, who had given it to her granddaughter on her twenty-first birthday. There was a Winchester Field Model 16339 shotgun, and Teddy Engebretsen and John Kvichak were released into the relieved arms of their families.

When they had the bodies loaded and were ascending once again into the air, Liam looked his last on the cabin, now engulfed in flames. He glanced at the woman sitting beside him, who had insisted on accompanying them that day. He had protested, but Wy had said, "She earned it, Liam. Let her go."

Rebecca had started the fire herself, on the floor in the middle of the cabin with a Firestarter log and a match. The wood, seasoned over thirty years, spread fast and burned hot, reaching up with greedy fingers to engulf first the walls and then the roof. He supposed he should have stopped her doing it, but he hadn't, and it was beginning to rain anyway, a gentle pattering on the bracken. A heavy gray layer of clouds building between the surrounding peaks promised more on the way.

None of them, in fact, had tried to stop her. They stood behind her, almost at attention, an honor guard, watching the flames lick across the floor, catch at the walls, crawl to the ceiling.

"Are you all right?" He said to her as the helicopter hovered over the canyon.

She looked at him. "I want to go home now."

"You heard the lady," he said over his headset.

The helicopter put its nose down and skidded across the sky toward Newenham.

Once during the flight he saw her looking out the window. "Easier than covering the same distance on foot," he said.

She looked at him, but she said nothing.

He put her on the jet to town that afternoon, foiling Jo's attempt to talk to her. "She's been through enough, Jo. Leave her alone."

"I will," Jo said, "but the jackals will be waiting at the gate in Anchorage."

They were; Liam and Wy watched it on television that evening, pictures of Rebecca Hanover shoving her way through a crowd of people with cameras and lights. WOMAN ESCAPES SERIAL KILLER BY TREK THROUGH BUSH, screamed the next day's headlines, and subsequent issues were given over to the stories of all the victims, including baby pictures, high school pictures, prom pictures and wedding pictures. Grieving parents and spouses were interviewed; Lyle Montgomery was photographed walking up to the door of Rebecca's friend Nina's house. He was the only person unknown to her who was permitted inside. He stayed half an hour and came out again, walking swiftly to his car, getting in and driving off at once, refusing to speak or even to look at the people calling his name. Still, the camera showed the tears rolling down his cheeks quite clearly.

The door remained locked thereafter, the shades drawn. Nina Stewart was photographed carrying groceries inside and the trash to the curb. *Hard Copy* snatched the bag one step ahead of the garbage truck Tuesday morning and had the extreme bad taste to open it on camera that evening, thus proving to an avidly watching public that Rebecca Hanover had been spared the additional trauma of pregnancy, if not the humiliation of having the news trumpeted on sixty-four channels. The next time someone pointed a camera at Nina, she flipped them off. That was aired, too, with a small blurred circle covering the offending digit.

The medical examiner's reports started coming in, and the circus moved to the second act. Most of the victims had had their necks snapped, and when Liam thought of those strong, hairy fingers closing around his own throat he wasn't surprised. "A quick death, anyway," he said to Prince.

"I'm sure that was a comfort to the victims," she said dispassionately. She wasn't much interested. She'd had her fifteen minutes of fame when Liam told her to take the interview with Maria Downey. The camera loved her, and shortly thereafter Liam's boss, Lieutenant John Dillinger Barton, called and offered her a job as the department spokesman. She had turned him down, saying only, "I'm not done racking up the cleared cases in Newenham yet. I'm not ready to spend my days talking to the press."

Much was made of how this serial killer had spread his victims out over the years. Lieutenant Barton was interviewed on Channel 2 News, and he managed to restrain his natural talent for profanity long enough to point out that Alaska's only other serial killer had been in action for fifteen years. Alaska was big enough to hide a serial killer's activities for a long time. The next day, the spokesman for the Alaska state troopers went on the air to apologize for Barton's remarks, and to say that he had not intended to extend an invitation to serial killers to set up shop in the Alaskan Bush. "Nope," said Prince, "not my kind of job."

Nine of the twelve women were identified. Three of them had been pregnant at the time of their death. "Didn't want to share," Prince said when this was discovered.

After three weeks the story died down, only to spring back to life when the killer was identified. It hadn't been easy. His cabin was on national park land. He'd had no permit and had built it on his own, so they hadn't been able to identify him through a title or bank paperwork. He had no friends, no family stepped forward, he didn't get mail, so it was something of a coup when a clerk in the Anchorage Police Department, after slogging doggedly through a mountain of retired paperwork, found a dusty file fallen behind a filing cabinet with the name Clayton Gheen on it. The clerk ran the fingerprints in the file, and came up with a match.

Clayton Gheen had a record going back to the time he was thirteen years old, mostly B&E and petty theft. There had also been two incidences of assault in the fourth degree. Neither girl had come forward to testify, and he'd walked on both charges.

"Abuse in his background?" Liam asked Prince as she was scanning the report, faxed from the Fairbanks post.

She shook her head. "If his father beat on him, it was never reported."

"And his mother just took off."

She nodded. "Doesn't automatically make him a serial killer, though."

Liam thought of his own mother, walking out when he was six months old. "No. What does?"

Prince looked up, surprised at the question, because Liam Campbell wasn't in the habit of asking questions which couldn't be answered. "When we have the answer to that, we'll put in for a raise."

"Works for me."

But he thought about it, off and on, for a long time afterward. He had distributed the contents of the pitiful little trophy chest Rebecca had found to the grieving families. One pair of the earrings, a ring and the crystal choker remained unclaimed, as did three of the bodies. Lost souls, lost to their families, lost to themselves, lost to him.

In 1975 Gheen had gone to work for BP in the Prudhoe Bay oil fields, working construction, and had moved to Anchorage. His record was blank after that until 1979, when he'd been arrested for aggravated assault. This woman had testified, and he had been due in court in Anchorage for sentencing in May of that year. He never showed. A bench warrant was issued for his arrest, but he'd never been found to be served.

Gheen was interviewed on Channel 11, where the pretty anchor punctuated every phrase with a nod and began every sentence with "Now." She asked him why he did it, her brows puckered with pretended puzzlement, her attention divided between Gheen and the camera lens. He stared at her bovinely. She spoke the names, rendered like the tolling of a bell, Merla Dixon in 1983, Sarah Berton in 1985, Paulette Gustafson in 1986, Kristen Anderson in 1986, Ruby Nunapitchuk in 1991, Brandi Whitaker in 1992, Stella Silverthorne in 1994, Christine Stepanoff in 1996, Cheryl Montgomery in 1997. Rebecca Hanover. The three unidentified bodies the medical examiner would only say might have been buried in, respectively, 1982, 1983 and 1988.

Won't you tell us, the little anchor asked prettily, who the other three women were? What were their names?

"Elaine," Gheen had said, and smiled.

Gheen's public defender had orchestrated the television interview. He went into court the following week and petitioned for a change of venue, arguing that his client could not get a fair trial in Newenham. Or anywhere else anybody watched television, Liam thought, a hard place to find, even in Alaska, in this age of satellite television. It sounded as if Gheen's P.D. would go for an insanity defense, but thanks to one of the few smart laws the Alaska legislature managed to pass in spite of themselves in recent years, Gheen could plead insanity all he wanted. He'd serve time in the Alaska Psychiatric Institute until his doctors declared him cured, from which time he would be incarcerated for fifteen life sentences, to be served consecutively. If district attorney, judge and jury did their job, that is.

Liam knew sincere regret that Bill Billington couldn't sit on a felony case. Almost twenty years—that they knew of—almost twenty years Gheen had been kidnapping and killing women. He fit no known profile, other than that he was white and male. He'd started his killing later in life than most serial killers, but that was only so far as they knew. He'd kept trophies. He hadn't stuck to victims of his own race, there hadn't been any apparent acceleration of murder toward the end, he'd kept his victims alive, some, it seemed, for years.

Liam had interrogated Gheen once before shipping him to Anchorage. "What went wrong?" he'd asked Gheen. "Why did you have to kill them? They run away? They get pregnant and you couldn't stand the thought of sharing? You hit them too hard, too often, and they up and die on you?"

Gheen had looked back at him, very calm, very still within his handcuffs and manacles and leg chains. His gaze was open and disinterested.

"Who was Elaine?" Liam said. "You buried her twelve times, she must mean something to you. Who was she?"

At that Gheen smiled, the same smile he would give the little anchor on Channel 11. "Elaine was my wife." His eyes went dreamy. "Elaine the fair, Elaine the beautiful, Elaine the lily maid of Astolat."

"She left you," Liam said.

Gheen smiled again.

"She never left me," he said.

Bill was back behind the bar, serving beer to Moses, who was also back and as cranky as ever. He'd been waiting on Wy's deck the morning after he got out of the hospital, and as far as Liam could tell, stifling an inner groan, it would take more than a bullet to slow him down. Liam, Wy and Tim went through the form five times that morning. Moses didn't even break a sweat. Liam lived for the day when he could say the same.

Amelia was buried in the Newenham cemetery, Darren Gearhart sobbing his heart out at the gravesite. Liam had to restrain Bill from assaulting him.

A few brief words from Bill had told Wy about Tim and Amelia. Wy asked him about her when they got back home that afternoon. "I liked her," Tim said, and made it clear that that was all he was going to say.

He at least had found a measure of closure by bearing witness to the disappearance of Christine Stepanoff. The remains beneath one of the wooden markers had matched dental records in Newenham. "She was really nice," he told Wy.

It was the first time he'd spoken of anyone from the tiny village where he had survived his childhood.

"She probably saved my life," he added.

The next time Wy flew into Ualik, she spent an extra hour on the ground while she knocked on doors. Two weeks later she gave Tim a package. "What is it?" he said.

"Open it."

He did, and found a brass frame enclosing the picture of a girl with narrow, tilted brown eyes, a long fall of straight brown hair and a laughing face. "Christine," he said, his voice a bare breath of sound.

"Her grandmother still lives in Ualik. She loaned me the negative. I just got it back from Anchorage today."

He gripped the frame tightly in both hands, his head bowed, his shoulders shaking. He said something she couldn't make out. "What?"

He raised his head and her heart turned over at the sight of his ravaged face. "Oh Tim, I'm so sorry, I—"

He barreled into her headfirst, the picture thudding into her spine when he threw his arms around her. "She looks like Amelia," he whispered.

She held him without words, grateful she could do that much, angry that she could not do more. Hot tears soaked into her shirt.

After a while he quieted. "Thanks, Mom," he whispered.

"Hey," she whispered back. "It's what I do."

She looked up and saw Liam standing in the hallway, watching, with something that wasn't quite a smile on his face. "You always figure out the right thing to do," he said later, "and then you do it."

She was taken aback. "You make me sound like Mother Teresa."

He laughed and hugged her. "Not hardly. Just Wy."

No one has ever known me that well, she remembered saying to Jo. Well, Jo had replied, what does that tell you?

You always figure out the right thing to do, and then you do it.

Prince had served her the court order the day after they got back from Old Man Creek. She'd run to Bill to get a restraining order in response, but it was only temporary. Natalie would appeal to her pet judge and they'd be right back where they started.

She thought of Moses. She wondered what her life would have been like with him in it sooner. She wondered what her life would have been like if she'd ever seen her birth mother sober. If her adoptive parents hadn't found her and kept her for themselves.

She thought long and hard of all of those things, she came to a decision and she laid her plans.

The knock came at nine a.m. the next Monday morning. Liam was at the post, Tim was at school. When Wy opened the door, a woman with clear eyes and clean clothes stood on the other side.

Wy took a deep breath. "Hello, Natalie," she said steadily. "Please come in."

At nine-fifteen the phone in the trooper post rang. Liam picked up the phone and John Dillinger Barton bellowed, "Congratulations, Sergeant Campbell!"

He sat very still. He was alone in the office, Prince off cruising the road to Icky in hopes of apprehending transgressors. "What did you say?"

"What, suddenly you got wax in your ears?"

This for Barton was almost playful. "Did you call me sergeant?" Liam said.

"I sure as hell did! Grabbing up a serial killer, especially one nobody knew was operating until a couple of weeks ago, and putting away thirteen of fifteen murder cases oughta be worth a piddly little promotion. Even those assholes down in Juneau gotta admit that! When can you get here?"

"What? Where?"

"Here, where the hell do you think? Jesus, Liam, wake up! You been promoted, I can bring you back to Anchorage, you're back on the fast track, boy! Get on a plane!"